Praise for *The Following Girls*

'Levene's sharply observed comedy mixes affectionate satire of the stylistic oddities of the time with an invigorating sparkle of real dislike for the petty tyrannies of parental and pedagogical authority: admirers of George Orwell will feel a chilly frisson of recognition at the scene in which the headmistress, Dr O'Brien, induces Baker to betray her best friend and fellow subversive, Julia'   *Evening Standard*

'The mind of a teenage girl is a strange, unruly, often hilarious place to be . . . Readers will grin in sly recognition at the petty tiffs, the codes of behaviour, the shared scorn for teachers, parents, schoolwork, and pretty much everything else . . . It's funny, boisterous and sharp'   *Sunday Telegraph*

'Levene's new novel has all the authenticity of a memoir, with her seamless knack for drawing characters that fully inhabit their historical setting. This is an acutely observed and witty portrayal of the school exploits and growing pains of a 1970s teenager'
The Lady

'Her protagonists are beautifully drawn, and the denouement is, if depressing, deeply realistic'   *Sunday Times*

'A chance to relive the days of double maths and ciggies behind the bike sheds'   *Good Housekeeping*

The Following Girls

LOUISE LEVENE

BLOOMSBURY
LONDON · NEW DELHI · NEW YORK · SYDNEY

Bloomsbury Paperbacks
An imprint of Bloomsbury Publishing Plc

50 Bedford Square
London
WC1B 3DP
UK

1385 Broadway
New York
NY 10018
USA

www.bloomsbury.com

BLOOMSBURY and the Diana logo are trademarks of Bloomsbury Publishing Plc

First published in Great Britain 2014
This paperback edition first published in 2015

Extracts on pages vii and 201 from *The Complete Works of George Orwell*, edited by
Peter Davison. Reprinted by permission of The Random House Group Limited
and the Estate of the late Sonia Brownell Orwell

Extracts on pages 70, 83–4 and 94 from *The Female Eunuch* by Germaine Greer. Reprinted
by permission of HarperCollins © 2006 by Germaine Greer

British Library Cataloguing-in-Publication Data
A catalogue record for this book is available from the British Library.

ISBN: HB: 978-1-4088-4289-8
PB: 978-1-4088-4290-4
ePub: 978-1-4088-4432-8

2 4 6 8 10 9 7 5 3 1

Typeset by Hewer Text UK Ltd, Edinburgh
Printed and bound in Great Britain by CPI Group (UK) Ltd, Croydon CR0 4YY

To find out more about our authors and books visit www.bloomsbury.com.
Here you will find extracts, author interviews, details of forthcoming events
and the option to sign up for our newsletters.

For my daughter Lily Mulvey

The Hate had started.

Nineteen Eighty-Four
George Orwell

Monday 24 February 1975

Chapter 1

The clock on the wall in Room 13 was striking four in the distance as Baker plunged a hand inside her blazer, slid open the flimsy cardboard packet and teased out a cheap cigarette. The jacket's lapels formed a felty cave that muffled the giveaway hiss of the match and Baker watched the toasted cloud from the first drag as it drifted swiftly upwards on the strong draught from beneath the cubicle door and out of the open window. Escape.

Someone outside had lost something. No one seemed interested. A sound of shoes hitting the floor, of loos flushing, taps running. The smoker puffed away, smiling, as another flotilla of perfect rings sailed off into the chilly spring air. Baker fidgeted into a less uncomfortable position on the loo seat: back to the wall of one partition, scuffed black lace-ups holding steady against the other, crepe-soled toes wedged either side of the roll of scratchy, papery paper with NOW WASH YOUR HANDS printed insultingly on every sheet. The top of the holder was scarred with a little pokerwork pattern of cigarette burns.

Baker's sideways pose created no tell-tale shadow in the gap below the door which had been left open a cunning inch or two and hung with a stolen 'Out of order' notice. She was safe for the moment. Invisible.

An angry sign about basic hygiene and the vague hope that

things might be left as one would wish to find them had been screwed to the back of the door but the lower screw had been removed and the enamel plaque could be swivelled clear to reveal a Rosetta Stone of fruity graffiti on the ancient grey paintwork. Mrs Mostyn was a slag, Amanda Bunter-Byng was a slag, Davina Booth was a slag, and cats liked plain crisps, apparently. The writing was fantastically small and neat and regular, some of it almost illegibly tiny – far too small to see if you were sitting on the seat: 'Snow White thought 7-Up was a drink until she discovered dwarfs'; 'Mostyn is a Snog Monster'; 'I must not obsess. I must not obsess. I must not obsess'; 'Ireland for the Irish: Peckham for the peckish'. The grey gap was nearly filled. Did Biro wipe off?

Baker pulled the cap from a new green ballpoint and began greedily colonising the remaining space with angry, anonymous capitals: POISON MRS MOSTYN. STRANGLE MRS MOSTYN. GAROTTE MRS MOSTYN. GUILLOTINE MRS MOSTYN. SUFFOCATE MRS MOSTYN. DECAPITATE MRS MOSTYN. EVISCERATE MRS MOSTYN. EXTERMIN-ATE MRS FUCKING MOSTYN.

A sharp tap on the door jolted Baker from her murderous trance. Panicked, she let the sign slide back into place. The half-finished cigarette hit the bog with a dying hiss while shaking fingers fumbled for peppermints among the dust bunnies cuddled up in her blazer pocket.

'Have you got the Maths master in there?'

Baker let off an exasperated sigh of relief as she got down from her perch and opened the door to the friendly figure of Amanda Stott who had a sheet of graph paper resting on the cover of her current library book (*Italian in 20 Lessons*).

'Don't bloody *do* that. Thought you were one of the goons or something.'

'Sorry. Didn't mean to *disturb* but it's mattresses again and I haven't got a bloody clue. It's due in tomorrow.'

'"Find the determinant of the following ma-trices",' quoted Baker, calmer now. 'Done my copy and handed it in already, sorry. Queenie had it last.'

Baker grabbed her bag and sidled out of the cubicle and into the cloakroom.

'God I hate Mondays.'

'Tuesday's just as bad,' said Stottie.

'Wednesday's worse. The exams start on Wednesday.'

Stott's younger sister Stephanie was loitering behind her. First years played hockey all through Lent term and every Monday afternoon you'd see another crippled crocodile limping back from a friendly, their knees buttered with yellow mud. Young Stephanie had a filthy pair of goalkeeper's pads stuck under her left arm and was tricked out in cupcake skirt, spiked hockey boots and a short-sleeved blouse with SS knotted in tidy chain stitch across her tidy twelve-year-old tits, reminding Baker that Miss Drumlin had threatened a double detention if she didn't sew a similar monogram on her own shirt.

Stephanie Stott was leaning against the great double row of sinks that ran back to back through the middle of the room, waste pipes all coursing into a great porcelain drainage ditch beneath. Irrigation. She stared hard at Baker. Her face was dusted with round purplish spots (the sulky, unsqueezable kind). Not just nose and chin but dotted evenly across the whole face like the blisters on the second side of a pancake or something catching in the *Beano*.

'Can't you just ask Miss Revie how you're supposed to do them?' asked the girl. Baker could smell the cough candy on her breath.

'Afraid not, young Steve. Been tried. Miss Revie has a degree in Mathematics from the University of Cambridge. Knows all about matrices: how to invert them, even knows what they're *for*, but she promised faithfully never to reveal the secret to a living soul. Swore a solemn oath. Not even for ready money. Not even for three and a half grand a year. *Much* easier to copy.'

'I'll *tell*.'

Baker powered up the scary stare that reduced grown German teachers to jelly, but the younger girl failed to wither. Perhaps she was short-sighted? Hardly ideal in a goalkeeper. Perhaps she knew Baker was on probation, knew how little it would take to tip them over the edge. Or maybe she just wasn't afraid . . .

'You've been smoking. Julia Smith says only *morons* smoke. It's a tax on stupidity, Julia says.' Stottie's sporty little sister worshipped the school games captain. Stottie gave an exasperated, 'She doesn't get it from me' shrug.

'Who gives a stuff what Julia Smith thinks?' sneered Baker.

'And you'll get cancer. Even says so on the box. Talk about *stu-pid*.'

'Very probably. Now why don't you buzz off and leave us alone. Proles aren't allowed in the Shell cloaks.' Baker deliberately translated her thoughts into the moronic school code – the only language they understand.

'I'll *tell*.'

But she did at last leave the room.

'Your young Steve's a bit of a prat. Is she adopted? Who knows? Maybe it's you who's adopted. She looks nothing like.'

Stephanie Stott had her father's burly build and the beginnings of her mother's blousy curves. Stottie, with her boyish frame and pixie face, looked like a doll beside the three of them, like they'd stolen her from somewhere. She was easily the smallest in the fifth – half the size of Linda Madeley who was on the far side of the cloakroom changing for netball practice. Baker watched her slither free of her nylon blouse releasing a gaseous whiff: half Body Mist; half body odour. Behind Linda loomed the beanpole shape of Oonagh Houseman who was trying to keep her back to the room, hoping no one would see how her mother had attached her treble-A bra to the top of her knickers with buttons and tape so that she didn't throttle herself every time she raised her arms for a save. As Oonagh reached under the bench for her gym shoes, the padded shell of white polyester gaped away from her chest. Why not just wear a bloody vest? Yellow wool in winter. Lacy cotton in summer. Vests. Baker frowned at the comfy memory.

Stottie had scampered off to the form room in hopes of catching Queenie and the one genuine piece of homework done by the sole member of the Beta Maths group who could make any sense of the prep (and her brother did most of it). The result was passed from hand to hand and copied over with sly crossings-out here and there to make the forgery look authentic.

Baker went across to her peg and huddled into her grubby blue regulation raincoat called, rather grandly, The Grantham and lined with its own peculiar plaid: a doleful chorus of greens and greys like the tartan of some extinct Highland regiment (Dress Grantham? Hunting Grantham? *Trench* Grantham?).

The girl changing next to her was sneaking her crucifix into the polished toe of her brogues. She twitched a glance at Baker.

'Don't look at me.' Baker was indignant. 'T'isn't me who nicks it all.'

Purse-belts and make-up and cherished gold-nibbed fountain pens and puzzle rings and illicit transistor radios went missing from the cloakrooms all the time. No one was ever caught, but then no one tried particularly hard to catch. Culprits meant punishment: suspensions, expulsions, *police* even (if the swag had any real value). 'Items of value must not be brought into school' said the Fawcett Code (the implication being that they would be stolen if they were), but it didn't go as far as 'No Stealing'. Odd really, mused Baker, the way they let it slide, made it the victim's fault. They were so strict in other ways, but the blind eye they turned to petty thievery meant that someone – could be the girl next to her, the crucifix-hiding business might just be a blind – was getting away with murder: a secret unflashable stash of cash and pens and lip glosses. Baker stared round the room: could easily be her, or her, or her . . .

It couldn't be a new problem. You even got it in Enid Blyton. Had all the sneak thieves over all the years grown up normal? Had they just grown out of it? Were they all in Holloway (nothing about that on the honours board)? Or did they take the values they'd learned at school with them into the outside world (like the Speech Day speakers always said) and spend lunch hours and tea breaks rifling through desks and lockers, fiddling their expenses and cheating the tax man?

There was an unread copy of the Fawcett Code pinned up on every cloakroom noticeboard. Drafting rules was obviously a tricky business. Stealing wasn't mentioned and you couldn't very well say 'No smoking' either, or 'No gambling' or 'No spitting' or 'No chewing tobacco' or 'Usury is forbidden in the lower school' because putting such things on the list of rules would admit that they took place. So the 'Code' was just general blather about keeping to the left in corridors and 'showing consideration'. A flyblown copy of the most recent edition was hanging alongside the upper school timetables. Baker groaned again at the thought of the next day's lessons. What kind of masochist scheduled netball at nine fifteen in the bloody ratbagging morning?

Bang in the middle of the corkboard was a plastic-covered copy of the school photograph and there on the back row were Amanda Baker, Amanda McQueen, Amanda Stott and Bunty, alias Amanda Bunter-Byng: the Four Mandies. They sat unsmiling in a sea of smiles, hair trussed madly into the side ponytails they'd given each other the moment Mrs Mostyn, perched just off-centre in her cap and gown, had completed her last-minute inspection. Stott Minor was sitting cross-legged at her feet in a stiff new blazer, her face caught mid-sneeze as if recoiling in horror from her closeness to the Snog Monster.

Baker hastily shouldered her book bag. With Queenie and Stottie off playing mattresses in the form room she was on her own and she was sure Bryony and that lot were talking about her. One of them stared across, then whispered something. The others sniggered and muttered things in aigy-paigy then laughed some more. Bryony (safety in numbers) wheeled round to face Baker, her chin orange with spot concealer.

'Girlfriend left you? No Bunty to play with?'

Baker turned to leave without answering.

'Better watch out,' persisted Bryony. 'Big Brother is watching you don't forget: Stephanie Stott's a right little tell-tale.'

It might have been worded like a warning but she wasn't really worried on Baker's behalf. She was glad.

'She wouldn't dare,' said Baker.

But she would though. Young Steve was kinky for the uniform, for the whole badges and prizes business, for her precious scholarship. And she didn't even mean any harm really – not in her own eyes. Smoking wasn't just unhealthy (said so on the packet, showed you on the lurgy lung leaflets); it was *Unschool*. The way Stott minor saw it, once Mrs Mostyn knew and you'd taken your punishment, *learned your lesson*, it would all be all right again. It wasn't nastiness in its weird little way, Baker could see that. Nastiness you could deal with. Nastiness and you could be nasty back.

As she sauntered down the stairs past the smart front lobby Baker spotted the headmistress's secretary shoving purple tulips into a surplus silver trophy (Greek Dancing and Eurhythmics) in readiness for the fifth form parents' evening. The main hall was cluttered with chatty groups of chairs and tables with jaunty subject flags on them, all lying in wait for Baker's dad.

Baker's dad hardly bothered to hide his disappointment any more as, one by one, the chances of certificates on the study wall melted away. Neighbours' girls were Queen's Guides or Duke of Edinburgh Awarded or pictured leotarding uncertainly from end to end of a four-inch beam in local newspapers. And Daddy's girl? Daddy's girl was in detention for putting half an onion in another girl's lunch box (it had been left over from Queenie's Quiche Lorraine – shame to waste it, said Queenie). The parents' evening would give him plenty of fresh ammunition, especially once they told him about the front lawn business. They couldn't prove it, thank God, but the net was definitely closing in. Maybe she could just not go home at all?

If she stopped off in the café by the station she'd be able to miss the 4.50 and catch the 5.10 or even the half past. There'd be no Bunty to talk to, but anything was better than going home. Dad wouldn't actually be back from the parents' meeting till gone 7.30 by the time he'd done the rounds of all the subjects but she knew that the sense of dread would be stronger if she went home. The house would still be humming with the aftershocks of the row they'd had at breakfast: why did she always *this*, why could she never *that*.

Stottie and her sister were still at the main gate when she got downstairs.

'Don't suppose I could stay over at your house tonight, could I?'

Amanda Stott's face gave a twinge of disappointment.

'Any other night would have been brilliant, but I've got a sodding piano exam. Mum's picking me up, then taking Stephanie to her gymnastics club, then dashing back here for the you-know-what.'

'Bum,' said Baker and slowly headed off down the hill to the station.

'You could come tomorrow . . .' Stottie called after her.

'You said *sodding*,' Stephanie Stott was saying. 'I'm telling Mum.'

Baker took out *Sons and Lovers* on the train so she could pretend not to be looking at the gang of girls from the school up the hill who were huddled round a shared cigarette at the far end, glancing across at her. They were all wearing platform shoes and trendy French-length skirts and two of them had blonde streaks in the front of their hair where the fringe flicked up – very Unschool. All of them had pierced ears and one had a phone number inked ostentatiously onto the back of her hand. The whole lot changed trains at the junction and made a point of walking to Baker's end of the carriage so that they could each take a passing kick at her ankles as they piled out onto the platform. Bunty would have kicked back.

Chapter 2

A big brown envelope was wedged under the front door addressed to Robert Baker Esq and franked 'Mary Kingsley High School'.

Baker was still in her coat, propping the post against the mirror above the hall table, when the key clicked in the lock and Mrs Baker came in, negotiating the door with two supermarket carriers and a shoulder bag bulging with papers from the office.

'You're back late.'

'Netball.'

'*Netball?*' An old-fashioned look. 'If you say so, sausage. Your dad won't be back till later. I nipped out at lunchtime and got him a nice pork chop but I didn't think we'd wait. Fancy an egg on toast or something? Boiled? Fried? Scrambled? Poached? Pickled? Addled?'

'You choose.'

Mrs Baker was heading off down the hall when Baker remembered about the initials for her games shirt, and yes, it was a bit urgent, and no, it wouldn't be just as quick to teach Baker how to do chainstitch.

'Won't take me a minute,' Mrs Baker sighed. 'Let me get tea out of the way.' Coat off, she began fussing around the kitchen, halving a grapefrut and putting Dad's chop on the grill in readiness for his return while simultaneously rustling up their own tea.

It was always busy in Mrs Baker's kitchen, even when there was no one in it. Every other tile had a daisy transfer, every surface was crowded with patterned tins. There was a toytown table with four matching yellow stools that stowed under it like something out of a caravan. A set of fancy plates too-good-to-use were hung in a row by the window next to a calendar with pictures of all the cats they had never had posing irresistibly in gumboots and Christmas stockings. Keeping them company was a spider plant which lounged from the ceiling in the macramé hammock that the eight-year-old Baker had made in junior school.

Baker watched the kitchen clock twitch nearer six thirty and felt her mouth growing dry at the thought of the evening ahead: a storm of reproaches followed by the usual one-way ticket to Coventry, with Dad relaying all instructions via his wife: Pamela Jean Baker; Pam; *Spam*.

'Pamela, *could* you be kind enough to ask Amanda if she has finished her homework. Pam love, could you ask Amanda to pass me one of those serrated spoon things.'

The grapefruit spoons were all part of her stepmother's 'dream kitchen' – what kind of nutter dreamed about kitchens? – and lived in the pantry with the rest of her equipment: a special flowerpot contraption just for cooking chicken, stainless steel dishes just for avocados, toy bolts that held on to your sweetcorn and a mad gadget with a butter curler at one end and a melon baller at the other (what more did a girl need?).

All of Mrs Baker's cooking was seasoned with a very heavy hand thanks to the giant thirty-pot rack of herbs and spices nailed to the wall by the back door. Very few of her pet recipes actually called for turmeric or fenugreek or asafoetida but she had taken to adding them randomly to things to keep the levels even. Baker's teatime scrambled egg tasted really weird and by the time she'd cut off the crusts and picked out the bigger bits of spice she'd gone off the whole thing.

'Are you not going to eat that?'

'I was going to ring Bunty.'

'Surely it can wait till tomorrow, for heaven's sake? You've only just seen her,' protested Mrs Baker as Baker picked up the receiver.

'No I haven't. She wasn't in school again today; she's been away since Thursday.'

'I expect she's poorly. Lots of bugs about.'

The twelve-year-old Bunty had missed the first two terms of the first year. Her dad had been transferred south from his firm's Edinburgh office and Baker's best friend-to-be had arrived at Mildred Fawcett out of the blue one Saturday on the morning of the inter-school tennis tournament. Baker had budged up to make room for the new girl on the spectators' bench and together they had sat through a semi-final in which a second year called Julia Smith, Stephanie Stott's pin-up girl, had made short work of a player from a rival school four years her senior.

'Blimey,' muttered the new Amanda as yet another back-hand whistled across the court to a parrot house chorus of cheers.

The precocious thirteen-year-old, her face and arms already freckled after a week of spring sunshine, tossed another ball and the two Amandas watched her easy stretch for the serve, watched the handful of fathers in the back row pretending not to see the sooty flash of gusset. 'Good shot!' Dad's voice cutting through the girlish trebles. 'Two-handed backhand,' noted Spam who used to play but didn't play any more.

Julia won her match in straight sets but the crestfallen away supporters began to look more confident when everyone filed back to the court after squash and sandwiches.

'Attagirl, Theresa!' shouted somebody and a tall blonde girl of seventeen strolled to the baseline, her ducky white tennis dress and fancy aluminium racquet announcing how seriously she played. Miss Drumlin had called both girls to the net and as she stooped to retrieve Julia's tossed wooden Junior Slazenger (rough), the two Amandas saw the smiling Julia lean across the net to the older girl and murmur something under her breath. Made Theresa blush, whatever it was, and made a complete mess of her ground strokes. She held her serve for the first game but Julia won the next five with ease.

'Come *on*, Theresa!' but there was a defeated note in the cries of the rival spectators and they were easily drowned out by the Fawcett fan club. Theresa kept pulling down the hem of her white frock and her serve had become so hit-and-miss that Miss Drumlin could barely contain her smiles as she logged each double fault. Julia Smith was smiling too as she swooped to grab yet another mis-hit and ping it neatly toward her opponent's feet but there were tears in the losing player's eyes and she fumbled the catch.

It was Julia's fourth match that day but, fuelled by lemon barley and custard creams, she was still playing full out and her game seemed to get faster and nastier with every point and her demoralised opponent was barely bothering to run for the shots by the end, concluding the final game with a sulky smash into the net. Bryony and friends, sitting cross-legged on the asphalt behind the baseline, all joined the mooing cry of *Jool-ya Jool-ya* as hands were shaken and the cup was presented, but Baker and the new girl didn't join in the cheers.

'Talk about gamesmanship. Could you hear what she was whispering to her?'

Baker shook her head.

'She'll go far,' said her new friend. 'Good prefect material.'

The summer term had started for real the following Monday and Baker managed to bag a double desk for the pair of them, forcing Stottie to chum up with Amanda McQueen. Baker and Bunty had been sitting together ever since (subjects permitting), spoke most evenings and spent Saturday afternoons at each other's houses planning their future when they would leave home, get jobs and share a big beautiful white bedsit somewhere. They were going to be each other's matrons of honour, godmother each other's children, take turns as mystery guests on their *This Is Your Lives* then, finally, grow old and tipsy sipping Napoleon brandy in a fancy apartment on the Boulevard St Michel. Or Something. Bunty had it all worked out.

Dad hated it whenever Bunty phoned Baker or Baker phoned Bunty and found things to do in the greenhouse whenever she came round but he was equally baffled by all Baker's friendships. The way Dad looked at it, friends were people you told jokes to in pubs or played squash with at clubs or 'had over' to mix drinks and talk bollocks about mileage. That's how his friends worked. Not to be holed up in an airless bedroom for hours at a time burning joss sticks and listening to some long-haired layabout with a guitar. And *talking*. What *about*, for heaven's sake? A question he asked every time Baker put down the receiver. 'You're with her all day.' He'd trained his wife to ask the same question but you could tell her heart wasn't in it.

Bunty's mother took twelve rings to answer Baker's call, then said she was very sorry, Amanda, but Amanda was unable to come to the telephone and actually Roy was expecting rather an important call and basically just get off the line. Baker hung up and went back to the kitchen.

'She any better today?'

Baker shrugged and after scraping her tea into the swing-top bin she picked up her book bag and nipped down the hall to the garage, closing the door silently behind her and switching on the light. She yanked the three darts from the centre of the board on the back of the door and, reaching up to the shelf that ran round the top of the room, pulled down an old snapshot of her father and tucked it under the wires by triple twenty so that it hung just over the bull's eye.

She was on her third round when she heard the crash of gears and brakes as Dad's Rover grouched to a halt outside, heard booted footsteps stamp against the doormat, heard the usual growl of greeting muffled by the evening kiss on his wife's cheek.

Baker froze, the dart still poised, as she watched the handle turn on the connecting door. It was always very stiff in cold weather and he had to shove it with his shoulder and the sudden jolt dislodged her last throw from the board and jiggled the photo free of the wire that held it, causing it to float unseen behind a pile of old *Cosmopolitans* (*What to do with an unemotional man*).

He stood on the threshhold, sheepskin coat over his three-piece suit. Older than his picture. As he turned from greeting his wife to confronting his daughter the rotation of his head seemed to wipe the smile away. Baker was still holding the dart up level with her ear and it was only the cross backward jerk of his head that reminded her that she was still taking aim at the deepening groove between his eyes.

'Out of there, young lady. I want a word with you.'

A hard, outdoorsy voice, a voice used to making itself heard above cement mixers and pneumatic drills, a voice too rudely big for the room. He didn't look at her as he spoke. His sheepskin bulk turned back into the hall and along the passage to his study and the waiting stack of prospectuses. Envelopes were starting to arrive almost daily now, the glossy brochures promising judo and ski clubs and language laboratories and filled with pictures of cheery, normal schoolgirls throwing pots or gathering excitedly round microscopes or breasting tapes with aertex A-cups. He'd found the old Fawcett prospectus in one of his filing drawers a few days earlier: 'Helping every girl to fulfil her potential' it lied. Did Amanda even have one to fulfil? He often wondered. Her mother hadn't.

The first Mrs Baker, Patsy, had spent over a month in hospital before Baker was born and during those idle, bed-socked hours had written a letter to her unborn child to be read on its four-teenth birthday in the event of her death. The envelope had been bundled together with her things when baby Amanda finally came home and Dad had kept it, unopened, in one of his desk drawers where nosy little Baker (aged fourteen) had found it. 'Dear Jeremy (or Amanda)' it began, *or Amanda*.

Patsy hadn't died (although Baker usually told people she had). Anything rather than reveal that Mummy had made a bolt for it when her daughter was three and a half after reading a copy of *The Second Sex*. It said 'This book will change your life' on the flyleaf and so it had: lots of people's lives.

Patsy had told Dad that she was off to 'find herself' and the initial search had been pretty bloody extensive to judge from the wide variety of postcards in Grandma's old shoebox – Marrakesh, Marbella, Trondheim. She only returned for the purposes of the divorce (and after Dad had blocked her signature on his handy new Barclaycard). He'd had no trouble getting custody. The estranged Patsy had been based at a psychotherapeutic community in the Basingstoke area for the duration of the court proceedings and the judge didn't hesitate.

His honour hadn't gone so far as to *forbid* access but he hadn't really needed to. According to Grandma there had been fortnightly visits in the early days, during and just after the divorce, when Patsy would get the coach up from Hampshire and take little 'Manda' out for the day but the bi-monthly screaming match with her ex-husband and the rootless tedium of funfairs and zoos and cartoon cinemas soon wore her down.

By the time Jeff appeared on the scene the visits were down to one a month. Patsy hadn't told Jeff about little Manda in the ad she had placed ('Aquarian, free spirit, having survived life's shit, seeks Scorpio male for adventure – non-smoking vegetarian preferred') and the longer their affair continued the more impossible the confession became. He hadn't looked like the paternal type, Grandma said (didn't exactly go with the territory for adventurous Scorpio males), and when he was offered a job in the Bahamas, Patsy tagged along – strictly no strings, she said (before he said it first). She could explain about Manda when they got there, she told Grandma, when they were 'settled', but she never did tell him in the end. Baker had found a long letter on airmail paper in Grandma's box, telling how she had taken a copy of *The Feminine Mystique* to read on that long flight to Nassau and the relationship was on the rocks before the ten days it took her to finish it. But never mind, wrote Patsy. The sun shone every day, the bars were teeming with adventurous Scorpios and she thought she might as well stay. Nothing to come back for. Manda was much happier where she was (Bob was always saying so).

Patsy Baker still sent the occasional postcard with a flamingo or a palm tree on it (just showing off, Spam said) and always remembered birthdays and Christmases with a series of bossy, butch 'non-stereotypical' toys all bought and posted by one of her pals back in Basingstoke: Meccano, a fishing rod, a soldering iron, a chemistry set. Was it feminism? Or were they all really for Jeremy?

It got to a point where Baker had stopped even bothering to unwrap the presents, just re-tagged them on the way over to her male cousin's every Boxing Day. This worked fine until two Christmases ago, when cousin David's gifts turned out to be *The Female Eunuch*, a speculum, a pocket make-up mirror and a Roneoed leaflet on where to find your cervix (north at the gusset and you couldn't miss it apparently).

It had been *Girl's Own* stuff from then on: a badge saying The Future is Female, a copy of *The Bell Jar* and, last Christmas, a subscription to *Spare Rib*. The most recent parcel had also contained a dog-eared copy of *Matriarchy: Myths of Motherhood* ('when we learn to disengage from the children we care for . . . we will be going some way towards true liberation' – thanks, Mum), and folded inside it was a leaflet from the Women's International Terrorist Conspiracy from Hell.

'They've got one of those in Wandsworth,' Spam had said when Baker unwrapped it.

'An international terrorist conspiracy?'

'No-ooh. A women's thing. I saw a fly poster: "The Wandsworth Liberation Workshop".'

'Might not be women.' Baker was annoyed now; Spam was taking the piss. 'Might be for everybody.'

'Leave off. Who else gets liberated?'

Funny bird, Spam. She worked in the office of a large building contractor and had first met Bob Baker at someone's retirement do. He married her ten years ago, just as soon as his decree absolute came through. Baker thought she could just about recall a pre-Spam era: a half-remembered smell of pans burned dry and some very vivid black and white memories of the day she came back from an outing to the zoo with her grandmother to find 'auntie' Pam in the sitting room drinking wine in a new white trouser suit. There had been tea chests full of newspaper in the kitchen and a new pink toothbrush in the rack.

Spam had grown up on the Falkland Islands wearing boots and something sheepish and waterproof and there was still an anorak-y aura about her even in her smartest clothes. It wasn't for want of trying. Three magazines were delivered regularly, like smokeless coal or gold top, and they told her what to wear, what to bake and kept her up to speed with fashionable problems (*Divorce: Is it ever the answer?*), fashionable vegetables and winning ways with curtains, and Mrs Baker read every word of every one of them. It was like she was taking a crash course – Womanhood in 20 Lessons? – or using the mags to help her pass unnoticed among women who genuinely gave a damn.

To do her justice, Spam didn't really seem to *care* all that much but she had a job in an office and had realised quite soon after arriving from Planet Pam that other people, other women anyway, cared a surprising amount. And you really did have to memorise all the ridiculous codes because they'd know you for an outsider straight away if you didn't, like a Nazi spy not knowing the Cup Final from the Test Match. Make the mistake of thinking that an outfit could last years – the way a man's suits did – and some cat from Dispatch would say how she'd 'always liked you in it'.

The magazines made sure that her trousers were all the right width, that her shirt collar was tucked out (or in, or out), that her page boy (dyed a slightly brighter brown) was the right length and that her make-up was all as it should be, which just at the minute meant khaki eye shadow and rust lip gloss. Just before heading out she would spray herself with perfume like Dad attacking greenfly. The scent was the one that advertised itself as 'a fragrance as individual as you are' – everyone was wearing it.

'*Three* squirts behind each ear,' complained Baker to Bunty.

'Blimey. You wouldn't need dogs if she went missing.'

'*I* bloody would. Big snappy ones who haven't had any dinner.'

Spam had not been able to have children of her own – which was a great pity (as Bob's mother, Granny Baker, was so very fond of saying) but Bob Baker never reproached her with the fact that there was no Jeremy to take to test matches and cup finals, no Jeremy to unpack the train set fussily folded in flannel on that high shelf in the garage where his childless wife ought never, in theory, to have found it.

Baker was never going to be getting that train set. When she was a child her father's gifts had seemed designed as a corrective to all the Patsy propaganda: doll's pram, toy sewing machine, even a toy washing machine – but the teenage kit was bossier still. Last Christmas it had been a set of heated rollers (as good as telling you your hair didn't look very nice).

Spam usually played safe with a new dressing gown or a book token (all the Mandies *hated* book tokens – like your family didn't trust you with the cash) but this year a big brown box had appeared under the tree a week before Christmas. Oh joy, Baker had thought, what delights would *that* contain? A facial sauna? A light-up make-up mirror? But it was such a wonderful present that she was almost disappointed: a typewriter. Just what she had always wanted (only you couldn't actually say that: sounded phoney). 'That'll be useful,' said Dad, spoiling it. Dad had given her a travel iron. His presents for his wife were bossy too – he gave her a set of bathroom scales one year, bloody rude (she took them back and swapped them for the cookery kind).

The magazines had made her a keen mushroom-stuffer. She served them once when Bunty came over, and when Bunty got all South Ken and smart with her Spam said that life was too short not to cook the food you liked to eat which had rather impressed Bunty.

'She's almost groovy in her own funny, body-snatchy little way: dull but not daft.'

'Hates me,' scowled Baker.

She never actually said as much, obviously, but Baker could tell. She sometimes glimpsed the sharp fall of her stepmother's face on a Saturday night if Baker said she wasn't going out or caught her looking at her via the mirror over the fireplace, her back-to-front features unfamiliar, unreadable.

But she did have her moments. Baker almost suspected her of a sense of humour. Every few weeks or so she would bustle back from her Saturday shopping expeditions with a present for Baker, clothes mostly. Her father, clocking the price tag before he'd even registered the colour, would flash a brief smile of pleasure at his wife's generosity, give her waist a squeeze, then pat himself on the back for picking the perfect stepmother but the actual clothes were always hideous: a red tartan mohair cape? A patchwork denim trouser suit? Spam never minded taking things back but Baker was always made to try them on first, do a twirl. 'Well I think it looks nice,' Dad would invariably say. 'Nice to see you in something smart for a change.'

'Not to worry,' Spam would say. 'I've got the receipt.'

The replacement things were always perfectly fine – like the whole trying-on nonsense was just an elaborate wind-up. Still, Baker had to admit that the typewriter was inspired. Spam had shown her which fingers went where and with constant practice ('Haven't you got any homework, Amanda?') she was up to 30 words per minute – 'w.p.m'. All she needed now was the speedwriting course and she *cd bcm a scrtry & gt a gd jb* (or so the ads promised).

The letters page of that month's *Spare Rib* had been very anti-seccy: 'The abuse suffered by the average secretary is tremendous. Making cups of tea, sewing buttons on jackets, booking holidays for the man's family.' The writer had signed herself 'Yours in sisterhood, a discontented secretary, Warwickshire'. Silly moo. Didn't sound too bad: more fun than just typing all day; more fun than double Biology. And at least you got *paid* which was more than could be said for the support staff at *Spare Rib* by the sound of it. There was an ad in the back looking for someone to help with layouts: 'No pay, no luncheon vouchers but opportunity to work in a non-hierarchical, non-competitive women's environment'. Thanks a bunch, sisters.

The supplier of the *Spare Rib* subscription had only once telephoned her daughter. Once. Christmas Day two years ago – the same year she sent the speculum. Spam was curling butter – or possibly melon – and Dad was on his knees in the corner of the sitting room telling a never-ending rosary of fairy lights in search of a dud bulb, so the thirteen-year-old Baker had answered. The long-distance voice was much posher than she had imagined – very like Grandma's. She'd expected something more Janis Joplin after all this time, druggier somehow rather than pissed (it was four in the morning in Nassau). Baker had let her rabbit on: *Manda* darling this, *Manda* darling that, she must be *so tall*, on and *on* about how tall she must be until Baker spoke, another version of the same voice.

'I think you've got the wrong number. There's no one here of that name. No one.' She hung up.

'Was that Auntie Janet?'

'Wrong number.'

She hadn't rung again. Or if she had, Baker hadn't answered.

When Dad had finally finished shouting through the details of his meeting with Mrs Mostyn and demanding exactly when was she going to start pulling herself together and God knew he'd done his best, Baker left the study and tiptoed back to the garage to rescue the fallen photo.

The inquisitive young Baker had first found it in an old suitcase full of junk that had been stowed inside the roof void above the garage door. There was a bundle of solicitor's letters – 'The respondent consistently refused to assist in the running of the marital home despite the petitioner working a 50-hour week to provide for her'; 'In June 1961 the respondent spent the entire quarter's housekeeping money on paying a local firm to construct a "menstrual hut" in the petitioner's vegetable garden' – gripping stuff. At the back of the bundle were half a dozen short, carbon-copied letters on the solicitor's letterhead: 'Dear Madam, Our client, Robert Leonard Baker, requests that any further communication be conducted exclusively via this office and that all attempts at contact cease forthwith.'

Baker had once asked her father if there were any pictures of her mother and he'd said no there weren't and why did she want one but there were loads in the hidden suitcase: Patsy on a slab at Stonehenge, Patsy in her wedding dress, Patsy with a brand-new non-Jeremy propped awkwardly in her arms like a doll being made to hold something. She had been quite pretty in a wholemeal hippy-ish sort of way: big eyes, light hair like Baker's, nice and thin. The best snap showed her on her honeymoon between the legs of the Eiffel Tower gazing adoringly at a person on her left, a missing person because the other half was on the sideboard upstairs: Dad staring right into the lens, oblivious to the smiling face at his side, the torn edge masked by the silver frame.

Baker retrieved the dartboard picture from where it had fallen and tucked it back in its hiding place. Older than any of the other snaps, it showed her father looking young, tanned, slightly cocksure, as if he had just got the photographer to laugh at some stupid joke. Not bad-looking really – if it weren't for all the little holes in his face.

Chapter 3

Bryony and Co. were whispering by the coat pegs again the next morning as they rolled their hand-knitted sports socks down to the ankle bone. There was a fashion for this – *fashion?* Mary Quant quaking in her boots. One of them had a magazine – some retarded girly thing – and there was a picture of a sissy-looking singer with feathered hair. He was actually quite dishy but Baker and the Mandies would rather die than say so. Bryony kissed the page then rolled up the forbidden comic and fed it into the dangling sleeve of her blazer. Another one of those accusing looks at Baker (as if she'd want the stupid rotten thing).

A herd of girls was storming up the cloakroom steps but their stampede was checked by a breathless fair-headed figure who charged through the group waving a sopping scarlet umbrella.

'Baker? Where are you, you slag?'

'Bunty? Oh, thank God you're back. Where the bloody hell have you *been*?'

'Squitters. Practically death's door. Hardly left the loo in three days: *nass-ty*. And all those loo books: *Pick* of *Punch*? What can the rest of it be like?'

Bunty's shoes flew to the far corners of the cloakroom as she kicked them off and two stray fourth formers scurried like puppies to retrieve them, picking up skirt, shirt and jumper as they fell.

'Thanks, doll. Really don't worry. They'll be fine on the floor.' But they picked them up anyway. It was a gift she had, like remembering birthdays and always keeping track of what your parents last said.

The lace on Baker's tennis shoe snapped as she tied it so she rummaged in her bag for her black plimsolls – same difference surely.

'How did it go last night?'

'*Car*-nage. The Mostyn told him about the front lawn and asked for another forty-seven offences to be taken into consideration, so I'm not allowed any telly and he's confiscated my make-up bag for some bizarre reason.'

'He'll have forgotten by Thursday. They always do. Mummy says if I don't pass the mocks I'll have to drop RE and Chemistry. Suits me, but the old man went ape. Money down the drain, old-old story. Meanwhile, *much* more importantly: did the wicked queen finally flog the piano?'

'Didn't dare. Came bloody close on Saturday though. Had three people phone up about the ad, but Dad put his foot down so Spam had to ring them all up and pretend one of the others had beaten them to it. She's not best pleased.'

The piano was a *bête noire* for Baker's stepmother. The brilliant white instrument had been bought for Baker at vast, unasked expense from a Bond Street showroom. Baker and Pam had both wanted the ebonised lacquer but that was before Dad's padification of the front room: orange raw silk lampshades, pearl grey emulsion, a solitary panel of William Morris wallpaper (just the one wall: like they'd run out of money halfway) and a trio of onyx boxes: tipped; untipped; extra strong mints. The piano was stuck there like a great big musical freezer, sheet music ('Imagine', 'The

Entertainer') strewn casually across the lid. Not that Dad played the sodding thing, and now neither did Baker. She could play by ear well enough, and was always surprised at how easily her fingers could pinch out the sketch of a melody, but 'Für Elise' was a very different story.

'Liberace she's not,' said Dad when she first played it. Supposed to be funny.

'You won't be safe until it's out of the house,' warned Bunty, 'mark my words. Some busybody at work will recommend a Mr Whatifski "who's made *such* a difference to young Melanie's fingering",' Bunty made a circle with finger and thumb and waggled her hand lewdly up and down 'and that'll be that. "Harder, Amanda! Faster! More *eggs-pression*!" Every Tuesday afternoon till you leave home – or shoot him.'

Bunty had got her kit on – all bar the socks, 'too bloody cold for socks' – and was rifling through the five pockets of her blazer in a panic.

'Bugger. Got any fags? Oh, thank God. Got a nasty, *nass-ty* feeling mine are on the dressing table. Mummy will be pleased. Oh well, lung leaflets here we come: lovely, lovely lung leaflets. I could paper a bloody house with lung leaflets. Be quite nice in a way . . .' She mimed the pattern repeat with the palm of her hand. 'Or beagles smoking – or beagles' lungs . . .'

She smiled at Baker and Baker beamed happily back. Not especially pretty – or so Bryony and that lot always decreed when they were doing their 'marks out of ten' thing. Looks was their main category – 'pretty' all the way down to 'nice personality' (consolation prize in life's lottery) but if you didn't rate as 'pretty' there was always 'interesting bone structure'. 'Wossat mean?' Bunty had demanded when she heard this. 'Like Quasimodo or something? Bloody cheek.' After looks came the rest of the marking scheme: dress sense; sense of humour; technical merit;

artistic impression; sustained tempo; and God knows what. Bryony had given Bunty's looks a grudging seven. Deep-set blue eyes (piss-holes in the snow, Bunty said), ratty hair still half-brown, half-blonde from her family's expensive winter holidays and unstraightened teeth. One of the front ones was slightly whiter and fatter than the others where her big brother Dominic had smashed her face with a cricket ball but it didn't detract from her appearance because it simply made you conscious of how very often she was smiling.

So, not especially pretty, maybe, but definitely *attractive*. Even Bryony conceded that – couldn't not: the evidence was inescapable. Bunty had *meaningful relationships*: boyfriends, several boyfriends, boyfriends with *cars*, *older* boyfriends who took her for dinner in trendy Chelsea hamburger places, gave her LPs or bottles of duty free scent. One had even bought her a camera.

'I rang loads of times. Did you not get a message?'

Bunty re-twanged the elastic on her ponytail while looking past Baker via the cloakroom mirror.

'Not a peep, but then Mummy's not a huge fan, let's face it.'

'Said you were out with "a friend" on Saturday. Anyone I know? And you can't have been at death's door if you were out. I thought you said you were ill.'

Bunty looked thrown then seemed to remember not to, a funny, keeping-a-straight-face look in her eye, the look she used when Mummy was being told lies about trips to the cinema or when homework had been left on the bus. Stupid lies for stupid people, not Baker.

Bunty's lips wriggled into a saucy grin.

'Only old whatsisface.'

'Anywhere nice?'

'We had lunch at some Italian dive near Harrods then he drove me back to his place.' Her voice lowered to a whisper, confiding suddenly – almost in spite of herself. 'His flatmate was *away* for the weekend.'

Baker made her eyebrows waggle up and down and waited for Bunty to answer her unspoken question, edging slightly closer so that Bryony, still over by her peg pretending to re-tie her shoelaces, wouldn't hear, but Bunty didn't elaborate, just pouted in a 'wouldn't you like to know?' sort of way and fiddled some more with her elastic. Baker so wanted to be cool but curiosity was building up inside her, like trying to hold your breath for three minutes under water and the whispered questions burst out before she could help herself: *did you let him, what did he say, will I like it?* But instead of answering – or even promising to tell all at break – Bunty carried on pulling at her ponytail.

'Come on. Stop playing hard to get, you silly moo.'

'I don't have to tell you everything. Besides, bit *tacky*. Nick asked me whether I would – obviously assumed I'd go gushing to the whole hockey eleven first chance I got and I said no, actually, I wouldn't and he thought that was quite mature actually.'

She looked back to the mirror, twisting her hair into a bun and skewering it in place with a hard-bitten HB pencil.

'Bunty!' there was the threat of tears in Baker's voice. Bryony was still lurking by the coats, obviously relishing the row even if she couldn't catch the words themselves.

'Nick calls me *Amanda* . . .' She turned to Baker. 'Get your own dirty stories.' And flounced from the room.

'Lovers' tiff?' sneered Bryony.

The cloakroom chatter dimmed as a big, cross prefect's voice boomed into the room. She was wearing her blazer over what were said to be her own clothes (a sixth-form privilege): grey serge skirt, grey tank top, white blouse – like a black and white photo of her fifth-form self.

'Get a move on, you lot.' She glared at Baker. 'Might have known *you'd* still be here.' Only seventeen but she wasn't a girl any more. She'd caught the tone of voice perfectly, like a toddler in a playgroup home corner moaning about mess in fluent mummyspeak. 'Pull your socks up. You're going to be late for Registration. Do me five hundred lines by Thursday: "I will not be late for Registration".'

'But we *will* be late for Registration,' countered Baker, happy to have any row that would jar her out of her shocked state. 'You just said.'

'Seven hundred lines. One More Word and I'll make it a thousand.'

'Make it two thousand. Enjoy yourself. Keep the change.' Baker looked archly up at her. 'Go on. I *dare* you.'

Always a lovely moment. Like a hand of poker in a film. The prefect longing to throw her weight about but knowing that she'd reached maximum what with Mocks coming up. Next week maybe, the Baker girl had been asking for it . . .

'I'm watching you. We all are.'

Stottie had finally tracked down the precious Maths master and was copying zeros and ones onto a sheet of graph paper. Once upon a time Amanda Stott had been rather good at Maths (she'd got her scholarship for being the only ten-year-old in the exam room who could multiply fractions), but she had wrestled in vain with the matrix business. Her mum hadn't left off about last night's bad report and was demanding to be told every grade from now on. The Maths monitor was grumpily gathering the last few sheets of prep.

'Come on, Stott. I've got to get this lot downstairs.'

Stottie crossed out one of the mysterious numbers and inserted a neat figure seven in its place.

'Can't have it *too* perfect or she'll smell a rat.'

'She'll smell a bloody rat anyway, you silly moo,' insisted Queenie, looking over her shoulder. 'You can't have *sevens* in matrices.'

'You can't? Why can't you? Is it just sevens? Can you have eights?'

'I don't *know*. You just can't. Or maybe you can but not in this prep you can't and if she finds out you're playing silly buggers then she'll twig it was copied and that'll knacker it for the rest of us. Cross it out again; put a one instead. One's safe – or zero. Zero's always good; they like zero.'

Stottie smiled gratefully at her friend and scribbled another 'O' into the inky mess: noughts and crosses played by a dangerous lunatic.

Baker spotted Bunty at the far end of the room but pretended she hadn't seen her. Strolling across to the classroom blackboard, she was about to pull a tissue from her pocket in order to update the chalk count in the corner (eighteen days to go till the end of term) when she spotted that their form mistress, Mrs Lorimer, a practical-minded woman, had brought in an off-cut of knitted dishcloth to wipe the board with since the real thing had disappeared. That was her little game, was it? Baker picked up the dusty white rag and dropped it down the back of the bookcase en route to her locker. The original felt brick thingy was still hibernating beneath a pile of dead leaves directly under the classroom window. Astonishing the amount of nuisance you could create with the simplest act of sabotage: the hunt under desks, the search for tissues, the selection of a volunteer to go next door ('Sorry, Mrs Rathbone, but Mrs Lorimer says can we borrow your board rubber?'). Hours of fun.

Amanda McQueen had, entirely against her will, been designated classroom noticeboard monitor and was standing on a desk posing menacingly with a staple gun like a lost Bond girl. The class next door had a trendy-looking collage of sunsets culled from back numbers of the *National Geographic*. Queenie's current display was composed of pages torn from the London A–D telephone directory with 'Call me' scrawled across the lot with one of her mother's old red lipsticks. Downright embarrassing, or so Mrs Lorimer felt as she made her way to the front desk and frowned for the hundredth time at the solitary blue carpet tile set in the otherwise grey floor. The room directly above had blue but none of their floor tiles was missing when she went to look (none you could see, anyway: Bunty had taken enormous care to pinch one from underneath the corner lockers). The form mistress looked up and noticed yet another drawing pin in the ceiling: a good twelve feet away. How did they *do* that?

'Amanda!'

Mrs Lorimer let out a wincing 'tut' as she remembered too late that all four heads would turn. Odd the way girls' Christian names washed in and out of fashion. Three of her grandmother's five brothers had married Dorothies: Dot; Dot; Dot.

'Amanda Baker. I daresay your father has spoken to you about yesterday evening?'

And Baker placed a bet with herself that she'd say 'new leaf' and she did. Good as gold.

Bryony and Vicky and Patricia were all admiring a centrefold inside Bryony's locker – same singer, different picture (different denim shirt, anyway).

'Excuse me, lads,' said Baker, squirming past the metal locker door. 'Oozat then, Brian?'

Brian. Tee hee. But it was their own fault really. Samantha started it – her and 'call-me-Jo' Josephine. As if you could just choose your own nickname. Well two could play at that game. And now the whole lot of them had a boy's name: Paddy, George,

Brian, Vic. All except Natasha. Natasha could easily have been 'Nat' but she wasn't. Natasha had only arrived a year ago, just after the Christmas holidays. She had been at some swanky 'international school' in Brussels or Bruges or Belgium or somewhere and had breezed in on her first day very, very full of herself, face and hands dry-roasted by a radioactive ski tan.

'I'm Natasha – Natasha Baldwin,' she gushed, 'but you can call me Stash.'

Except no one did of course. Bunty christened her 'Tash' and it stuck (what with the dark hair and everything).

The assembly hall was already nearly full as Baker and Bunty took the seats that Queenie and Stott had run ahead to save for them, only they had to budge up and let Baker sit at the other end of the foursome, as far away from Bunty as she could get. There were still two empty rows in front of them, thanks to an extended lecture being given by Mrs Rathbone to her half of the Lower Fourth on the importance of punctuality in later life.

That was one of the Rathbone's running gags, that codswallop about 'preparation for later life', the idea that this artificial planet they'd created, with its nutty rewards and punishments, with its poxy little pecking orders and traditions was some sort of model village version of the world beyond its chain-link fencing. The idea that once you let yourself yield to the joys of Mildred Fawcett, let her into your life like Jesus in gown and kick-pleated tweeds, you could be re-made as a separate species, *femina Fawcettiana*, merely by being banged up in the same institution for seven years. Did Holloway make the same boast?

Mildred Fawcett had begun in 1900 as a far smaller school, but had grown steadily from the original thirty pioneers. After the war, when more and more girls were demanding to stay on for their Higher Certificate, the trustees had decided that the old junior and senior schools should be split into three sections, but to this day not one of the staff had tumbled to the fact that every boys' school in the district knew their precious sixth form as 'Fawcett Upper'.

The assembly hall was lined with oak panels – Dr O'Brien's 'Wall of Glory' – prefects, captains of games, the odd scholarship. Nothing later than 1952, mind you (when the space ran out). Were they even real, these Sidebottoms, Trubshaws and Pratts? They made them up, surely? Or had they just bought a job-lot of sign writer's samples? *Scrote*? That was just being silly.

Lower Four R were finally clacking across the parquet, a blur of blues. All those different materials – serge, Courtelle, botany wool, nylon, flannel, not to mention the many, many different vintages (and wash temperatures) – meant that there were a dozen shades of Fawcett blue: matchbox; spaghetti wrapper; salt bag; Rothman packet. Not forgetting knicker – and bruise.

The miniskirt, still all the rage when Baker started in '70, had resulted in a diktat that all hemlines should be one inch from the floor when you knelt down but it was a tricky bugger to enforce: 'On your knees, Upper Threes!' – not really how the goons saw themselves. Fashion had now swung the other way which made a sizeable fraction of the second year very groovy indeed as their entire kit was several sizes too big – 'Mummy says I'll grow into it'. Mummy bloody well hoped not, actually, but it lasted longer and Mummy secretly preferred the shapeless silhouette and had an inbuilt horror of seeing her daughter's perfect young shape in anything too obviously form-fitting. Mummy pined for the days of bust-binding and the Liberty bodice and was ready to thank heaven fasting for the six-month craze for thick black tights and granny boots.

One sure-fire way to wind everyone up was to wear everything much too small. Queenie, a veteran of the prep department (alias Fawcett Under), was still skinny enough to fit into her original blazer, a saucy little bum-freezer in faded blue flannel which she had grown into and out of since her mother first bought it when she was seven. The goons, who spent more time and energy belly-aching about hemlines and hairstyles than they did on *Macbeth* or matrices or petty larceny, were horribly torn about this. Making do and mending had stained their thinking like beetroot on a powdered egg omelette, but it drove them all good and mad just the same.

The alternative strategy was to get everything in the largest possible size: growing into things was never an exact science, after all, and large was very very large indeed – it had to be. Every form had one – a walrus in blue serge wearing sizes you normally expected to see being pulled out proudly by slimmers of the year in mumsy magazines at the dentist. *Glands*, they usually said, or *big bones*. How big? There was a skeleton in the Biology lab and it was hard to picture it inside Rosemary McReadie. That neat, bleached pelvis would be lost underneath those forty-six-inch hips ('death helped me shed twelve stone').

Brian and the lads preferred to wear everything on the small side: skirts on the short side, shoes on the high side, purse-belts pulled unlunchably tight, in hopes that wolves would whistle at them. But nothing too rebellious, nothing detention-worthy and all very much as per The List which was pinned inside the special glazed noticeboard on the wall of the entrance lobby along with the names of governors and where to muster should the whole putrid place go up in flames. The List told you where to buy it, how many to get, which styles were acceptable, but it was quite an old list because it still had 'gymslips' as an option.

The only shop in England authorised to sell the uniquely terri-ble outfit worn by the girls of Mildred Fawcett didn't find there was much call for gymslips and finally stopped stocking them in 1969 (stopped stocking stockings too), but they were still on the blessed List and the local Oxfam shop had them: only 20p; irresistible; one step closer to the St Trinian ideal.

Baker's stepmother hadn't minded the gymslips – pleasantly traditional; safely girlish; undeniably practical – and she said as much in her reply to Mrs Mostyn's letter which had heavily hinted that a skirt be bought.

It had been two years now since anyone had worn a hat but, like gymslips, they still featured on The List: felt in winter; straw in summer; which was fine if Daddy drove you in but an incitement to riot on the top of a local bus and the School Council vote against had been unanimous. Mildred Fawcett MBE, would be turning in her grave.

The current head (Desiree Mary O'Brien MA Oxon, PhD Lon) generally excused herself Tuesday assemblies. The excuses varied but whatever it was – important calls, pressing matters, *other business* (a cigarette by the open study window) – appeared to involve a great deal of strong tea and shortcake biscuits. Proceedings were directed instead by the dreaded Mostyn, Snog Monster and all round graffiti-magnet. This morning the deputy head was a vision in violet Crimplene beneath a crumpled nylon wig.

'Looks *zackly* like Ted Heath in drag.'

Baker and Stottie had begun a silent game, safe in the knowledge that Miss Gleet would never dare pull them up for it. 'Talking in assembly' was a recognised crime but 'playing Scissors Stone Paper' definitely wasn't. Braver souls than Miss Gleet had been known to go for 'mucking about' but it still looked pretty bloody feeble spelled out on the printed pink detention form.

They carried on with the game. Baker could see the slightly alarmed look on the mistress's face as, count after count, their two hands made identical shapes – until it dawned on the silly cow that the three shapes were coming round in order: stone, paper, scissors, stone . . .

Baker altered her strategy: scissors, scissors, scissors, scissors, to leave her mind free to wonder what the hell Bunty was playing at, while Stottie alternated stone and paper and the Mostyn got stuck into one of her god-awful readings.

Dr O'Brien usually liked to rustle up her morality tales from scratch, using raw ingredients from the *Daily Telegraph*. Not the juicy bits – like the story about the jilted lover who posted baby rats through the letterbox while her rival was away on the Norfolk Broads for three weeks. Nothing fruity. Just common-or-garden tales of polio victims playing the oboe.

Mrs Mostyn preferred the ready-made musings to be found in *Gladsome Minds*, a slim green volume packed with convenience food for schoolgirl thought, homely homilies that could be relied upon to bridge the gap between *Non Nobis Domine* and the netball results. There was a moral – there always was – to Mrs Mostyn's dismal stories: pride being skin deep or beauty going before a fall. Some rubbish.

The first hymn was 'I Vow to Thee', omitting the slightly belligerent second verse. Mrs Mostyn still missed the bone-buzzing hum of the organ (out of commission since Founder's Day 1969). Even with the pedal down the baby grand was simply no match for copper-bottomed hymns like 'Jerusalem' or 'Those in Peril'.

The Mostyn's next task was to announce that a first year called Mary Field had been chosen to represent Surrey in a chess competition and as a result the staff room had voted to award her a blue enamel badge with 'School' printed on it. Surprised applause in the first year ranks. Young Miss Field hadn't breathed a word about her chess habit, fearing (rightly) that it wouldn't play well with the Upper Third. But a 'School' badge? Nice one.

Mrs Mostyn handed the prize over with her left hand while crushing the girl's metacarpals with her right. Blue was the first rung of merit badging. Green came next, then red, then yellow, then, finally, white – but no one ever got white, just as no one was ever given full marks for an English essay (always something to strive for). The entire school badge collection lived in a roll of green baize in a tambour-fronted cupboard in the school secretary's office, along with a whole card of virgin badges in various shades marked simply 'Leader', a stillborn brainchild of the head before last that had been voted down by the staff room. Rather a pity, thought Mrs Mostyn.

The founding headmistress had originally intended there to be only *one* white merit badge to be awarded in truly exceptional circumstances to the Fawcettian *par excellence*. There were in fact *two*, left over from 1949, a vintage year when the legendary Mallinson twins had been joint head of school, taking it in turns to welcome visitors with confident, painstakingly-elocuted votes of thanks. At least, Mrs Mostyn paused in her happy daydream, one *assumed* they were taking it in turns ... they were identical, after all. Identical in *most* respects, at least (only *one* of them got into Cambridge). One never knew, twins did lark about so ... Mrs Mostyn had yearned for a twin: the *fun* one could have had.

Yellow merit badges were slightly easier to come by but there were still only four of them in circulation at any one time like Orders of Merit or Companions of Honour or Garters. Someone had to leave the school or die or elope with their orthodontist (in the infamous 1962 case) for a Yellow to become available.

Mary Field's chess gong would normally have been it for school news. There had been a happy time when the names of those in detention were read out to shocked silence, a real black cap moment: 'The following girls ...' but Dr O'Brien's arrival had put an end to the practice on the grounds that the additional humiliation was 'unnecessary and inhumane' (or so she put it at the policy meeting). But she too had probably seen the smirks and heard the admiring giggles as the same naughty names were recited week after week, heroines of the wrong sort of school story.

O'Brien's unwillingness to draw attention to the undesirable element meant that Mrs Mostyn wasn't able to give her next announcement the weight it deserved, but the assembled girls sensed at once that something significant had occurred. Eliza Warner was to be head of Nightingale House with immediate effect. There was a puzzled burst of applause as the captain badge was handed over and Eliza (who had been sitting in the second row of prefects) now took the empty seat alonside the Head in the first. The seat where Alison Hutchinson usually sat.

'What happened there?' whispered Baker.

Stottie shrugged her shoulders. A hushed hum filled the hall as the girls puzzled over the substitution.

'*Silence*! Well done, Eliza. I'm sure that *you*' (the tiniest telltale emphasis) 'will be a fine example to the younger girls. So important.'

Mrs Mostyn preferred not to read out the sports news herself: always a lowering change of tone after *Gladsome Minds*, she felt, and in any case it was good public speaking practice for the sixth form. Today's results had been delegated to the school's games captain and Julia Smith, now seventeen and darling of the Lower Sixth, was standing alongside the Mostyn, waiting to divulge. She would have scored quite high on the Bryony Scale, noted Baker: tall and slim with that wavy auburn hair and perfect white teeth – but 'dress' would have let her down. Ever since her triumph in the tennis tournament she seemed to be forever playing or refereeing or coaching or cheering on some game or other, tricked out in a sort of mongrel kit. This morning it was a divided skirt, leotard and hockey boots finished off with her grandmother's old Fawcett cricket sweater, a hangover from the pioneering 1920s when all sports were fair game and the domestic science kitchen was a carpentry workshop.

'She wants a cravat with that,' hissed Stottie as she sized up the ensemble, 'or spats.'

Over the sweater Julia wore a fashionably junior-sized blazer, heavy with its six-year crop of enamel: tennis (natch), deportment, netball, a yellow 'School' badge and *all four* personal survival medals which proved that she could, if required, retrieve bricks from deep water or make a rudimentary float from a pair of Winceyette pyjamas – so likely. As the orderly queue for lifeboats formed on the promenade deck to the sound of 'Nearer My God To Thee' and the steady scrape of deckchairs being rearranged, there Julia would be in the icy North Atlantic, personally surviving on a balloon of stripy brushed cotton.

The lower school inter-house netball semi-finals had been won by Fry and Stanhope (Curie and Nightingale being rubbish at team games). The head girl, in pride of place at Mrs Mostyn's right, tried her best not to cheer too keenly because the head girl was also head of Fry House. This development had been unforeseen and did not, technically, contravene the Fawcett Code but it had smelled a lot like pluralism to Queenie: 'Or do I mean nepotism?' she asked when the double promotion was announced. 'One of those. *Greedy*, either way. Head girl *and* house captain? She'll be invading Poland next.'

Fry and Stanhope. Who the hell was Stanhope, anyway? Baker had once put a motion to the School Council suggesting an update of the house names. Her cousin's school had houses named after the conquerors of Everest said Baker, face suspiciously straight. Mrs Mostyn, who had been the presiding member of staff at the meeting, pointed out that Mildred Fawcett, who christened the original houses in 1900, wanted specifically to celebrate (Mrs Mostyn could no more split an infinitive than dangle a participle) *specifically* to celebrate *feminine* achievement. Fair enough, conceded Baker, but could they not celebrate something a bit more up-to-date: like four great women composers, say, or artists? Mrs Mostyn had looked at the girl very sharply. What a ghastly little smart-aleck she was. Was she being facetious? Surely not, but Baker's proposal had kept her awake that night just the same. She managed the four artists eventually (just do-able if one allowed sculpture and included Kate Greenaway and Beatrix Potter) but *composers*? Not possible.

Julia still held the floor. The previous afternoon's league match had been against St Ursula's who had made mincemeat of the home side. Julia Smith might have finessed the odd tennis trophy but Mildred Fawcett had never really been an especially sporty school. The small suburban site had only space for three courts, hockey was a twenty-minute hike away and the results were invariably 'disappointing'. Julia certainly looked disappointed. Stephanie Stott and the Under 13s had 'done their best' but they had been trounced 14–1 by the superior fire power of the local convent. The fourth form sat on its hands and there was even some booing from the fifth (like Guernseys in a far-off field) but there wasn't a peep of complaint from the goons: a blind eye; a deaf ear. The girls needed an outlet and it might, God knows, put a bit of heat under the Under 13s. Very *Unschool*, of course, not to clap, but no more than the eleven little slackers deserved. You could tell Julia thought so, as she grinned approvingly at the front row of the gallery.

'But the good news,' Julia raised her slightly husky voice, immediately stilling the outbreak of chatter, 'is that Penny Drummond of Lower 5P has been picked to join the Surrey Under 16 ladies fencing team.'

Frabjous abandon in the ranks, even though Penny Drummond's skill with a foil owed bugger all to Mildred Fawcett and a very great deal to her long-suffering father's willingness to spend his weekends driving to tournaments in draughty sports halls in places like Leicester and Ashton-under-Lyne.

On and on it went. Out of the corner of her eye Baker could see Bunty stroking purposefully at the ladder on her knee, coaxing it down her calf. Bunty's legs were nine out of ten (always something to strive for).

'Very well done, Penny. Everybody,' smirked Julia 'didn't she do well? Hip-hip?'

'Ra-a-a-y!'

'You can do better than that!' Like some tosser in a pantomime. 'Still can't hear you!'

Baker looked along the cheering row: schoolgirl complexions livid with spots, crooked teeth reined in by the sinister glint of their braces, crooked hair held in check by clips and slides and loops of elastic. A chemist's shop aroma of (permitted) cough sweets and Victory Vs and Fisherman's Friends. The proles in the very front row were wetting their little selves: shouting louder to please Julia. Young Steve Stott's face was almost bruising with strain.

'Hip-hip?'

'R-a-a-a-a-ay!'

And Julia was smiling now – her mouth was, anyway. Baker watched the older girl scanning the rows of screaming blue murder, then suddenly Baker caught her eye and Julia seemed to pause mid-grin and one sleek auburn eyebrow arched higher than the other. The practised move made her look smugger than ever. Baker pictured pinning the pale, pretty Julia to the garage dartboard, taking aim again and again and again, arrows sprouting from all over her stupid face. Treble twenty would be right between those unsmiling blue eyes.

Mrs Mostyn was also watching Julia from behind her upswept spectacles while pretending to straighten the skinny ribbon bookmark in her hymnbook, marvelling at the girl's unteachable gift for bending a crowd to her will. Look at them all: had them in the palm of her hand, *eating* out of it.

When the storm had passed, the Mostyn rose effortfully to her feet. She closed her eyes and there was the hint of a chant in her lah-di-dah tones as she gave her godless recitation of a prayer selected from her other book, a brown one: leader snot; witch art; usual stuff. And Baker watched as Brian and the chaps made signs of crosses over their navy V-necks. They weren't Catholic or anything – wouldn't be in the hall if they were. Catholics bothered God in their own mysterious way Tuesdays and Thursdays in the first floor music room. Jews Mondays and Fridays. Jews. Were there hymns for Jews? wondered Baker. And if not, why not? There were all-purpose hymns surely? They weren't *all* stood up, stood up for Jesus. And the God was supposed to be the same. Were angels kosher? The Old Testament had angels. Baker turned to ask Bunty but then remembered that she wasn't speaking to her.

There was a special board for house notices outside the assembly hall and Eliza Warner's name was already in place on the list.

'What happened to whatshername?'

'Stole an eye shadow from Woolworths or something, so my little friend Bryony tells me,' murmured Queenie. 'Suspended for the remainder of the term pending a governors' meeting, so Eliza gets promoted.'

'Which reminds me,' said Baker, 'I found a use for that bogus badge.'

Baker had been to a church jumble sale a few weekends earlier and while rootling in a box of dead men's buttons had unearthed a whole blazer's worth of random school badges, King's Manor by the look of them (nowhere else offered lacrosse). Baker was wearing 'Lacrosse' herself but the treasured white 'School' badge deserved a better home and where better than the head girl's lapel?

'It's still there. She's got so many she hasn't even noticed. Left her blazer on a bench yesterday and I seized my moment: there was just space under "Hockey".'

Chapter 4

The rest of the form had charged out of the hall towards the rain-glazed exercise yard but Baker dawdled in the lobby, putting off the horror that was Tuesday morning games. Games. Games used to mean quoits and hoops and bean bags covered in brightly coloured burlap. Fun and games, *proper* games and Sports Day. Baker cuddled the memory. A whole field alive with chatty six-year-olds in vests (summer ones) and navy knickers, running up and down holding spoons with eggs in them. One mad, marvellous year lovely, clever Miss Gatsby who was new and wore flick-ups and lovely green glass beads and who always gave the winner a big, soft freesia-scented hug had combined the dressing-up and three-legged races so that the finishing line of small girls in outsize tea gowns and vast picture hats looked like a drunken vicarage garden party.

Races over, it would be time to wriggle back into a dozen different red ginghams in a hundred different dress patterns and tidy all the different hairstyles: braids and bunches and tails – low ponytails, high ponytails, *side* ponytails – and those of the little coloured twins whose heads were ploughed and scattered with fuzzy-felted fields, a plaited scarecrow on duty in the centre of each square.

Ribbons re-tied, buttons buttoned and they would all flock round the trestle tables spread with beakers of fluorescent orange squash and paper plates of unfamiliar biscuits (the kind that said on the top how nice they were). And pretty doll's sandwiches – pink and white, yellow and white – the sliced bread so plump and soft that tiny fingers left dimples in the bright white dough, penny-sized munches missing from the discarded crusts.

Even netball was a game in those days but it was mortal combat now – especially the way Bryony and her lot played it. It wasn't a *sport* either, was it? Not really. You never saw netball on the telly, grown-ups didn't play it, there weren't clubs for it like golf or tennis. Nobody ever went on a netballing holiday – except possibly Miss Drumlin. Miss Drumlin was painfully keen on sport of all kinds and played lacrosse for Middlesex. At least the Mandies very much *wanted* it to be Middlesex (may actually have been Surrey but where was the fun in that?)

On a normal Tuesday, Miss Drumlin would pick her pets to be the four team leaders who would then pick *their* pets plus the straightest shooter and the tallest girl in the class – not necessarily in that order – before finally divvying up the lumpy, butter-fingered leftovers who'd have to take whatever position remained (wing defence was usually the last to go). But not everyone could play. Give or take a flu outbreak, there should (in theory) be four girls left over from a class of thirty-two: a Mandy-shaped four-some who could loiter on the sidelines and pretend to practise passing.

But first came PT. Ugly, jumpy, stretchy movements led by the ugly, jumpy, stretchy Miss Drumlin. The Drumlin had been delayed that morning by a prole with a nosebleed. There was no Fawcett matron. Instead the role was shared by Miss Drumlin and a scary ex-hockey international called Mrs Bremner who haunted the touchlines in a judo suit or (if wet) re-sorted the lost property cupboard armed with a gaily-striped Thermos traditionally believed to contain a fortifying blend of Horlicks and cherry brandy. Neither mistress had any patience whatever with any sort of ailment, be it headache, sore throat, growing pains or, in one nasty but mercifully not life-threatening case, scarlet fever ('Don't *fuss*, Melanie! It's just a heat rash!'). And Mrs Bremner gave painful periods very short shrift and kept elaborate note of the menstrual cycle of all regular sufferers. Cry off too often and she would consult her precious chart – '*Again*? So soon?' – and threaten letters home and internal examinations by the school doctor until the pain subsided and the poor hockeyphobe agreed that yes, do you know, yes, perhaps the aspirin had done the trick after all.

Julia Smith had been drafted in to deputise while the Drumlin dealt with the bleeding junior. She had hung her blazer on the chain-link fence and led them all in a round of star jumps, side bends and toe-touchings. Baker thumped a few jumps on the slippy tarmac, picturing all the bones of her feet – tarsals, metatarsals, malleus, incus, wossname – fanning out beneath her weight as she landed, then gathering themselves back together for the next spring. Clever old Bunty and Queenie had both pleaded asthma and Stottie was planning a painful period. All three had retreated to a spectators' bench in the gulley that ran alongside the netball court behind the chain-link fence and Baker stopped bouncing and joined them, making a point of sitting at the far end next to Queenie.

'My kid brother's kinky for basketball,' said Queenie. *Kin-ky*. Just the way she said it in her posh mummy's voice made you smile. 'We've even got a hoop in the garden. Right over the daffs. Car-nage.'

'Basketball?' marvelled Bunty. 'He must have shot up.'

'Naah. He's no taller. Just jumps a lot.'

Once her victims were red and sweaty enough, Julia let them get on with picking their teams while she retrieved her blazer and loped across to the shivering Mandies. She squatted down to be nearer their eye level and you could see the blue thread of her Tampax and a few stray pubes peeping out from the wash-faded six-year-old gusset of her regulation knickers: *gross*. Did she play games *before* she got the curse, or had 'becoming a woman' made her instantly fit for everything promised in the ads: disco dancing, fell walking, snorkelling?

'What's the story this time, you lot? It's always the same four of you, isn't it? Must be catching, whatever it is.' She addressed the group but it was Baker she was looking at: doing the eyebrow thing; daring her to answer back. 'You'll feel heaps warmer if you get moving.'

'Says you.'

'You're asking for trouble, Amanda Baker. I've got my eye on you.'

The prefect bounced easily to her feet and strode off towards the sixth-form common room, nodding to Miss Drumlin who had finally staunched the flow and was ready for action once more. The Mandies got up from their bench and began half-heartedly passing their leaden leather ball back and forth.

'Amanda!' The games mistress didn't bother to specify but Baker knew at once who she meant and turned to face her, cocking her right shoulder forward to show off the monogram, the tiniest smile fluttering across her face at having sidestepped another lecture but it seemed that Miss Drumlin was no longer concerned about embroidery.

'*Those are gym shoes.*'

Baker looked dumbly down at her black canvas feet.

'The lace broke on my others and I couldn't . . .'

Miss Drumlin was not interested in Amanda's feeble explanation and immediately launched into her usual moan about the vital importance of having the Right Kit. (*Vital?* It was only netball for Christ's sake, not a bid for the South Pole.)

The Drumlin droned on while Baker stood transfixed by the browning bloodstain on the front of the games mistress's shirt. It had seeped into the open weave like a giant version of the mark left on that little square of gauze you got inside a sticking plaster. Some nosebleed. Could you have projectile nosebleeds? Baker hoped so.

Miss Drumlin had raised her voice.

'Are you even listening to me? Anyone would think you actually *liked* getting into trouble.'

Baker, roused from her trance, glared back at her and the shocked look on her face – 'wooden insolence' was how Mrs Mostyn usually described it – caused Miss Drumlin to cut the wigging short and issue a red card instead: Amanda would go straight to Dr O'Brien and jolly well explain herself.

Baker heard someone else's voice begin to stammer with panic.

'Dr O'Brien? But I've got the right ones upstairs. I can run and get them.'

Miss Drumlin did not want to hear Amanda's pathetic excuses, Miss Drumlin was sick and tired of Amanda's deliberate disobedience and Miss Drumlin was very surprised that Amanda was still taking this attitude after everything that had been said to Mr Baker yesterday. Very surprised.

Baker lobbed the ball hard at Bunty and marched slowly round the edge of the court in the direction of the main building. She tried hard not to let the fear show, but the thought of the evening ahead was making her pipes freeze. There would be another icy plunge of the heart at half six as the parental key ground into the lock. Spam would hide upstairs again or find some reason to clear out the kitchen cupboards or pop to the corner for an evening paper or a block of ice cream and leave Dad to spell out his disappointment and contempt in that cold, speak-your-weight voice and dream up some more threats and promises: not allowed out; not allowed pocket money; not allowed television; not allowed to phone Bunty. Anything he could think of. All because of a snapped shoelace. As she bent her head into the breeze, she could see Spam's exquisite satin stitch lettering upside down on her chest, the capitals given three dimensions by two shades of blue silk. Must have taken a lot more than a minute but it was all a waste of time. It was plimsolls today. Probably hair tomorrow or fingernails or tights or shoe polish. The happiest days of your life? Please God no.

There was a traffic light thingy on the door jamb of Dr O'Brien's study but no light at all came on when Baker knocked. It was never especially reliable. Queenie, who had quick fingers and long, sharp nails, had once tweaked out the three coloured filters and swapped red and green over in the hope that prospective parents would open the study door and find the head sneaking a crafty fag or picking her nose or adjusting her 18-hour girdle. A pleasing thought. Baker knocked again: still no answer. Where was she? Off teaching? Out cold? Baker took a seat on the bench in the lobby and stared at the wrong shoes: stupid *fuss*, honestly.

The lobby was home to a dozen glazed notice cupboards. Not everyday bread-and-butter notices – teams, chess clubs, term dates, that kind of guff – but long-standing ones, yellowing typewritten things no one thought to look at any more. Which was a bit of a pity. Although each frame had a keyhole they were never actually locked. A compass point (or a Queenie fingernail) could open them easily and Baker's lovely new typewriter had the same sort of lettering.

School governors now included Dame Myra Hindley, Dr Harold Crippen, Sister Ruth Ellis (MA Cantab) and Magda

Goebbels. Once in a while a visiting parent at a loose end, too early for their ghastly get-to-know-you with the head, might double-take and chuckle but none had blown the whistle so far.

There was a copy of The Fawcett Code here too, but they had left this as it was – it was already a joke. In the next frame along, under 'News' were two cuttings from the local paper. One showed the cast of last year's *Importance of Being Earnest* taking a bow. The other was of a row of assorted females holding a large shield, and there on the end, in her dinky little skating skirt, was a slightly younger Bunty. Like the school had taught her to skate.

The main wall outside the head's study was hung with portraits of Dr O'Brien and the six previous incumbents: shingled, four-eyed frights in gowns and collars and ties, all looking like Eleanor Roosevelt with toothache, with perfectly round black spectacle frames over their beady eyes – as though the pictures had been vandalised. You half expected a Hitler moustache or two and a few blackened teeth. Had they even needed those creepy little John Lennon glasses, or did they just bung them on to look intellectual? All six were at their desks, all desperately trying to cultivate an air of brainy benevolence – hence the book at the elbow. A pipe might have helped.

Bunty always said that Miss Eileen Pinto MA Oxon (1928–1935) seemed the nicest. All the others looked as if they didn't take sugar. This was one of Bunty's yardsticks, the first question she'd asked about Spam – and one of the first points in Spam's favour.

Dr O'Brien's picture was at the far end: not a huge success. The artist was in regular demand for his ability to do impressions of impressionism without sacrificing the all-important Good Likeness, but the lurid pink of the gown that came with a London PhD (*Anglo Saxon Place Names in Pre-Conquest Charters for Kent*) had somehow infected the whole painting. There were fashionable dabs of green about the face but, with so much Permanent Rose on the palette, some of it had, inevitably, got into the cheeks, giving the subject a faintly gin-soaked look not helped by the water glass on the desk top. The eyes, hard black buttons of eyes stuck in the paint like coals in a snowman, followed you round the room.

Still no sign of the original. The bell rang for the next period and the stairs were filled with a thundering blue mass hurtling from room to room. They didn't look at Baker (not cool to stare) but Baker was ready to be looked at just in case: slumped against the wall, bored look in place, chewing invisible gum, betraying no sign of the sick fear inside.

Her father really really would kill her. Yeah yeah, it was only plimsolls, but he'd be sure to start anyway. Symptomatic, he'd say (a word he'd taken a fancy to lately), *symptomatic* of her whole *Att*-itude. She could already hear him saying it while he snipped her face out of photographs, could already see it typed in carbon on a nasty little solicitor's letter. Just as she could vividly imagine the O'Brien bitch mooing on about Last Straws and Baker's new 'contract' with the school, drawn up after the whole lawn fiasco.

They still hadn't got any proper proof that it was Baker who had smuggled in the squeezy bottle full of Domestos and doodled rude words across the headmistress's hallowed turf, but yesterday's little chat with Dad meant that everything would have to be just right from now on, shoes included, or she'd be expelled and then what? An awkward, career-wrecking glitch in her academic record, a nasty moment in job interviews ('What happened here, Miss Baker?') when they spotted the obvious step down from the glories of Fawcett Upper to one of the bottom-feeders of the educational stream. It was all very well Dad salivating over the glossy brochures, but none of the schools he lusted after would want her.

There *were* places that specialised in hoovering up trouble-makers (even bad girls had to go somewhere). Most of them probably just did it for the money, happy to overlook any number of unfortunate episodes if it meant plugging that embarrassing gap in their cash flow. Other places genuinely relished the challenge of a difficult pupil: new leaves in blotted copybooks. Schoolmistressing was nothing if not a means of showing how bad mistakes could be corrected: a practised blade down the stapled edge; a nifty dab of ink eradicator: good as new.

Queenie was one of the last to trickle by, feet heavy in her trendy shoes, a soft rattle from the mass of lovebeads on her wrists. After checking that the coast was clear, she ambled across to the staff pigeon-holes and began pulling piles of prep from their slots and filing them randomly on different shelves, ending with a sheaf of fourth form geography homework (*Explain the influence of climate on farming in either South West England* **or** *The Fens*) which she posted wholesale down the back of the unit.

'Any joy?'

'Not a peep so far.'

'Probbly asleep. Don't worry. They can't expel you just for plimsolls.'

'They won't need to. Dad's dying to send me to another school. Keeps going on about fresh starts. Another bloody prospectus came this morning. I was down early and I saw it on the mat. Said "Elm Hill" on the envelope, sounds like a loony bin.'

'Elm Hill?' A silent whistle from Queenie. 'He'll hate it: no uniform, lots of *Aaaart*. And besides, you can't leave Fawcetts, Bunty would pine.'

'Wanna bet?'

Queenie's questioning look went unanswered. Queenie would never understand.

'They always get wound up after parents' evenings. Mine were on about boarding school when they got back yesterday, but it never comes to anything. What did your stepmother have to say? Did she go as well?'

'Spam? Don't be daft. Just hides in the kitchen with the radio.'

Not strictly true, admitted Baker to herself as Queenie zipped back up the stairs. She'd brought Baker a hot chocolate after she'd gone up to her room: 'Cheer up, sausage. He really worries about you, you know.' But then Spam hadn't been in Dad's study for the speeches, hadn't seen the look on his face.

Just when she thought the last straggler had passed, Baker heard the springy, scuffing tread of tennis-shod feet coming up from the ground floor towards the lobby: Julia Smith.

'Down to see the Doc? You'll have a long wait. She's at a conference – at least that's what it says on the staff noticeboard. Miss Drumlin won't want you sitting here twiddling your thumbs. I'll see if I can dig her out.'

What business was it of hers? Interfering cow. Julia bounced off but, before she could return, the Snog Monster, Mrs Mostyn, emerged from the staff room. She didn't spot Baker at first and carried on talking over her shoulder as the door closed slowly behind her.

'Mark my words: Sir John and the other governors will want to take the firmest possible line, whatever she may like to think. I shall see to it personally.'

She stopped short as she turned the corner on her way to the pigeon-holes. What, pray, was Baker doing there?

Snog Monster. Legend had it that the nickname, older than anyone could remember, referred to an Ordnance Survey field trip to the New Forest or somewhere on which the Mostyn had been spotted in the waxed cotton arms of a National Trust ranger during a camp fire singsong. Can't have been true, thought Baker, looking at the old bag's Crimplene bulk. You could fit two skeletons inside that mass of flesh, *easy*. But the name had stuck. Even the first years used it.

Mrs Mostyn squinted, nonplussed, at the pigeon-hole that Queenie had emptied then turned tutting to Baker as she stammered out her story.

'In trouble again? I had rather hoped that your father would have had the chance to talk to you very seriously after the little chat we had yesterday evening. I don't think I have ever seen a parent so disappointed. In any case, you can't stay here all morning.' Powdery jowls dangling playfully over the top of the tie-necked blouse. 'Dr O'Brien has quite enough to do on her return without your plimsoll nonsense. Is this a free period? Come with me. You can do a detention right now in the Geography Room: plenty to do.'

Much as Baker abominated the Snog Monster, anything was better than O'Brien and a letter home. With any luck this summary detention from Mostyn wouldn't clock up a nasty little pink slip, so Dad needn't find out. And the actual detention itself would be worse if the Drumlin had any say in the matter because the Drumlin always found filthy physical things for you to do like washing tennis balls or whitening goalie pads or chipping Juicy Fruit off the bottoms of chairs.

Baker tailed after the Snog Monster to her lair. The box pleat beneath the baggy arse of her skirt flapped from side to side as her veiny great legs scuttled along the corridors, like the back end of an elephant on a nature programme. On she trundled, past the Music Room where first years were wrecking 'The Skye Boat Song' (one of the treats being lined up for Founder's Day) and past the Art Room whose masterpieces spilled out on to the noticeboards of the corridor outside. None of them was current, indeed most seemed to have been there since Baker and her father and Spam had come to that fateful open day when Dr O'Brien sold Dad on the idea of Fawcett and 'the rosy path of golden possibilities'. Nearly all of the art was signed 'Dora Hardcastle' who was clearly nothing if not versatile: portraits, landscapes, the odd abstract and a stomach-turning still life of a Bakewell tart and what the Mandies had agreed could only have been a Scotch egg (Bunty's favourite).

'I blame Cezanne,' sneered Queenie (whose mum dragged her round galleries every weekend while Daddy played golf).

'I blame Mrs Chiffley,' said Bunty. 'I'd know those Domestic Science leftovers anywhere.'

'Where is Bakewell?'

'Bakewell's *a place*? I thought it was just a cooking instruction.'

Mrs Mostyn shared the Geography Room with a Miss Combe. Miss Combe had only graduated in 1970 and was keen to bring all that she had learned to the classroom. Out had gone capital cities, map-drawing, imports, exports. In had come pebble formation, ox bow lakes, meanders, town planning and 'acid rain'. Miss Combe had her own cocoa bean, her own crumbs of bauxite and a special dinky apparatus to prove, after two weeks of drips, that rainwater would wear holes in limestone or similar – just in case the students thought she was making it all up, presumably. Far quicker simply to *tell* them, reflected Mrs Mostyn, or chalk it on the board, or give them a *sheet* about it.

Her keen young colleague, physical geographer to her unpainted fingertips, had mentioned with pride that the upper third in her last school could all parrot the chemical formula for sulphuric acid. Doubtless. But could any of them name three cities in West Germany? fretted the Snog Monster. Or say where pineapples came from? Or find Minsk? Mrs Mostyn liked her girls to have a good basic grounding in old-fashioned human geography – capital of Albania; neighbours of Switzerland; countries through which the Rhine flowed; uses of palm fibre, yam, that sort of thing – what Mrs Mostyn liked to think of as the *useful* sort of geography that enabled one to take an intelligent interest in people's holiday stories, or overseas postings.

Mrs Mostyn's pet detention was the never-ending business of updating the school's stock of atlases. Half of these dated from 1944, the other half 1955, and the world was not what it was. Dr O'Brien had very generously offered to replace them all – Miss Combe was mad keen – but Mrs Mostyn, who begrudged spending school money every bit as fiercely as she begrudged spending her own, had resisted: *unnecessary* expense; nothing that a few duplicated cut-outs or an extra-fine nib couldn't put right. Besides, new atlases would have meant New Geography and she was determined to hold out against this for as long as she possibly could. None of the scholastic publishers bothered with proper political maps any more, so it was by no means certain that the old copies would be replaced with anything suitable.

Miss Combe didn't seem to care for maps at all, or map-reading. Such a skill, such a pleasure, so *satisfying*. Mrs Mostyn mused miserably on the ignorance of Miss Combe's current Fawcett first formers. Not one, *not one* could read a real, grown-up map and the simpler one tried to make it, the worse it seemed to get. Only last week Mrs Mostyn had sketched a diagram of the Indian railway system and more than half of her upper thirds assumed there were no stations between Bombay and Madras just because she hadn't marked any. A 32-hour non-stop train journey? Dimwits. Made you wonder why they even bothered with an entrance examination – they'd let in anybody.

Mrs Mostyn opened the door to the Geography Room and showed Baker to a large desk already laid out with a stack of dog-eared old atlases and three trays filled with trimmed and coloured countries which were to be glued over any anachronisms. The Belgian Congo was Zaire now, Basutoland was Lesotho, Rio de Oro was Spanish Sahara, etc. The biggest change was French West Africa, which used to be a big bad blob of bottle green but was now a picaninny hairdo of a dozen little countries: more border controls; more wars; more capitals to learn.

Baker stared at the offending outline, as green and random as an English pasture – though much larger. Heaps larger. And should you be in any danger of forgetting how much larger, the publisher had included a scale map of the British Isles in the bottom outside corner of each page (although the double page spread of New South Wales had a scale map of old South Wales – some sort of cartographical joke).

Africa had undergone so many changes that on some pages the whole continent had to be papered over with the replacement that Mrs Mostyn had drawn and duplicated and which the upper thirds had cut out and coloured in using the poshest possible aquarelles which blended surprisingly well with the old coloured plates.

Baker picked up one of the atlases, took one of the new Africas, buttered it with the paste spreader and held it carefully above the page before dropping it in place, draping a blank sheet of paper over it and smoothing the whole lot down. Bye-bye Belgian Congo. Bye-bye Tanganyika. Odd how some borders were straight and others wiggly. Rivers? Rock formation? A drunken cartographer? They never told you stuff like that. And why didn't Ethiopia put up a fight when the French and Italians and Brits came and divvied up their whole coast into private Somalilands? And Lesotho and Swaziland, tiny pimples on the chin of South Africa. Barmy. Like granting political independence to Clapham Common.

Mrs Mostyn watched Baker stick down her first map (neater than expected) and returned to her marking: thirty-two second year exercise books containing labelled sketches. The previous week's homework, a cross-section of an oil refinery, had been an a la carte dog's breakfast of laziness and ineptitude, but they at least had the excuse that oil refineries were hard to draw. This week's, 'A Typical Home in Malawi' (née Nyasaland), was a simple enough assignment: a thatched roof of palm fibre shaped like a giant half coconut on top of a cylinder of wattle and daub. Only three labels and a drawing any toddler could do, yet nearly all of them contrived to make a mess of it. 'Use a ruler when labelling' wrote Mrs Mostyn's red pen for the eighth time. Was it, in fact, typical, this hairy brown igloo? wondered Mrs Mostyn to herself. Or did the modern Malawian live in a concrete bungalow and use their palm fibre for something else entirely? (it had many, many uses after all).

Baker was actually rather enjoying her punishment. Even the sticking-in business was quite satisfying, fiddly but not difficult. She had a funky little rhythm going: take Africa, butter Africa, position Africa, stick Africa: simple; automatic; mindless (in the sense that it left your mind free to go where it liked). Every duff bit of 'see me' C minus homework and they warned you that you might end up stacking shelves in Safeways or copy typing but how bad could it be? Probably quite nice.

She never really minded detention – better than lessons anyway. She had once spent a very pleasant lunchtime punish-ment removing graffiti from a batch of upper fourth French books. Someone had written 'POINTLESS' in enraged capitals down both margins of a spread on the proper use of the past historic but the verb rubbish was all still perfectly legible. Why did it need to be removed? *Pour encourager les autres*? Or because no one must ever know that the past historic had been invented by Rampton and White because there simply wasn't enough French grammar to fill a textbook otherwise. Baker hadn't been the first to set about those pages with the ink eradicator: there were bleachy blobs in the margin where other uncomfortable truths had been blotted out. French got off pretty lightly. A few of the other textbooks had been past saving, like the History primer where all the line drawings of historical figures had had their heads filled in with turquoise felt tip: Smurf Thomas Cranmer; Smurf Ignatius Loyola; Smurf Bloody Mary.

By the time the bell went for break Baker had edited twenty-three atlases. The Snog Monster seemed almost pleased.

'We'll worry about Ceylon another time,' she conceded, indulgently. 'And I hope that will teach you to wear the right shoes in future. Off you go now. I need to memo Miss Drumlin and I have to get your pink slip done for Dr O'Brien.' An almost nasty smile as she saw Baker's flinch of surprise: 'You didn't think you were going to get off that easily did you?'

Chapter 5

It had actually been a Miss Drumlin detention that brought the four Mandies together in the first place. Some row about name tapes had prompted her to keep the four first years behind, sorting lost property in the hockey hut one afternoon, and when they'd finally finished they had all scurried guiltily down the road to the out-of-bounds Victory Café. Bunty, who'd already eaten most of Baker's Cornish pasty at lunchtime, had scoffed an entire toasted sandwich and was on her second glass of Tizer when her face suddenly fell as she spotted the multi-chinned profile of Mrs Mostyn gliding past the station at the wheel of her little snot green Morris Minor and drawing to a halt just beyond the bus stop. She walked back to the café and stood on the other side of the glass and stared at them. It had reminded Baker of the zoo but she wasn't sure which of them was the animal.

Mrs Mostyn beckoned to them with a fur-lined hook of kid glove which then uncrooked and pointed to the car. Waving aside their buts and can'ts about violin lessons and trains to catch, she had driven them back to the now empty school. A trio of girls from a rival grammar who were draped against the record shop window had watched, laughing as she bundled them into the back and stuck up two fingers as the Morris pouted off up the hill.

Eating toasties in local cafés had never featured on the Fawcett not-to-do list but a staff meeting was hastily convened (Mrs Mostyn, Dr O'Brien and a passing Biology mistress who had stayed late to refresh the formaldehyde round the yellowing pickled baby). The three had decided that punishment of some kind was definitely in order and the offence was roughly translated into 'Unschool behaviour'. All four sets of parents had been telephoned to come and fetch their errant daughters. Mrs Stott and Mrs Bunter-Byng pitched up first and led their daughters to the school gate with wait-till-I-get-you-home faces, although new girl Bunty had seemed oddly relaxed for someone in so much trouble.

'Thought you'd be out getting Dominic.'

'Dress rehearsal.' Then a smile (a very small smile, like a coin left in the powder room) for Mrs Mostyn.

'*Hamlet*,' she explained.

Bunty had opened her mouth to add 'Gertrude' but a warning glance made her think twice.

Baker's dad had been out at a site inspection so Spam had come on the bus and the pair of them had been given a lift home by a very bad-tempered Mrs McQueen. There wasn't much chat, each woman mentally concluding that the other's child had been the ringleader. Mrs McQueen was driving very fast in order to get back to her afternoon card party.

'Do you play at all?'

Spam's face, reflected in the rear-view mirror, was being kept unnaturally straight.

'Poker? Used to, once upon a time.'

'Canasta. We get together most Mondays.'

Baker could see Queenie's mother sneaking glances at Spam, at the documents spilling from her bag, at the butch bunch of home and office keys in her hand as they pulled into the drive, saw her mentally crossing Mrs Baker off the list.

'*All four of you?*' Dad hadn't seemed sure whether that made Baker's first ever detention better or worse. 'What are their names, these new mates of yours?'

'Amanda.' He thought she was joking until Spam explained.

'I wanted Jane.' The strangest look on his face. 'Jane Margaret. My mother's names,' and retreated to his study without another word.

'Do you reckon she *knows* she's the Snog Monster?' Queenie was thoughtfully detaching slabs of chocolate from around a break-time Mars Bar with her front teeth.

'Probbly,' said Bunty. 'Somebody must have spilled that bean by now; it's been going on for years. Probbly flattered. There are worse nicknames. Fuckface is worse.' (Fuckface taught Physics.) 'Sheepshagger's much worse.' (The Australian domestic science teacher.)

'Hardly any point *having* a name,' concluded Baker. 'Only gets changed. My baby cousin was christened Kate: no Katherine, no middle name, no nonsense. Made no difference. Likes to be called Twinkle. *Twinkle.*'

'If I have a boy, I'm going to call him Bill,' said Bunty.

'Billy Bunter-Byng?' spat Queenie. 'Don't be bloody daft.'

'Yes but it won't be Bunter-Byng will it? I'll be Mrs Wotsit.'

'Mrs Charlton?' Baker hadn't meant to join in but she couldn't help herself. Nick Charlton. The man with the obliging flatmate.

Baker stuck her head round the corner of their playground hiding place to check for passing goons. A mistress and two prefects patrolled the perimeter fence all breaktime and every second or third circuit they were supposed to hike over to the bike shed (not all the way, just close enough to make them all stub their fags out).

The corrugated iron structure was hidden away at the far end of the yard, not exactly *convenient* for the (three) cyclists but then it had been something of an afterthought. Back when the school was first established the sainted Mildred had dreamed vaingloriously of a brave new world in which all of her girls motored to school or flew in personal gyrocopters (the founder was a big H.G. Wells fan). Even constructing something as prosaic as a bicycle shed had seemed a betrayal of the bright future promised.

Julia Smith was one of the prefects on duty (the bloody girl got everywhere). She was heading towards the Mandies' hideout but doubled back when she saw Baker's head poke round. Her orange ponytail swinging cheerily as she skipped back down the slope. A self-consciously sporty walk.

'Xerxes,' said Queenie. 'If I have a boy I'm definitely calling him Xerxes.'

'Boys have all the fun,' agreed Bunty.

'Or Atahualpa. And if it's a girl, I'm calling it Dido.'

'Dildo?'

'I want four girls,' decided Bunty.

'And wotcher gonna call them?'

'*Amanda*.'

Even Baker smiled.

'Yeah, but what if you get boys?'

'Four boys? No thanks. I shall leave them on a hillside like the Spartacuses. And I'm definitely not having a bloody Dominic. Did I tell you he's got a girlfriend? Mummy's furious – jealous probbly. Her darling boy.'

Darling Dominic. Daddy had wanted Dominic to go to boarding school but Mummy couldn't bear to part with him, instead agreeing to drive the fifteen-mile round trip across London twice a day to get him to and from a school that snobby old Mr

Bunter-Byng approved of. Dominic not boarding meant that Bunty couldn't be made to either. Not that her mother hadn't tried: 'You'll love it, darling. I did. Heaps of fun.'

'So what's this girlfriend like, then?' Queenie asked.

'Dunno. I was still stuck in the loo when she popped round. Calls herself Soo with two Os, like Sooty's little friend. Mummy says she's *common*. Heard her on the phone to Aunt Marcia. Not "people like us", whatever that's supposed to mean. Calls him Dom, Mummy says – Mummy hates that, she's such a snob.'

'Do they have a meaningful relationship?' nosed Queenie, wasting no time.

'Probbly. Sounds the type. Lots of buttons undone apparently. "Damaged goods" according to Mummy – this is all to Aunt Marcia. She tells me nar-sing. I was earwigging on the extension. "Damaged goods", honestly.'

'You know Brian's got a boyfriend, don't you?'

'Has she indeed? Meaningful?'

'Dunno. Tash told me – she gets quite chatty on the bus. Still at the planning stage, she reckons. Snogs and feels but no shags *yet*, she says.' Queenie nibbled on her chocolate some more. 'Says she's giving him her virginity as a seventeenth birthday present.'

'Christ on a bike. What's she gonna give him for Christmas? A kidney?'

Spam never spoke about virginity – she wasn't the 'little chat' type. A pack of Dr Whites and a (larger) box of tampons had appeared in Baker's wardrobe as if by magic about three months before the big day and that was pretty much that, apart, obviously, from Patsy Baker's increasingly nutty Red Cross parcels.

Stottie's mother was too obsessed with the grades and certificates earned by her scholarship-winning, smart-blazered offspring to say much about birds or bees, and Mrs McQueen rather felt that the school was being paid to take care of that side of the syllabus, but Bunty's mother (who was over fifty) had a bit of a thing about 'damaged goods'. Virginity or (at worst) *apparent* virginity was like the cellophane on a packet of fags or the tiny stamp sealing a deck of playing cards: its loss undermined potential resale value ('discard if seal is broken'). A still unravished girl like Amanda, who really was quite presentable if she'd only make the effort, ought to be able to take her pick – but of course Mummy hadn't been told about any of the Chelsea boys. Bunty always said she was going to the cinema with Amanda Stott, knowing full well that it would take a fairly major domestic emergency – another war; cat death; navy knickers in the white wash – for Mrs Bunter-Byng to ring Stottie's house. The Stott girl was pleasant enough but Mrs S wasn't really PLU. Queenie's mother was more her thing: Queenie's mother had an Hermès scarf knotted around the handle of her bag; Queenie's mother played canasta.

The Bunter-Byngs had driven past Château Stott one Easter on the way to the airport: one of those terraced dog boxes on the old London road, ugly and made uglier by the nubbly tide of pebble-dash that had backsurged irresistibly through the suburbs just before the war. Cladding was what they all did now. Uglier, if that were possible.

The Stott house (did Mrs Bunter-Byng but know it) was equally nubbly on the inside because Pa Stott had rough-iced the walls and ceiling of the ground floor with Artex decorative plaster. Did it himself (not the best idea he'd ever had). It was painfully rough to the touch, and if by any chance – tiredness, Lambrusco, an unexpected slap in the face – you stumbled against a wall with bare skin, the surface left an angry graze. The ceiling hadn't worn as well. Pa Stott did that himself too, but hadn't done whatever needed doing before combing on the gunge so that when Amanda let her bath run over, the sitting room ceiling had come down in one crispy white piece, like a giant table water biscuit hanging from the light fitting. The builder called to fix it nearly died laughing, Stottie said.

'Here.' Bunty poked Baker with a chocolate flake. 'Take away the taste of that detention.' For all the world as if they were still on speaking terms.

'Fattening. You eat it.'

'Please yourself.'

Baker tucked the flake behind her ear. Bunty sighed crossly and began licking the sides of a large, ripe banana.

'Oh blimey, look at her,' laughed Queenie. '*The Sensuous Female* rides again.' (Bunty had bought a copy of this at the airport last holidays when Mummy wasn't looking and they had all borrowed it in turn: *After you have mastered the Penis/Mouth ploy, add the Hummingbird Flick and the Silken Swirl.*)

'Put it *a–way*, Amanda.'

Baker scowled as she transferred her unwanted chocolate bar from her ear to her book bag. You became an expert banana-licker and then what? Some bloke would see you at it and immediately start chatting you up. All because your winning way with a piece of fruit had told him that sucking people off was your idea of a good time, and then you'd be obliged to deliver on your promise. Practically trades descriptions. Advertising standards.

'You're making a rod for your own back. It's like learning shorthand: if they find out you know how then they'll make you do it.' Baker was very careful not to address this to anyone in particular and her eyes avoided the banana-munching Bunty.

'And then he'll tell everybody,' said Queenie, 'or write it on the side of the bus stop. That's what my big brother did. Toe rag.'

'No! Who was it?'

Queenie frowned. 'Someone in the Lower Sixth if you must know – and before you ask I'm not telling. Bad enough Nigel telling bloody everybody. Poor cow.'

Queenie went back to the remains of her Mars Bar and there was an awkward silence with all three of them wanting to know but not wanting to ask, all three of them slightly shamefaced at Queenie coming over all mature about telling. Too juicy not to (you'd have thought) but she didn't. You had to admire that – but you didn't have to like it.

Bunty caved in first. 'Bet it was Moggy Giles. Dominic got off with her at his last school dance. Access all areas, Dominic says.'

'I'm saying *nar-sing*.'

'Her sister's nearly as bad. Only in the Upper Fourth.'

'It'll be the whore moans,' said Baker, pulling *The Female Eunuch* from her bag and reading out the bit she had marked: '"Irritability, nightmares, bed-wetting, giggling, lying, shyness, weeping, nail-biting, compulsive counting rituals, picking at sores, brooding, clumsiness, embarrassment, secretiveness."'

'Yup,' nodded Queenie, tearing cautiously at a hangnail. 'Yup. That about covers it. Apart from the bed-wetting – though I'm sure that will come.'

Stottie was unconvinced. 'Yeah, you *say* that, but our Stephanie's showing no signs of any of it – apart from the compulsive counting lark, *ob*-viously – does a lot of that. Counts Smarties.'

'Counting Smarties is *normal*,' insisted Bunty. 'She's definitely got the spots though. Does she count those?'

As Bunty spoke the bell rang for the end of break and the girls in the playground below the bike shed began funnelling back inside.

'Did you do the German homework?'

'*Am Zahnartzt*. Who in their right mind would go anywhere near a German dentist? They never teach you anything useful; grown-up courses are miles better,' said Stottie '"Two more gin and tonics and a pack of your finest rubber johnnies."'

'Spam's firm are talking about sending her on a Spanish course,' said Baker. 'She can't wait, but Dad says she's wasting her time, says they all speaka di English anyway and you could learn the important bits on the plane from a phrasebook: "This shower does not work; this wine is undrinkable; these vegetables are not cooked." Dad *hates* hotels; doesn't matter where we go: it's never "what a lovely room" or "this is delicious".'

Tuesday's German lesson was spent revising the dative while the German mistress ran back and forth to the staff room in search of the lead for the overhead projector so that she could show them some slides of the Schwarzwald (which was going to take time as the missing cable had been wedged down the back of the radiator).

'How come we haven't got a dative?'

'Cutbacks.'

'It's like the goose step: they just do it to make life harder,' said Queenie. 'Character-building.'

'*Aus, ausser, bei, mit, nach, seit, von, zu, gegenüber*,' parroted Baker, unanswerably.

'Two can play at that game,' whispered Stottie. 'Please remember every day, neuter plurals end in A.'

'In March, July, October, May, the nones fall on the seventh day.'

'Father Christmas goes down an escalator backwards,' trumped Queenie.

'Do what? You're making these up,' hissed Baker.

'Am not. Something to do with musical keys? Or Chemistry? Might have been Chemistry.'

'Thought you gave up Chemistry?'

'*Zackly* my point.'

'*Why* did you give it up?' asked Stott, who had already whizzed through the dative exercise and was drawing an elaborate Greek key pattern all round the cover of her rough book.

'It became necessary.'

Queenie was still in the proles when she developed her loathing of the periodic table, reacting first with blank disbelief then with blind panic to the news that she was expected to commit this seemingly random sequence of numbers and initials to memory.

'You don't have to learn logarithms or cosines. There's a little book. It's like being made to memorise a bus timetable of somewhere you don't even live. In Greek.'

'But there is a logic to it,' insisted Stott. 'Look at it. All the metals go here ...'

'Arsenic,' suggested Baker.

'No need to be nasty,' Bunty, straight-faced, 'she's only trying to help.'

German was followed – just in case any of it stuck – by forty minutes of French conversation practising the future perfect (*I/you/we will have murdered Miss Gray by next Tuesday*).

'Not what I'd call conversation.' Stottie was off again.

Stottie, who had a knack for languages, was mid-way through teaching herself Italian in twenty lessons from her library book. It was taking slightly longer than promised but it was still a hell of a lot quicker than French.

'"*Quel est votre sujet préféré*"? Is that really their idea of a conversation? I mean, picture the scene: you, Roger Vadim—'

'Jean Paul Belmondo,' purred Bunty, 'he looks dir-ty.'

'A corner table in a bistro, checked tablecloth, candle jammed into a wine bottle, an accordion wheezing away in the distance as you sip your Napoleon brandy. "Tell me, chérie," he murmurs, lighting another little yellow French fag while you hummingbird flick your banana, "*avez-vous des soeurs ou des frères*?" I worked it out. A thousand French lessons: one a week from the age of seven; one a *day* the five years we've been here. *Madame*

Dupont va a l'épicerie? It's a total con. We should all be bi-bloody-lingual by now. A *thousand* hours down the bloody buggering drain. I've spent more time one-to-one with French teachers than I have with my dad. Far more.' Stottie stopped, sad suddenly. 'And why *French* anyway? *Loads* more places speak Spanish. Loads more *people* speak Russian. Did money change hands?'

'"The language of international diplomacy" Miss Gray says.'

'Oh yes, very likely. Has Miss Batty got a folder on that in her careers file? Data Processing, Dental Nursing, Diplomacy.'

Miss Revie was flicking through the matrix prep as they barged their way into Room 8 for Beta Maths.

'Jolly well done everybody, getting all the matrix homework in, not bad, not bad at all.'

Had Miss Revie spotted the massed cheat? Not a chance. She tamped the sheaf of sheets against her desktop. Would the Maths monitor be a sport and hand them all back? And they must all remember tomorrow's exam and the need for constant revision and could they all turn to the section on Topology and could someone please tell her the maximum number of odd nodes in a traversable system? (Surly silence.) Anybody?

Miss Revie's good mood swung back to minus one. Hopeless. Thank heavens she was getting the Alphas next year, at least a few of them had an inkling, but God preserve her from fifteen-year-old girls who couldn't do Maths, whose boring binty mothers could never do Maths, whose boring binty mothers had deliberately inoculated their daughters with their own superstitious dread of fractions, graphs, set squares, protractors and the entire contents of the Oxford Mathematical Instruments set, together with their pea-brained belief that Mathematics, like red hair or cystic fibrosis or a third nipple had some bona fide genetic component. This lot looked indignantly at each batch of equations as if the sums had been delivered in error, and the cheeky ones came right out and said, in their Neanderthal, proto-Benthamite way, that they were never going to *need* differential equations, Miss Revie, not in Real Life. As though the ability to find the determinant of a matrix, dissect a rat or parse a compound sentence were just so much excess baggage that would weigh them down on their breakneck race through life and must be hurled from the back of the sledge at the earliest possible opportunity.

Miss Revie slumped down in front of the projector and picked up her pack of felt-tips.

'Can you all turn to page seventeen.'

Baker opened her Maths book at the Topology chapter. There was a picture of a TV set next to a Dalek and a caption pointing out that they were topologically equivalent, plus a short hymn in praise of the London Tube map.

Bunty was flicking crossly through her own textbook. 'There's a whole chapter on Practical Mathematics in the back here,' she hissed, 'all the stuff I can do: compound interest, percentages, how many bathroom tiles to buy. All that malarkey. Not even on the syllabus. I'm *never* going to *need* this rubbish.' Bunty was almost squealing with frustration as she unconsciously trotted out Miss Revie's unfavourite phrase. 'There already *is* a bloody Tube map. And if they wanted a new one they're never going to ask *me* are they?'

'Not with your job in the diplomatic corps, *chérie*. Far too busy.'

Baker leaned back in her chair, opened her rough book and began writing 'KILL JULIA SMITH' in very small capital letters over and over and over until it filled the page. That bitch was everywhere. By now she would have run the Drumlin to earth and told her that Baker hadn't managed to see the headmistress and the Drumlin would probably bring it up in the Thursday staff meeting and Mrs Mostyn would add her two pennyworth and they'd phone Dad or write to Dad or fire off some smoke signals to Dad to say that Baker wasn't keeping to her side of the 'contract' and it wasn't the plimsolls it was the *principle* of the thing and he would shout and pull his face into cross, crumpled shapes and tell her she was just like her bloody mother.

One day, thought Baker, one day he'll trot out that rubbish again about apples not falling far from trees, he'll say it again and I will murder him and it will all be Julia's fault. Fucking Julia. Her Biro went through the paper. No one else hated their parents this much. Unless they did. Maybe they did? Maybe that was why people sighed at sentimental pictures and cried at *The Railway Children* ('Daddy! My daddy!'). In mourning for the families they hadn't had.

She could see Dad's Monday night face in her head, see the girlishly long cowlick of hair flopping sweatily forward. She could see his teeth (you couldn't as a rule), chubby and yellow like sucked buttermints and stained with strong tea and tobacco that silted up the grooves where they met. She could feel the germy sparks of spit that flew around whenever he started shouting. *Father-like he tends and spares us?* Oh really?

'So,' Dad always said when he finally finished, 'have you got much homework?' Like someone had pulled a string at the back of his neck.

Queenie had had a lot of talking dolls when she was small. She brought them all to school once: Ken (Barbie's boyfriend), Stacey (their chatty chum), and evil Captain Black off some *Thunderbirds* thing and the Mandies spent a happy breaktime making up a dolly drama.

'I think mini skirts are smashing; Barbie and I are having tea; Oh dear. What shall I wear for dinner?' said Stacey who sounded just like the Queen.

'We will take our revenge,' vowed Captain Black.

'Let's go listen to Barbie's records,' drawled Ken in a desperate bid to lighten the mood.

'Everyone will die,' warned the Captain, implacably.

Barbie had a talking boyfriend, a talking friend, a talking enemy but no sign as yet of a talking dad.

'You're not going out like that, are you?'

'Have you written a thank you letter?'

'Take that stuff off your face.'

'Apologise to your mother.'

'We will take our revenge.'

Chapter 6

'I hate my stepmother.'

'Well just eat the potatoes.'

Queenie was poking suspiciously at her lunch plate with a fork. 'Is this really what they eat in Lancashire?'

'Probbly. All food has to be named after somewhere. Well-known fact: Bakewell tart; Oxford marmalade. All cheese. Biscuits.'

'Biscuits?'

'Lincoln, Shrewsbury, Bath Olivers, Nice, Garibaldi.'

'Gari-baldi? Wezzat?'

'Near Nice.'

Bunty peered hungrily at Baker's plate. 'Are you not going to eat that?' She smiled a little guiltily at Baker – like they were still friends – and began helping herself to the untasted hotpot.

'Your stepmother can't be *all* bad,' said Queenie. 'Not if she wants shot of the piano.'

'Yeah, but she isn't doing it for my sake, it's not about me. She just wants a bigger telly and there isn't room.'

'I don't see why you want to get rid of it. I wish mine was as nice,' gushed Stottie. 'And you're really *good* – you can play anything.'

Baker looked down at the remaining yellow discs of potato and pinkish shreds of meat in their puddle of brown grease.

'Spam makes hotpot: *special* hotpot.'

Queenie sucked air in through her teeth. 'Never good news, "special". Special fried rice is always a no-no: peas and prawns and what have you; chopped up leftovers. Nass-ty.'

'It wouldn't be so bad if she could bring herself to stick to a proper recipe. It'll *look* normal and then you'll discover too late that she's put curry powder in it, or raisins. She puts raisins in *salad* for Christ's sake.'

Queenie shuddered. 'I tried to get Mummy to write the day's menu up on the kitchen blackboard. You feel such a prannet *asking* all the time. Sounds rude: "Wossis then?" and what with the Cordon Bleu course it's always Allah something, so it's not like you could guess or anything.'

'Mine doesn't do recipes, thank God,' said Bunty. 'Just grills steak, mashes potato and heats up frozen green things. Delish. And if Dad's off broking somewhere we have hoops on toast and Antarctic Roll.'

'Arctic, surely,' corrected Stottie.

'Same difference.'

'Even Spam's specials are better than this Lancashire muck. And another thing: why am I eating off lino?' Baker banged her hand on one of the fake marble tiles glued along the tops of the trestle tables. 'Like eating off the floor. Feel like the bloody dog.' She pushed her plate away untouched.

The others had moved on to pudding which was tinned fruit and a small brick of ice cream.

'OK guys and gals, mums and dads,' yodelled Queenie, a yellowish cube pronged on her fork. 'Time to Name That Fruit.'

'Yam,' said Bunty. 'Yaaaam. Has many uses: ceiling tiles (obviously); animal fodder; the hollowed-out rind can be used as a primitive drinking vessel, and any leftover fibre can be used to thatch a rude hut.'

'Talking of which . . .' whispered Baker, 'have you clocked the Barnet?'

A second year called Nina, who until last Friday had worn her hair in two mousey bell ropes, was sporting a new brown bob.

'Shame,' said Stottie.

'Typical home in Malawi. Maybe it's her Geography project.'

'Lot of trouble to go to.'

'Do you think her mum cut it?'

'Naaah.' Baker timed the world-weary sip from her water beaker like a mummy downing gin. 'Very tidy woman our Nina's mother. Irons jeans.'

'They keep their car in a cosy,' said Stottie, who lived on the same road. 'If it really *is* a car. Never seen them actually *drive* it anywhere . . . Might be a dirty great car-shaped thing made from cornflakes packets and Fairy Liquid bottles for all I know.'

The room rang with the sound of two hundred sets of cutlery scraping two hundred cheap green and pink and yellow plates, two hundred ravenous chatterboxes all talking with their mouths full. The Nina person stood uncertainly with her tray in the middle of the dining hall, engulfed by the hellish din, a look like headache on her face. Baker turned to watch the girl walk across to the corner where packed lunches were eaten and sit down opposite a smiling Julia Smith. Her again. Were there two of her?

Baker let her head nod forward and watched the corner of the room from behind a safety curtain of fringe. Julia had taken a foil triangle of processed cheese from her plastic box. You were supposed to peel those by pulling the dinky red tag but Julia just ripped away the corner with her thumbnail and squeezed cheese into her mouth. G-*ross*. Nothing about *that* in *The Sensuous Female*.

'Would you say she was pretty? Attractive?'

Queenie looked at Baker in surprise.

'Don't you start. You'll be awarding points out of ten next.'

'You lose points for ginger. Brian's very firm about that.'

'Don't see why. Strawberry blonde's all right.'

'I wouldn't eat a strawberry that colour. *Apricots* possibly . . .'

'Apricot blonde? Sounds like a shampoo.'

But it was too nice a name for shampoo, argued Baker. Shampoo was dry or greasy or damaged or difficult: flyaway, unmanageable, problem, lifeless. Terrifying the amount of self-loathing you could pack into just washing your bloody hair.

'Spam only buys Normal.'

'I warm to Spam,' smiled Bunty.

'Is it my imagination or does she keep looking at me?'

'Spam? Spam's *here*?' Bunty stared about her in mock panic.

'No, stupid, Julia Smith.'

The others were now staring over towards the corner.

'Cornflower-coloured eyes. You'd get points for those,' conceded Queenie.

'Cornflowers come in pink too, I'll have you know. Daddy has them in his *mixed bedding*.'

And everyone laughed. The way they always did laugh when Bunty did her funny look. Hard to know exactly what triggered it. 'Bedding' would probably do the trick on its own but 'mixed' and Bunty's fruity voice clinched it. 'Mixed bathing' and they'd be splitting their sides. Even 'mixed doubles' got a chuckle. And 'ladies doubles', 'ladies' anything come to that.

Baker's gaze turned to the other side of the refectory.

'I think our Brian should grow a moustache over Easter. Like that bloke in *If*. Save a packet on cream bleach.'

'Miaow.'

They'd all laughed but Queenie crossed her legs (not a safe moment to go to the bog with Baker in this mood).

'Hello, you lot.'

The Mandies looked up to see Beverly Snell, the English monitor.

'How are your novels coming along?'

Beverly was having a fairly easy term of it as Miss Gleet had said they could, if they wished, wait until after the Easter break before handing in their novels, although she would be permanently on call to stick her oar in, change the ending and rewrite the whole thing in a style she preferred – 'consulting' as she liked to call it.

'So much more fun than essay writing,' gushed Beverly. She squeezed herself, unasked, on to the very end of their bench. 'Mine's called *The Hope Chest*.' No one was listening. 'It's set in the wild west and it's about a young schoolteacher. All her family die of scarlet fever and she's making a quilt out of all their old clothes.' No response. 'Memories of when they were in the covered wagon.' Still nothing. 'Mummy's idea. Miss Gleet says it's very *evocative*.'

'That's one way of putting it.'

'I've written twenty thousand words.'

'Wossat in pages?' Queenie called after her as Beverly headed for the cloakroom. 'Twenty thousand words? Silly moo.'

'GTP,' said Bunty. It was short for 'Good Team Player' and it wasn't a compliment.

Baker looked at her watch.

'Off we trot.' She scraped the remains of her hotpot onto the top of the stack of plates. 'Triple English? They want locking up.'

Miss Kopje, the librarian, who had a knack for such things, had spent the previous August wrestling with the upper school timetable. For three weeks her dining room suite was loose-covered with pencilled charts and scraps of coloured paper, but there had been no getting round it. Nothing to be done. There had been a 'terrible glitch', a 'ghastly blunder' with the blocking (as the deputy head had put it when she broke the news to the staff room) which meant that three of the Upper Shell's five weekly English lessons would now all take place one after the other on Tuesday afternoons. The girls weren't too thrilled about this but Miss Gleet had burst into tears at the news. A repeat prescription for lithium had taken the edge off the pain and then an old college chum had suggested the energy-saving wheeze of having her fifth formers write a novel to use up the final four weeks of term.

Queenie had called hers *Wanted on Voyage* and it was all written in postcards. 'The Gleet eats up that kind of tripe with a spoon,' said Stottie, enviously.

'Bloody gets on your nerves though. Has she let you read it? Really, *really* hard to tell who's wishing who was where.'

Baker's novel was called *The Snapdragon Harvest*.

'You can't call it that. She'll know you're taking the mick.'

'She loved it. Look: "Intriguing title" it says here. Liked the plot summary as well: young woman meets rude man; rude man fancies young woman, becomes less rude, young woman marries rude man. I didn't mention "Rude Man" in my plan, obviously, just some rubbish about self-discovery, love and loss and a dark family secret – practically wet herself. I didn't tell her about the twist at the end either.'

Miss Gleet was going to hate the twist. It occurred four pages before the end – the bit in the 'true love' stories when the scales fall and it dawns on the heroine that Rude Man is not, in fact, an overbearing, sadistic pig but the love of her life. The bit when she thinks she's never going to see him again just as the taxi turns round or the telegram arrives or she finds the first class plane ticket tucked into her knicker elastic and yes, reader, she can have him after all, that bastard she didn't want in the first place. *That* was where Baker was putting her twist.

'I nearly called it *The Forgotten Wishbone* but then she really would smell a rat.'

'Mine's called *Thirteen for Croquet*,' said Bunty as the four Mandies slumped into the back row of desks, 'and I'm killing *everybody*.'

Miss Gleet had a new top, stretchy and zebra-striped and she was wearing a fashionably chocolate-coloured lipstick to celebrate ('Secret Squirrel' according to the label).

'What's black, white and brown round the mouth?' whispered Baker.

'Quieten down, everyone,' sang Miss Gleet.

Stronger medication was definitely an improvement: 25mg with the midday meal and she was nicely relaxed by Registration. Relaxed enough to spend the first thirty minutes of the triple English marathon reading to the Upper Shells from a novel selected from the rather limited supply in the school book cupboard. *Jane Eyre* would make a change, Miss Gleet felt (young woman meets rude man). Miss Gleet had no recollection whatever of reading out the exact same passage a fortnight earlier, but there wasn't a peep from the Mandies, nothing from Brian and the gang either. Brian and Paddy both had Charlotte Brontë sitting on their desks but were busy playing Hangman in their laps. Baker slipped the *Eunuch* from her bag and tucked it inside *Jane Eyre*. The Gleet, who'd read English and Drama at university, always insisted on acting out all the parts. Helen Burns was done in very snotty Scots.

'I wish she'd do "The Green Eye of the Little Yellow Dog" again,' yawned Bunty under her breath. 'I liked that one. I hate school stories.'

Baker was miles away in the land of the *Eunuch*.

'*Female students are forming a large proportion of the arts intake at universities*,' said the *Eunuch*, '*and dominating the teaching profession as a result. The process is clearly one of diminishing returns: the servile induce servility to teach the servile.'*

Those who can't, teach ... Baker stretched out her finger and teased a pencil across the desk and into her hand. Miss Gleet was doing Mr Brocklehurst now in an all-purpose, whippet-keeping, northern accent. Her eyes stayed glued to her text and didn't see Baker underlining the bit about servility.

'Education cannot be and never has been a matter of obedience.'

'Beverly, if you could gather in the books and if the rest of you could carry on with your novels. I have a few errands to run. I shan't be long. I'm leaving the door open and Mrs Rathbone is next door if you need anything.' A warning.

The Gleet left a trail of scent behind her as she swept from the room. Queenie gave an educated sniff.

'Ugh. *Je Reviens.*'

'Not if I see you first.' Bunty, quick as a flash.

'What *is* black, white and brown round the mouth?' remembered Stottie.

'A nun eating—'

'Ssshh!' hissed a girl by the door as a stray goon paced past.

'G-ross.'

'Give it a rest, can't you?' sighed Queenie. 'I thought the new top looked quite swish.'

Brian and Paddy were still on the same round of Hangman which they managed to keep going almost indefinitely because they cheated, drawing shoes and bow ties and scrubby little penises on their condemned men so that the game lasted longer and no one ever really lost. Paddy's word was *dirndl*; this was going to take time.

Baker got out her English file and opened it at the most recent chapter of *The Snapdragon Harvest*. She had made the mistake of handing it in for comment and the carefully typewritten pages were now awash with the Gleet's shrill red ballpoint.

It was late spring which she loved and dreaded. **Why dreaded?** *She came upon the great bank of snapdragons and her heart quivered with brightness.* **What does this mean?**

My lamb! **Really?** barked Miss Gleet.

There was a cold correctness in the way he put his bicycle in place that made her heart sink. **Why?** *Her innermost soul shrank within her in a coil of torture. He was looking at the snapdragons disconsolately and the white tilt of his neck, slender and firm, gave her a sharp pang that resonated to the depths of her soul. She sensed the very quivering stuff of life in him.* **Over-use 'quivering'.** *Down to her bowels went the hot spasm of fear. Her mouth parted with suffering and her heart was scalded with pain.* **Ouch!**

She lingered to gather the snapdragons, tenderly, passionately. **Be more sparing with adverbs** *wrote the Gleet, censoriously. The love in her fingertips caressed the peachy bursten blossoms,* **Bursten?** *the passion in her heart came to a glow upon the petals but why had she the dull pain in her soul?*

'Why must you always be fondling things?' he cried, in his musical caressing voice.

Interesting but overwrought quivered Miss Gleet. Lawrence would be disappointed.

The only Mandy who took the novel business even remotely seriously was Stott. Stott had nearly finished *A Mind of Her Own* which was about a fifteen-year-old runaway with a drunken father who goes on the road with a pair of juvenile delinquents.

'What was the Gleet verdict?'

'Only shown her the plan so far,' said Stott. '"Gritty." Gritty! Wait till she sees it. The gang bang'll make her hair curl.'

Bunty and Stott both had a free last period on Tuesdays. Bunty had made a run for it, but Stottie had hung around in the library and was now loitering by the school gate in hopes of catching Baker on her way home and renewing the offer of the spare bed.

'Sorry about yesterday. How about tonight? Cheese on toast for tea.'

'I'm not a big cheese person. How did the exam go?' The question was automatic but the answer bloody wasn't. The Handel Suite in G had gone quite well considering and she was fairly pleased with the Scarlatti Sonata and the Beethoven adagio was a breeze but the contrary motion scales were a bit of a nightmare and she hadn't done herself justice in the sight reading (not having Baker's flair for it) and so she only got merit and Mrs Stott was really disappointed. Mrs Stott had bought a bar of milk chocolate all ready to give to her and had given it to Stephanie instead.

Baker fought hard to stifle a yawn.

'But merit's brilliant, surely? No one ever gave me merit.'

'Yes but Steff got distinction for her grade three last year.'

'Stephanie's going to get very, very fat by the sound of it.'

'Do come round. We could make a Rice Krispie cake – you used to love that.'

'Not allowed out, sadly.' Dad's curfew was practically a blessing.

Baker got home to an empty house and found the second post on the doormat: yet another brown envelope. She left it lying where it was, then made a tactical retreat to her bedroom. There would almost certainly be one of Spam's spazzy little notes on the kitchen worktop: *Be an angel and sort out a few spuds/grate cheese/pod peas/curl butter if you're back in time, sausage. Fondest P'* but that only worked if Baker made a bee-line for the biscuit barrel and Baker wasn't hungry.

She was fast asleep over her Scripture revision when she heard the slam of the front door, shortly followed by the resentful rattle of saucepans as Spam, still in her coat, lit the oven and began peeling two pounds of King Edwards while her husband lay on the sofa with a can of lager and the second post until his supper was on the table.

'Who was your letter from?'

A defensive look in Dad's eyes while the rest of his face chewed chop.

'You know perfectly well what it was, the name was on the envelope. It's another brochure from another school.'

'Lots of girls like to make a fresh start in the sixth form,' said Spam, 'and it's got masses of facilities: swimming pool; judo; language lab.'

What went on in language laboratories, wondered Baker, were there rats in mazes?

'You'd soon make new friends.'

She'd bloody need new friends after this morning, and she remembered with an unhappy shiver the unfamiliar snotty note in Bunty's voice. *I don't have to tell you everything.* Since when? It wasn't as if Baker specially wanted any of the grisly details about Bunty's dirty afternoon: it was the principle of the thing. And she'd have to tell somebody . . . Stottie? Or Queenie? Queenie was a bit of a dark horse. Lots of people told her stuff. Surprising people.

The phone rang during the news headlines, interrupting Baker's miserable musings.

'Who on earth can that be?' tutted Dad. 'It's gone ten.' (Though he never went to bed before the *Epilogue*.)

'It's for you.'

'Hello, babes.' Bunty's voice. Bunty's lovely husky smiley voice. 'Sorry about this morning. I could see Brian earwigging and besides,' whispering now, 'there wasn't much to tell.'

There was the sudden sound of the television as someone opened a door and Bunty's voice took on a coded, cagy quality.

'Yeah. Slightly disappointing, very, er, *short*.'

'Sweet?'

'Not specially,' a cough, '*premature*.'

'Oh.'

'Can't talk now,' the huffy thump of her sitting-room door being closed, 'nothing to write home about, basically. I just wanted to say sorry for being a silly moo.'

'Silly moo,' echoed Baker, pressing her eyelids together and beaming with relief.

'Ni-night.'

Chapter 7

The usual horde of wage slaves poured on and off the train at the Junction next morning, giving Baker the chance to grab a corner seat and light a cigarette, at which point the woman across the aisle tutted off to the other end of the carriage and flumped down next to Julia sodding Smith. Julia Smith. Again. Did she even come to school by train as a rule? She looked up from her book and nailed Baker and her cigarette with an unreadable stare, the blue flannel shoulders giving the slightest possible shrug, a 'you give me no choice; you brought this on yourself' shrug.

The long, bare legs looked downright obscene in the commuter carriage. You could see the bowler-hatted man on the other side of her admiring the smooth ivory thighs running parallel with his pinstripes. Julia leaned back slightly, legs parting an inch. It wasn't about sport at all, was it? Just an excuse to wear a shorter skirt. She had taken a tiny scrap of paper from her bag and was scribbling on it left-handed. Baker puffed stubbornly at her cigarette. No sense not. Too late now.

Someone had left a magazine behind on the seat opposite: *Ads and Admen*. It was like stumbling on an enemy code book: *Playtex to launch bra aimed at 15–24 year olds who want to make the most of limited resources*. The glossy black and white pages were packed with snaps of beardy blokes in snazzy ties with five-point plans for persuading the British housewife that life would not be complete until every family member had a range of products that only they could use. His'n'hers soap, his'n'hers fags. They even had cheeses of their own: manly mature for the dad, low fat for the mum and novelty triangles for the two point two kids (and Julia). No dog or cat cheese – not yet anyway.

According to *Ads and Admen* there was going to be a new bubble bath campaign which would be designed for the young teen market, advertised in magazines called things like *19*, but read by Lower Fourths in a hurry. The new product was called Three Wishes. The cheap scent, oil and soap it was made of separated out into layers of orange, red and yellow gunk, which meant you had to shake the bottle hard before using, then offer up your three wishes. Baker stared at the carriage ceiling wishing she was thinner, wishing she was twenty-two, wishing Julia Smith would get off her back.

Julia got out of the far door when the train stopped and breezed along the platform to the exit, the pleats of her divided skirt lapping against the back of her thighs beneath the shortie blazer, her not-especially-limited resources bouncing revoltingly as she walked. She walked very fast. In a hurry to get to O'Brien presumably: spill beans, let cats out of bags. Another letter home.

Baker swam wearily against the tide of passengers surging up the stairs to the platform and grumbling at her for bucking the morning trend. She paused just beyond the station entrance to peer in through the steamy windows of the Victory Café and check if Bunty was at one of the tables. Sometimes, when Baker managed to catch an earlier train, they would meet there and spend half a blissful hour and forty pence on two teas and a buttered bun, composing dirty limericks and watching the office workers milling past, the same faces almost to the minute, on their way to take up their places in the 'real world' as Mrs Mostyn liked to call it.

The café clock read eight fifteen. Baker almost ran up the hill to the school gate and just caught Bunty in the empty cloak-room, about to head off for Registration.

'The balloon's about to go up.'

'A balloon? We have a *balloon*? Now you tell me. Not a word about it in the prospectus. Can you get a badge for it?'

'Stop wittering, woman. Julia Smith just saw me having a fag on the train.'

'Her again? Is she following you? Are you following her?'

Baker didn't smile but then maybe Bunty wasn't joking – hard to tell after yesterday. They were back on speakers right enough, but it still wasn't quite the same.

The two of them sneaked back into the cloakroom after assembly. Free periods were supposed to be spent in the library but the librarian taught first year elocution on Wednesday mornings (Browning, Belloc, Little Yellow Dogs) so there was only the slimmest chance of discovery.

The cloakroom smelled powerfully of gym shoes and wet fish. Wednesday's domestic science project was to be rollmop herrings, 'a nourishing and economical supper dish' according to Mrs Chifley but an odd choice for a class of girls who'd never know-ingly eaten a piece of fish without batter on it.

'It'll be tripe next.' Bunty was curled up on the windowsill on top of the radiator. Not a proper window, more of a vent really, designed to make escape impossible – you never saw windows like that on houses. She yanked it open and lit one of her new cigarettes with a flourish. The packet had drawings of flowers all over it and the fags themselves were unusually long and thin with a band of daisies marking where the filter began. Cigarettes for girls.

No dog fags yet (beagles didn't count; beagles would smoke anything). But they already had children's fags. Not just the tiny white sugar ones. Baker remembered once buying cousin David a whole chocolate smoker's set for his birthday: chocolate pipe, chocolate tobacco, a box of chocolate matches, a pack of chocolate fags rolled in edible paper and a huge chocolate ashtray all nesting in custom-moulded dimples in a big cellophane-fronted box. Everything but chocolate lungs. There was no girl's equivalent. No flowery packs or pink sugar cigarette holders. Nothing to be going on with until you could pass for sixteen and buy the real thing (not that the old man in the fag shop ever cared). Smoking was your destiny, one of the things grown-ups did, like Scotch whisky and headaches and indigestion tablets.

You didn't wake up on your sixteenth birthday with a royal flush of adult kit (fag in one hand, pack of three in the other), not like one of Mrs Mostyn's tribes where you got locked in a typical hut while the tattoos healed. In deepest South London the signs of adulthood were awarded in stages like personal survival badges: sherries at Christmas; a dab of lipstick on the bridesmaid; a trendy aunt offering you a few puffs after the wedding. They knew you'd end up with the whole set eventually, but they liked to pick and choose: one minute they wanted to keep you in vests and socks and sandals and ponytails and take-that-stuff-off-your-face-Amanda; the next they were on at you for being 'immature' when you didn't play nicely about the nine-to-four school day plus homework, plus netball practice. A 50-hour week? Miners struck for less.

'You're supposed to leave the last third.' Bunty waved her cigarette at Baker's Rothman which was almost down to the filter. 'Says so on this little card thingy – "leave longer stubs and take fewer puffs" – buy more fags, in other words. I mean, how come they carry on selling them if it's so bloody bad for you? How come your parents carry on doing it? "Wish I'd never star-ted, dah-ling."' Mummy in the room all of a sudden. 'But Mummy says the same about plucking her eyebrows and that doesn't give you cancer – or does it? Maybe it does . . .'

Bunty lit another cigarette from the remains of her last one – not quite the look the brand manager had in mind – and flicked the still-glowing stub out of the window.

'At least Spam leaves you alone.'

Bunty was always saying that, pretending to envy Baker her semi-detached stepmother who didn't do cosy chats and had the grace to take a back seat at parents' evenings and who wasn't forever bursting into your bedroom to tell you how much deodorant to use or how your father would be *so* proud if you'd only pass Grade Seven or finish in the top fifteen or stop shaving your legs with his safety razor.

'I think Mummy sees me as Gloria Bunter-Byng Mark II: new improved, with added flavour, fewer calories, bigger tits, more miles per gallon,' she giggled. '"Don't make the dweadful mistakes I made dah-ling." Explains everything: not being allowed to give up Chemistry, piano lessons. Everything. Her latest wheeze is for me to leave after O levels and do one of Mrs McQueen's crappy Cordon Bleu courses, then get a job cooking directors' lunchicles in the city somewhere. With luck I will look so fetching dishing up the *boeuf en croute* I'll be able to truss and stuff a spiffy little company director and drag him back to the family cave. Never mind whether I'd like it or not. I don't want to be a bloody skivvy.'

Baker was due a termly careers check-up that afternoon: a quarter of an hour locked in the sick bay with Miss Batty and her leaflet collection.

'Tell her you're settled on nursing, that's what I said. She has *loads* of leaflets on nursing so she feels useful. And you only need about three O Levels cos they teach you it all anyway, so she can't say you're aiming too high like she does when you say fashion designer or airline pilot.'

'I could always say teaching, I suppose.'

Baker pulled out the *Eunuch* and began quoting the bit about teachers and servility.

'*Only one third of teachers are still at work after six years in the job.* All that training down the drain.'

Bunty yawned. 'Baker dearie, could you possibly, just once, read a book and then just keep it to yourself? Just to please me?'

Baker caught her breath: what a rotten thing to say.

'Sor-*ree*. Pardon me for breathing.' Was she really that boring?

'No, doll, don't take it the wrong way but I really mean it. Whenever you read anything you never stop banging on about it. Like Dr O'Brien reading out bits from the paper in assembly – gets on your nerves. Deadly. Nick hates it when I read anything out.'

Nick again.

Bunty shrugged and smiled. An automatic there-that-didn't-hurt smile and she was all ready to change the subject and no hard feelings. Bugger that. Baker took an angry, actressy drag on her fag and hit right back in a shouty whisper.

'Sod right off. *Boeuf en croute*'s about all you're fit for. It's *important*. It's not just boring stuff you can't be bothered to read.'

Bunty did her cute 'sorry' face – only not so cute. Must have worked once upon a time when the hair was blonder and curlier, the eyes bluer and larger in that cheeky baby face. A daddy's girl – you could always tell: they gave it away whenever they tried to win you over by turning on one of those pathetic doggie-in-the window looks. Mummy's girls worked on a different principle: deceit, bribery, guilt. Baker had herself down as a mummy's girl – just minus the mummy.

Bunty wasn't giving up. Nonono Baker was quite right. Bunty

knew *zackly* what she meant. Sorry to snap, sorry for being a cow. Falling over herself to be nice. Did Baker want a nice chocolate biscuit? Nice fag, then? And please do lend her the book because yes-no-absolutely, God, no, didn't want to end up dishing five star *pommes dauphinoise* to James D Right Esq.

'Talk about getting off on the wrong foot. You'd end up tied to the stove if you cooked to that sort of standard. Lousy cooks like Mummy have a much easier life. Start boning and rolling and they'll expect it nightly: "What's for dinner, darling?", "*Entrecote chasseur, Sachertorte* and a spot of *fellatio anglais* to follow."'

'And Stottie thought those language classes were a waste of time.'

And Bunty smiled again. Not the daddy's girl simper this time but a proper smile, like a toy with a light on inside.

'Couldn't your dad get you a job breaking stock or something?'

'With my maths? You're barmy.'

'Yeah, but you can do *sums*. Oonagh Houseman wants to be a doctor like her dad and she's a semi-moron.'

'So? Probably an advantage. My GP's a halfwit. *My GP's a halfwit. He wears a halfwit's hat.*'

'I reckon you can take this whole daddy's footsteps lark too far,' said Baker. 'My dad's a surveyor and no power human or divine is going to get me into that lark: wandering in and out of hot huts in hard hats all day, drinking tea and quantifying aggregate or whatever it is he does on his "projects". I don't want any job that has its own headgear.'

'Except Queen,' said Bunty, 'and policewoman, ob-viously. What *is* aggregate anyway?'

'You get it in football.' Queenie had just arrived from double Art. 'Leeds United are on it.' She squinted across at Baker's advertising magazine.

'Three Wishes, eh? What would yours be?'

A funny look on Bunty's face, like she'd been asked this one before and always got it wrong.

'Smaller tits, longer legs and a Lamborghini. How about you, Baker baby, what are your three?'

'Roxy Music,' she lied.

'There's *four* of them. Five, possibly.'

'Yeah, but not the *bald* one, *ob-viously*.'

As the Mandies jostled back out into the corridor towards their History lesson, Baker saw Julia coming in the opposite direction.

'You can't go on meeting like this,' muttered Bunty in come-to-the-casbah tones. Cow. Like she was jealous or something.

The sixth-former stumbled along the crowded corridor and deliberately bumped Baker with her tote bag as she passed and, before Baker could speak, crackled a folded scrap of paper into the side of her bag. Bunty stared after her in surprise.

'Getting a bit bolshie, isn't she?'

Baker was almost fighting for breath, heart racing.

'She's put something in my bag . . . a note.'

'Oh shit. Wossit say?'

Baker's voice was cold, dry.

'*I don't have to tell you everything.*'

She dumped her bag on a desk in the far corner and, with her back to the blackboard, began reaching into the side pocket for the bit of paper Julia had put there, trying and failing not to catch on the torn skin around her nails.

'Amanda!' Mrs Horst's cracked soprano rose above the buzz of arriving Upper Shells. 'Bags over here please. Test today, don't forget. Pencils are provided.'

The note was in too deep and the Horst would be sure to think it was a crib and confiscate it and read it. But read what? If Julia had reported her to O'Brien what did she need to send a note for? What was she after?

Mrs Horst began going over the previous week's homework – a freehand map of Ancient Egypt – and itemising her disappointment: colours too strong; not coloured enough.

'*Print* place names, please and make a note of my corrections. Very nice, Joanna.' (This in an undertone to her pet.) 'Only one S in Rosetta, Davina.' But today's special treatment was reserved for Bunty.

'Was this supposed to be a joke, Amanda? Because I can tell you here and now that I am not amused by it.'

Girls on all sides craned to see the map in her hand.

'It's topological, Mrs Horst.'

'It's to be done again.'

And all at once Bunty lost her rag, her voice getting louder, her face getting redder as she demanded what the hell was wrong with it. Any fool could see it was Egypt (it had 'Egypt' written on it for one thing). North, South, East and West all worked, Thebes was south of Rosetta (only one S). It was only supposed to be a basic outline. It wasn't as though they were all planning to go there on a hiking tour for Christ's sake. If they were, they'd buy a proper map, wouldn't they? Or hire a native guide, or get the tour bus, or a *ta-xi*.

Suppressed giggles (*ta-xi* clinched it) and a thrill of anticipation breezed round the room. Mrs Horst had gone very pink. Her lips were trembling with unspoken retorts and ingenious punishments, but Bunty was unstoppable. Straight to Dr O'Brien's office? That suited Bunty just fine. The Horst had asked for 'A Sketch Map' – Bunty jabbed at her prep diary with a furious finger. S-k-e-t-c-h. If she wanted pages copied from the atlas then she should have bloody well said so.

And with that she shimmied out from behind her desk, extracted her tote bag from the mound under the blackboard and stormed from the room.

'Great telly,' muttered Queenie.

You could see that Mrs Horst was at a loss as she weighed up the pros and cons of a. keeping her cool and handing out the multiple choice papers or b. chasing after Bunty and rugby tackling her before she reached the blasted headmistress. O'Brien could be tricky. She was frightfully keen on 'cross-fertilisation' as she called it, and Bunter-Byng's lazy little map might be exactly the sort of thing she was after. The girl would be punished for discourtesy but the damage would have been done ...

Mrs Horst grew up in a world where a mistress would have left an exam room without a qualm if the need arose. The girls would all have been 'on their honour' not to cheat, sighed Mrs Horst to herself, but leave this fifth form zoo without supervision and you could definitely wave goodbye to 'exam conditions'. And yet there'd be no time left for the progress test at all if she risked delaying the start till after her return ... Her dilemma was resolved by the History monitor taking the pile of test papers from the front desk.

'Shall I hand these out, Mrs Horst?'

Oh well. With any luck O'Brien would be out in any case. As the class settled down to its test (*Mark Antony was defeated at a. Trasimene, b. Trebia, c. Actium, d. Antirrhinum*), Jennifer Horst returned to her chair and set about tearing the offending map from Bunter-Byng's book together with the companion half of the sheet at the back: as if it had never been.

Trying to present a calm front, she made a circuit of the silent room, oblivious to the frantic semaphore of signs and pointings as Upper Five A collectively upped its average. The mistress noted with unworthy satisfaction that the foreign-looking girl whose name she could never remember was circling her answers instead of cancelling them with the neat vertical line specified in the exam board's rubric, thus invalidating her entire paper. There was always one. It would be a useful object lesson to the rest of the class when the results were pinned up: nought out of forty: naughty. But Mrs Horst was rather ashamed at the pleasure it gave her to contemplate the tearful scenes and caught the girl's eye, giving her head a cross little shake. The silly creature frowned at her paper and hastily rubbed out the ring around answer a. and circled d. instead: Mrs Horst *was* a sport. The mistress sighed again and turned away. What was the point?

'Fifteen minutes have gone, you have five minutes left.'

Mrs Horst gazed out of the window at the rainy spring sky. She was still itching to go downstairs and collar the Bunter-Byng baggage: give her some lines or some copying to do, some rocks to break – Mrs Mostyn wouldn't have hesitated. Mrs Horst's heart was still drumming hard from the girl's assault. It didn't use to be like this when she did her B.Ed. Nobody had mentioned not letting your pupils smell fear; riot, rebellion, gross impertinence, third party, fire and theft hadn't really been antici-pated, not in *fee-paying* schools. The better type of girl knew how to behave and even the charity pupils were no trouble, a few rough edges but generally pleasant enough and keener, if anything. Nowadays one could scarcely tell the two tribes apart. Bunter-Byng didn't have a scholarship. Her grandmother had been one of the original thirty Fawcettians but it made no odds. The girl was discourteous at the best of times, and as for that lunatic tirade about the lazy so-called map she'd drawn ... Almost as though she were *trying* to get herself expelled from the room, or miss the test ... This worm of doubt arrived too late. Damn. By now the girl might be regaling the head with her topological tosh. Damn, damn, damn.

Test over, Mrs Horst returned to the chalkface. Could anyone tell her the three causes of the *Graeco–Persian* wars? Anyone?

Not a single hand raised.

'Amanda McQueen, let's have *one* cause shall we? One reason for Xerxes' invasion . . .?'

'Boredom?'

'Don't be flippant, Amanda. *Examiners* don't like it.'

Mrs Horst began drawing an outline of the Grecian coast (after eighteen years on the job she could do this blindfold) and sketching edited highlights of the Battle of Salamis with coloured chalks. She then called Bryony to the front to have a stab at labelling the arrows. She tried not to ask Bryony *every* time, but the lazy fool was always good for a laugh and this morning she excelled herself. Mrs Horst got little enough in the way of amusement but Bryony Cotter insinuating Hannibal into the Athenian high command was definitely one for the album. Did they not listen to a word one said? Then the grisly realisation dawned: in the previous week's multiple choice the barmy answer (it was fun to include at least one barmy answer, Mrs Horst always felt) had suggested Hannibal as a potential leader of the Allied fleet. *Maddening* how quickly such tiny seeds of misinformation could flower, infinitely more robust than the real thing – like dandelions (and just as hard to uproot). She waved Bryony back to her seat and began automatically filling in the missing names. Again.

Mrs Horst hadn't exactly planned a teaching career but it had seemed a terrible pity to waste her degree. One never admitted as much at parties, at interviews, even in the staff room – it sounded so small-minded said out loud – but the old notes still came in very handy. It would have been perverse not to make use of all that knowledge, all that blotless underlining and labelling. And teaching had looked like an attractive option at the time because she had, foolishly, made the mistake of seeing her chosen career in terms of what the world at large always thought of as perks: the pension; the annual sixth-form trip to Rome or Athens or

Crete; those fabled long holidays. In fact the sixth-form trips were growing rowdier and less manageable by the year, and as for the holidays, one forgot that they would need to be taken at a time when the museums and galleries of Europe (as well as the cafés and beaches and camp sites and swimming pools of Europe) were full of schoolchildren, and the guidebook-guzzling parents of schoolchildren doggedly introducing their offspring to each foreign land just as they'd introduced them to chicken pox.

Mrs Horst looked out at the sullen sea of unresponsive faces. The remaining three Amandas were all together on the back row. They'd retrieved their bags from the heap and one of them was quite obviously hiding a book or magazine of some sort inside her historic atlas: Amanda Baker, already on the brink of suspension or even outright expulsion according to the last staff meeting. Disruptive. Destructive. One more slip and the girl would be suspended. Should she say something? A report would have to be filed. Meetings with O'Brien. Meetings with Mostyn. Meetings with parents, even. Angry, guilty, defensive, customer-is-always-right parents. Ghastly. She struggled to picture Mr Baker. Had he been there on Monday night? Fathers didn't always come, but it was always unpleasant when they did. They behaved like someone sending something back in a restaurant: this isn't what I ordered. Finally she took a deep breath, strode down the aisle and twitched Baker's copy of *Ads and Admen* from inside her book. She could decide later what action to take.

For the last five minutes of the lesson the History mistress tried her hand at a pep talk. They must all do their very, very best. Mrs Horst thought of Hannibal sending his men into battle at Cannae – a seamless flow of oratory: inspirational; passionate; hortatory (*hortor, hortari, hortatus sum*).

Baker yawned openly. Go through all your notes, droned the Horst, for the millionth time. Learn your dates and spellings, read the question, go through your answers scrupulously. Everyone will die.

Bunty was already at the head of the tuck shop queue when Baker got there (an adoring first former had let the older girl push in).

'Blimey, that was quick.'

'Want one?' Bunty took a hungry 100-calorie bite from her chocolate snack. 'No? Please yourself.'

'Was O'Brien not there?'

'No she was there all right, just couldn't be bothered. "I'm not interested in this nonsense" – her very words – apologise to old Horst-face, re-do map, go to tuck shop, go directly to tuck shop. Fancy a fag?'

'See you round the sheds in a minute. I've changed my mind about getting some chocolate.' Baker picked up a disgusting great marshmallow biscuit thing and waved it (a funny look from Bunty).

Baker watched her friend shoulder through the quad door and out of sight before binning her unwanted biscuit and fleeing back through the refectory to the ground floor cloaks.

The room's two-tone grey paint job switched from gunmetal to dishwater at about tit height with a black gloss tide mark where the two shades met. The shiny grey ceiling was beaded with chilly white dishes of light, a dozen at least, but the thick glass of the shades and the thrifty wattage meant that they had small impact on the gloom (not a light to read name tapes by). Beneath the coat pegs hundreds of outdoor shoes and plimsolls lay trapped inside the wire-fronted benches like lace-up lab rats.

Baker slipped into one of the cubicles, delved into her bag and finally unearthed Julia's scrap of paper. The note had been written on the inside of a chewing gum wrapper, the letters scratched onto the chalky surface of the foil's white lining, its edge serrated like a blade, a minty smell still clinging to the inside. Just one line in rough capitals – as if written with the wrong hand: 'MEET ME. ORGAN LOFT. TOMORROW 1.15'. No signature. No chances taken.

The school organ had breathed its last before Baker even started. The retirement of the only mistress who could play it and the lack of interest shown by even the more musical Fawcettians meant that the restoration fund was a long way down the head's list of priorities (above 'redecorate sick bay' but some way below 're-turf vandalised front lawn' and 'query twinning with Dusseldorf').

The 'loft' (really just a room full of dusty pipes) was secured by latch and padlock – but the Mandies (who habitually checked all doors and routinely hid any key they found) had made short work of that, thanks to the tiny screwdriver on Queenie's multi-purpose knife. Dry, warm, slightly spooky, it ought to have made the perfect breaktime hidey hole, but the floor was almost all plasterboard and there was only really room for one bum on the joists – last thing you wanted was one of your size fives poking through the assembly hall ceiling. The bike sheds and loos made safer (if chillier) hideouts.

What did Julia want a meeting for? Why didn't she just report her to Mrs Mostyn and be done with it? Had she had a change of heart about shopping her to the Drumlin? Or had she decided to dream up her own punishment instead?

Such a lot of girls left after the fifth form that anyone left standing was automatically made a prefect, whether or not they were Good Prefect Material, and some of them could be downright sadistic. The previous year's Upper Sixth had ganged up on a scholarship first former they'd all taken a dislike to: Claudia something, very tall, very swotty, played the bass recorder. They had decided that her old man was a dustman and threatened to tell everybody and would sing the special song whenever she walked past, pinching her hard where it wouldn't show. Made her cry. She left at the end of her first year. Turned out her old man was nothing of the kind, not an *actual* dustman anyway, no dustman's hat or anything. Just worked in an office in the cleansing department.

'Did he live in a council flat?' demanded Bunty at the time.

'Denbigh Avenue? Doubt it.'

'And what *are* gorblimey trousers?'

Julia knew that Baker was within an ace of getting thrown out (*I've got my eye on you*), knew she had only to report her for smoking to get her suspended at the very least but what did a meeting in the organ loft have to do with it? What was she after? A pep talk? It could hardly be blackmail? Or could it?

Chapter 8

Queenie wasn't the only girl who'd given up Chemistry. Lured labwards by the promise of a white coat and the mad scientist fun of drawing fantastical Professor Branestawm experiments with their nifty little plastic stencils, the would-be chemists soon became baffled by the alphanumeric soup of the periodic table. Trouble was that it wasn't especially popular with staff either – as Dr O'Brien had long ago discovered. Any Chemistry graduate with half a brain got a job pouring test tube contents into beakers in 'industry' (if the photos in the ICI leaflets in Miss Batty's filing cabinet were any guide). The dregs of the university Chemistry faculties assumed teaching would be an option once they graduated, but they had little stamina for the work and even less aptitude and seldom lasted more than a year or two.

Mildred Fawcett's last upper school Chemistry mistress had left mid-term under something of a cloud. Her replacement, conjured into being at terrifyingly short notice, was, quite unprecedentedly, a man.

'Male?' marvelled Queenie.

'Definitely says *Mister* Mars on the noticeboard. Emergency appointment, apparently. Started Monday but he's been ducking assembly, jammy bugger'.

There was no one in the lab, male or female, when they filed in. Stott grabbed the back bench and the three Mandies settled down to chat.

'Have you worked out what you're going to say at your careers interview?'

'I'm considering Hairdressing.'

Miss Batty had lent Baker a copy of *Modern Careers for Girls* to prepare her for that afternoon's advice session. It was fifteen years out of date.

'"The true hairdresser,"' read Baker, '"must have an innate artistic sense and a creative flair . . . physical fitness is essential for this career."'

'It always says that,' said Bunty. 'What if you had a wooden leg?'

'A one-legged hairdresser? Don't be daft. Do you know any one-legged hairdressers? I rest my case.' She continued flicking through. 'How about Dentistry? "Physical fitness is essential, as is first-class eyesight." Doesn't say anything about hairdressers needing perfect eyesight.'

'Aha. Well that's Tash's feather cut explained.'

'I might just say Secretary. Got to say something.'

'Secretary? You can do better than that.' Stottie all peculiar and serious as per usual. 'You're so lucky – you could do *anything*.'

Brian, Vic and pals had set their hearts on becoming secretaries – *bilingual* secretaries. Strange the way they all wanted the same job – not like they could all save desks for each other. Baker looked across to the next bench where the gang were sitting.

'Do you think they're all from another planet? Like that film with all the creepy blonde kids.'

'*Village of the Bland.*'

'They're definitely telepathetic. Look at them.'

All six had pulled their blue science overalls as tight as they would go and secured the ties in the same slipped reef knot on the left side. Crossed legs all coated in an identical mildew of ash grey stretch nylon, lips subtly smeared with a lick of Vaseline from the same slim tin.

'Did you really say Nursing at your last Careers thingy?'

'Yeah,' laughed Bunty, 'kept the Batty quiet.'

'And what d'you really want to be?'

'Wanna be a Bunny.' Bunty rolled her torso, emphasising her cup size.

'You're a silly moo, you are. You said you didn't want to be a skivvy and a Bunny's just a skivvy with ears. And all those old leches. And all that *wiping*. Bad as nursing.'

'Yeah, but the tips are bigger. Nobody tips nurses, just cheap chocolates, and anything beats typing, whatever Bryony says – even if it is bi-bloody-lingual. What the hell do they do all day, anyway?' continued Bunty. '*Cher monsieur, merci pour votre correspondence, wollen sie im Schwartzwald spazieren gehen? Quel est votre sujet préféré?*'

Not that Bryony's secretarial fantasies went anywhere near the actual typing side. Bryony pictured herself in a maroon pencil skirt and blow-dried page boy, booking plane tickets, travelling to business conferences, buying duty free scent and alien brands of aspirin (in fluent French, obviously). Not messing about filing documents or opening post or reconciling petty cash. There would be people for that (monolingual people). There was usually a boss in Bryony's picture: young, blue-suited, a man of distinction (big spender).

Still no sign of Mr Mars who was, as they spoke, panting up the hill to the front gate. The arrival of a male Chemistry teacher had unsettled the senior common room. The only men's lavatories were the one in the Music block and the brick outhouse used by Mr Dingle the school caretaker. The existing staff agreed that the simplest solution would be to reallocate the headmistress's private privy. And do you know, actually, yes, Dr O'Brien had in fact given the matter a great deal of thought and no, she concluded, it would set a potentially dangerous precedent to give ground to that extent, dignity of the office and so forth, and Dr O'Brien decided that, on reflection, the walk to the Music block would do their new colleague no harm at all.

Derek Mars had underestimated the time it would take to get from his designated lavatory (blue paper, most amusing) to the main building. Pins could have been dropped as he finally crossed from the lab door to his bench beneath the wide, green blackboard. The tweed jacket and old whatsits tie were regulation issue but the cut of his cavalry twill Sta-Prest strides was unexpected.

'Ooh,' whispered Baker. 'Do clock the trousers.'

'Gorblimey,' said Bunty. 'How does he get them on, do you reckon? Do his feet unscrew?'

Baker, suddenly inspired, got to her feet and began to applaud. The new master's face quivered suspiciously. Was this normal? No one had said anything about this in the staff room. Other things, yes, but not this. The rest of the class joined Baker (say what you liked about them, they were a game crowd) and he reached the front bench to a respectable ovation. He signalled his puzzlement to a girl whose spectacles and keen-as-mustard front row seat inspired confidence.

'It's traditional, sir.'

Was it? And how would he ever find out? The staff room was still falling silent whenever he entered it – he half suspected them of passing notes.

Derek Mars had had every intention of giving up teaching. His very first job after qualifying had been at a large Church of England school: single sex, selective, *absurdly* well-equipped. The head of department was a former Rugby Blue and regularly bullied the headmaster and board of governors (not a BSc between them) into buying whatever kit he fancied: infra-red mass spectrometer, electron microscope, you name it.

The boys assigned to Derek Mars had been loud and large but they weren't delinquent or idle. They passed exams, moved on to good technical colleges, a few even went to university. Big, brash, hairy, confident, sarcastic boys, boys with a sixth sense for weakness, boys who twigged at once that Mr Mars was not a master to fear or obey.

The headmaster had called him in for a fireside chat at the end of his first term (said it was 'routine' but none of the other new masters was summoned) in which he was told he would soon 'learn the ropes'. Did he play golf at all? He'd said no but the old fool persisted with his fatuous analogy – *yips*, forsooth – and bleated on about how it was probably just honeymoon nerves and would all come out in the wash – rather an off-colour metaphor mixture, Derek Mars felt.

But he never did 'find his form', never did lose that feeling of almost weepy panic when faced with twenty pairs of unforgiving adolescent eyes, seasoned critics of the genre who'd seen the whole thing done better and more persuasively elsewhere, who saved their plaudits for virtuoso performers like Harris with his tricksy little packets of gun cotton.

By his second year even the new intake had been primed to watch for his nervous stammer, his clumsiness with laboratory glassware – 'C-c-c-careful sir!' Mars was barely taller than his second form students and was skinny with it. They called him Stinker, apparently. The can't-be-bothered dullness of the sobriquet was depressing in itself. The department head rejoiced in the name of 'Flash' Harris thanks to his meretricious antics with primitive explosives.

And as Derek Mars inched through the syllabus with his middle school mediocrities (a senior colleague had nabbed the

A streams and Flash Harris creamed off the sixth form) he began to feel more and more as if he'd been written into one of those plays his mother took him to, dry as common room sherry, that told of misanthropic schoolmasters who couldn't understand why it was that boys never teased them or sent them Christmas cards or asked them which girl to ask out or which horse to back. Harris had all of that: faintly louche, avuncular (but not like any uncles Derek Mars had ever had).

Stinker had only just survived his second year, kept going by the comforting thought that he had given notice. He'd spent both Christmas and Easter holidays applying for jobs but was only offered the humblest bottle-washing lab work with lousy hours, the meagre salary notionally enhanced by promises of early promotion once he 'knew the ropes' (more blasted ropes).

After six miserable months freelancing for a plastics factory the memory of the classroom faded, and fifteen weeks' holiday, a near-decent salary and a guaranteed pension looked a lot less unattractive. Perhaps if he taught at a prep school? Or tried girls? Girls would be a lot easier, surely? Biddable, underlined neatly, copied nicely, didn't spill things – or set fire to anything.

The short stint in plastics made his CV look scrappy but his mother had been unwell and her three-month decline could be twitched back and forth like a skimpy fitting room curtain to cover the awkward gap in his professional life story. The Mildred Fawcett interview panel appeared impressed by his filial devotion and cooed awkwardly like doves in tight shoes when the cancer was mentioned, although the O'Brien woman (no fool) did wonder why he hadn't asked his old school for a sabbatical of some kind ...? Derek Mars managed not to stammer over the reply which had been copied out in neat in his memory: how he hadn't wanted to leave St Christopher's in the lurch (how considerate) and how he very much wanted a new challenge (if Dr O'Brien had had a pound for every deadbeat job-switcher who'd dredged that one up she could have bought herself an electron microscope). He learned afterwards that they wouldn't have cared too much what he said, given that the bulk of middle school chemistry was being taught by a physics teacher keeping one chapter ahead.

His appointment had alarmed the existing staff but his first few days gave no cause for complaint. He didn't grumble about his chair or the size of his locker and he didn't smoke a pipe or monopolise the coin operated phone ringing up his paramours or his bookmaker. Dr O'Brien relaxed: he'd do (just about). At barely twenty-five you might have expected a bit of horseplay with the younger mistresses but he didn't seem the type and in any case his oddly elderly, mother's boy wardrobe of turned-up trousers and Terylene ties had beta minus allure, had he but known it.

'Stinker' had been ragged rather about his new job by the chaps at the bridge club, who assured him that anything in trousers (turned up or otherwise) would be of interest to this closed order of bluestockings and he was almost looking forward to a smattering of feminine attention.

The chairs in the staff common room were newish and cheap: bony arms, little padding and generally uninviting – very much like their occupants. He'd chuckled inwardly at this happy comparison (one to remember for the chaps). The Fawcett SCR spent most of its free time marking homework, carping about the girls or toiling over the *Daily Telegraph* crossword – very much a joint effort (although from the few conversations he'd had he wouldn't put money on any one of them being able to complete a puzzle single-handed: *Some insane roman (4)* – 'Oh of *course*, Edith, how clever of you!').

When he arrived for work on his second day he had been part gratified, part terrified to note that one or more of them had taken to wearing large amounts of very strong scent – or so he thought until he spotted a can of air freshener on the windowsill by his armchair. His allotted chair had originally been chummily close to another group but had been moved and now sat in surly splendour in the far corner of the room. Peculiar creatures. Perhaps it would be more prudent not to ask about this applause business.

The clapping in the chemistry lab had continued for well over a minute but they'd stopped at last and he took his place at the front bench. The blackboard behind him was entirely taken up by a hastily drawn diagram showing the procedure for making distilled water with 'please leave' implausibly scrawled in the bottom corner in girlish roundhand. No sign of a board rubber . . .

'So. How was life on Mars?' asked Queenie, who had joined the three chemists in the cloakroom after her domestic science lesson.

'Absolute Stinker,' said Bunty.

'In every sense,' snarled Stott. 'A whole class given double prep over a missing board rubber? Bit extreme. I mean what has he got in reserve? What's his nuclear option if we all set fire to the fume cabinet again?'

'"The following girls will report to the staff room for the shagging they so richly deserve,"' said Queenie in her Mostyn voice.

'I think I'm going to be sick,' said Bunty. 'Imagine that lying on top of you: even his eyebrows have dandruff.'

'Married?'

'Leave off. Did you see his shirt when he took off his jacket to wipe the board? Only irons collar and cuffs and front. Wives wouldn't get away with that.'

'Maybe he's looking for *lurve*. Can't have Miss Drumlin, she's married to Middlesex lacrosse. The Gleet might suit, smarten him up a bit anyway. Bet the Gleet irons sleeves. She'd soon put a crease in his underpants.'

'As the actress said to the bishop.'

'Yeah, but at a price. The Gleet's neurotic, Mummy says. Do better just having a bit on the side with Mrs Chiffley, fatten him up at least.'

'Only if he likes rollmop herrings,' said Queenie who was humming 'Born Free' as she scraped her fish down the loo. 'I'm releasing them back into the wild.'

'Where is Rollmop?' wondered Bunty.

'Sweden somewhere. Just outside Britvik.'

Everyone laughed and Bunty grinned. Anyone else would want the punchline but Bunty just wanted more jokes to be told.

Chapter 9

Baker had arrived early for her careers appointment and was sitting outside the sick bay, trying to think of something that would really get up the Batty woman's nose (Mountain Rescue? Merchant Banking? Minesweeping?), when her eye was caught by an unfamiliar movement at the far end of the dark narrow corridor. Julia Smith, entirely alone in the lobby outside the staff room, was turning cartwheels. Over and over and over, so fast and smooth that the rubbish didn't even fall from her pockets – centrifugal? -petal? She came to a halt outside the headmistress's office and Baker held her breath, waiting for the knock on the door, but Julia merely tossed back her shiny auburn hair, straightened her pervy little skirt and jogged back up the stairs without a glance.

Miss Batty herself was still finishing up after her last music lesson. The Lower Fourth had evacuated the Music Room at top speed, leaving her to tidy away thirty-two copies of 'Summer is Icumen In' and making her late for her session in the Careers cupboard. She was in no hurry, methodically refolding the sheet music and stowing it all neatly in the correct folder in the glazed cabinet by the piano.

Miss Batty had been at Mildred Fawcett ever since she got her B.Ed. *Fionula Batty MA Oxon: Music and Careers* said the prospectus. The ad in the *TES* had only said 'Music Teacher', but her predecessor (hired by La Fawcett herself to teach pianoforte and deportment) had drawn the short straw when the need for careers advice became ever more pressing and it had been decreed that the twinning of the roles should continue. Deportment lived on as a badge awarded to anyone with a clean blouse and unladdered tights but the encyclopaedia-balancing days were long gone.

Miss Batty's immaculate assumption from Lady Margaret Hall to Fawcett Upper meant that she knew almost nothing about the job market so they sent her on a course: two days of lectures and slides in Leicester somewhere at the height of the Proms season. It was largely common sense and most of the work was done for you by the trusty old 'Careers Archive' which consisted of the leaflets contained in three drawers of a four-drawer filing cabinet (the bottom drawer having been requisitioned by Miss Drumlin for the sick bay log, a bottle of Lucozade and half a pint of nail varnish remover).

Miss Batty had also inherited a long shelf of books called things like *A Career for Your Daughter*; *Challenging Careers in the Library World*; *Working With Animals*; *Rosemary Takes to Teaching*; *Pauline Becomes a Hairdresser* and *A Career for Women in Industry?* (the question mark said it all).

Miss Batty locked the Music Room's Steinway and sped along the dingy admin corridor to where Baker was waiting. She saw the silhouetted student take something from her mouth and stick it under the seat of the bench. A rebuke was in order but Miss Batty hadn't the heart. You couldn't see the beastly stuff, after all, and fifteen minutes flew by quickly enough as it was.

'Amanda Baker? Go on in. It isn't locked.'

The room was hardly wider than a corridor and was almost filled by a narrow steel bedstead made up with knitted cotton blankets and a foam pillow pessimistically draped with blue paper towels in readiness for another projectile nosebleed. There was a canvas chair and one of the rickety folding desks used for public exams wedged between the bed and the wall, under the window, but Miss Batty preferred not to use the diagnostic end of the room – *How long have you had this urge to be an articled clerk?* – and made do with a clipboard and a pair of tip-up chairs just inside the door.

Baker sat down on one of them and stared blankly at the ancient WAAF recruitment posters hung either side of the filing cabinet. The uniformed smiles did little to lighten the sickly mood established by the green gloss paint and the small temperature chart with its panicky notes in Biro (Normal, Feverish, Summon Assistance). The walls at the bed end were otherwise bare, apart from a large map of the world placed at eye level to distract first and second formers while the creepy little man from the health authority took their hands and made them squeeze his thin old thigh while he gave the German Measles and BCG injections (even the proles knew what *that* was about). It was a map of the wrong world, mind you, West Africa was still a big green blob.

'What are the red pins for?' Baker's question interrupted Miss Batty's recitation on the importance of keeping options open.

'What? Oh that: old girls who have worked overseas.'

There were three pins.

'Had you thought of working abroad? Perhaps in the services?'

Golly, this was depressing, thought Miss Batty. Always the same jobs. A few girls each year would set their hearts on wireless operation or dental nursing or speech therapy (there was quite a vogue for this among Miss Kopje's 'ragged rocks' contingent). One, sometimes two girls per year settled on a career in medicine (or thereabouts), two or three would plump for teaching. The air hostesses tended to come in pairs, dreaming of staff discounts and poolside pina coladas. Miss Batty's fiancé had suggested she run a book in the staff room, the distribution of girlish wishes was so predictable, but you'd still need to keep a weather eye on the trends. Fashion Buyer had fallen from favour – it was really only one up from 'Can I help you, madam?' the fifth form had decided – but working in an office (surely the dullest life imaginable) was always popular, particularly since the advent of the 'personal assistant' and the bi-lingual secretary. Miss Batty occasionally helped out with the French conversation mocks and the idea of one of those tongue-tied eskervoos querying an invoice or a ship's manifest always made her laugh.

Received Careers wisdom had it that every subject dropped, every examination flunked, meant another option sealed off. And yet one did meet (or read about) lawyers who hadn't studied Latin, photographers who had given up Chemistry. The idea that one needed the periodic table to make sense of a dark room had always been one of her predecessor's trump cards, but no one ever called her on it: did David Bailey have a Chemistry O level? Of course he didn't. Silly sausage. But Miss Batty was still trotting out the same speech about 'doors closing', complete with cautionary tales of old girls whose dreams had been blighted when potential employers spotted their ignorance of South American exports or trigonometry. *Woolworth's* would be whispered, as if the future were not Mildred Fawcett's 'rosy path of golden possibilities' but a hostile terrain strung with tripwires.

Ask the pre-preps in Fawcett Under what they wanted to be when they grew up and their horizons were limitless: film star, lady astronaut, princess, Lassie … but it was a career mistress's duty to rein in such ambitions. Vet? Try kennel maid. Restaurateur? Try catering supervisor. Floristry? Now you're talking. It was like pick-a-card-any-card. They thought it was random, thought they'd got fifty-two to choose from, but they still took the one they were supposed to take.

Miss Batty had once thumbed through a copy of *Careers for Boys* in Smith's. Such a lot of careers – airline pilot, stonemason, stockbroker – far more than would have fitted into her filing system. Was there a *Careers for Dogs*? Plenty to choose from: police work, mountain rescue, modelling, drug squad not to mention any number of openings in pharmaceuticals . . .

Baker's surprise announcement put an end to Miss Batty's rueful reverie.

An *actress*? Was the girl mad?

'Should be under A,' said Baker in her only-does-it-to-annoy voice, but Miss Batty was still too taken aback to even register her rudeness and besides it very definitely *wasn't* under A. Animals (care of), Army, Air Force, Air Hostess, Au Pair: yes. Astrophysicist, Astronaut, Arms dealer, *Artiste*: no. Not even Accountant (although Accounts was there). And definitely not Actress. Stupid girl.

Cold water poured out in an unceasing stream from Miss Batty's unpainted lips. It wasn't steady work. Even good actresses could spend a lot of time unemployed – 'resting' they called it (she smiled at this point, as if she had just made a joke). Only the *very best* became really famous. Which couldn't conceivably be you, ob-viously. Not *you*. Someone else.

'I didn't know you even *liked* acting, Amanda. You weren't in the school play – the drama schools would almost certainly expect that.'

As if anyone who enjoyed acting would have wanted to be in the school play, thought Miss Batty: *King John* (were they out of their minds?). And the whole production dominated by the Remove prefects and the elocution mafia.

'I suppose I could try to get some leaflets from Rada ... or maybe Lamda would be better ...' Miss Batty gazed disconsolately at the bulging A–K drawer, wondering if it would really be worth the bother of yet another pink folder. No one had ever asked about Bookbinding again ...

'You asked me what I wanted to do. That's what I want to do.' Baker was quite pleased with her chosen career. Saying 'Nursing' would have made it too easy. Nice to make 'em sweat. What would Miss Batty know about drama?

The mistress looked sidelong at Baker as her fingers trod across the files in the top drawer, noting the greasy dark blonde rats' tails, the skinny shape under the ridiculous gym slip, the complete want of grace in that Stanley Spencer slouch. Actress? Talk about aiming high.

Miss Batty thought of the actresses she sometimes spotted in the reasonable little restaurants wallpapered with signed photographs where she and a theatre-going chum would eat rigatoni and discuss whatever play they'd been to, marking performances out of ten (*could do better; this is not what you were asked to do*). Sometimes an actress one had just seen in costume looking enraged, seductive, murderous, tormented, would be at a nearby table in a smart silk shirt, snapping tiny bites from bread sticks with her capped white teeth while smarming waiters brought undrinkable complimentary liqueurs smelling of bath essence.

Had those actresses ever had one of these careers chats? And if they had, had the part-time careers mistress fired back with a yes, gosh yes, definitely Cicely, Dulcie, Maggie, of *course* you should act. I will never forgive you if you don't go for that audition. Change your name, dye your hair, straighten your nose, cap your teeth, sleep with whoever you must but don't, don't I *beg* you, deny the stage your genius. Was that what they said?

Of course it wasn't. They said 'Take a typing course' just as Miss Batty was about to do.

If they were really determined on a stage career no amount of discouragement would put them off but was it really just about confidence, about only the strong surviving? Did talent count for nothing? And Miss Batty wondered how many art mistresses and elocution teachers were just the bruised remains of women who wanted to be something else. She never played the piano any more. Not properly.

Chapter 10

Most of the Upper Shell had slept badly on Wednesday night because most of them had stayed up till the small hours belatedly revising for Thursday's mocks, but Baker's sleepless night had been spent dreading her meeting with Julia Smith.

Baker had been packed off to bed after the *Ten O'Clock News*, but a broken thermostat on her bedroom radiator made the room unsleepably hot and she was still awake at midnight, listening to the noises of the house. Spam was already cold creamed and hot water bottled in the master bedroom and Baker could hear the master himself brushing his teeth in that angry haphazard way that left white specks all over the bathroom mirror, followed by a long gargle that echoed hideously in the tiny tiled room. Ablutions completed – his word – he locked and bolted the front door and she heard his slippered feet climbing back up the carpeted stairs, like the sound effects in a radio murder mystery.

Nothing had been said during dinner about her morning's detention so no one could have rung Dad with the glad tidings and Baker began to think the Drumlin had had a change of heart about reporting her to O'Brien – until she arrived at Registration next morning.

'Amanda!' Form mistress Mrs Lorimer, assertive for a change, delivered the news that Baker was wanted in the head's office

PDQ. She felt her shoulders going into spasm. Was this just Drumlin's little shoe fetish again or had Julia told about the fag on the train?

Dr O'Brien was on the telephone but Baker got the green light straight away and was signalled into a chair but remained standing, scanning the decor. O'Brien had overhauled the study the first week she took over as head, covering her predecessor's green emulsion with a smart silver stripe and replacing the Japanese woodcuts with a selection of really pervy prints: *The Wreck of the Medusa*, Judith beheading Holofernes and an oleograph of St Agatha holding a silver tray and absently caressing one of her plump white breasts, like a pornographic pastrycook. They were all on the wall facing the headmistress's chair (where visiting parents tended not to spot them).

Pride of place on the left wall (which they could see) was given to a pair of schoolgirl still lives. One was a photo-realistic trio of school badges: 'Squash', 'Vice' and 'Racquets' – had she been taking the piss? The other featured two lemons on a blue and white Cornishware plate. It was actually rather good: bold purplish shadows under the fruit and a real sense of the glaze on the china. The rubbishy Art Room paper had bubbled badly against the mount and a fine dust of yellow powder had trickled along the inside edge of the frame. Fine art; cheap paint. The typed label said *Dora Hardcastle* (who else?) *1965*. It wouldn't last another ten years.

Dr O'Brien had finished her call and was disinfecting the receiver with a cloth soaked in surgical spirit, a now-have-a-rinse smell that did nothing to ease Baker's nerves. Nor did the head's plummy, chummy manner.

'Sit down. Sit down.' Why did grown-ups always think it was jollier when you said things twice?

'See you're admiring Dora's lovely lemons.' Dr O'Brien turned her head towards the wall on which they were hanging and peered blindly at the yellow blur through heavy duty reading glasses worn on a chain round her neck.

'*Such* a talent.'

'What happened to her?'

'*Happened?*' The head looked perplexed: a fatal stabbing? a premium bond win she hadn't been told about? 'Oh I see, yes, yes, I see: *career-wise*. Very happy, I believe. Twin boys. He's a chartered accountant, or so she writes. Pity in a way. She'd have made an excellent art teacher.' Those who can *and* those who can't? Bit greedy.

'Now then, now then: to business.' She put the duster and the surgical spirit bottle in a desk drawer, let her glasses fall from her face to hang like a tortoiseshell trapeze against her paisley bosom and turned to Baker with lips pulled into a wider line.

'I have had a letter from your father this morning. I believe Mrs Mostyn had quite a heart-to-heart with him at the meeting on Monday but there were still a few points he wanted to raise with me.'

Baker looked at the letter in O'Brien's hand and felt her intestine curdling into a plumbing emergency – a vile, sour, sore, horribly familiar feeling. After four years of double Biology, she could actually picture all those villi going into reverse, flooding her gut with squittering panic the way they always did when anyone at home mentioned school or anyone at school mentioned home. She tried so hard to keep it all separate. They were *supposed* to be separate: different buildings; different food; different languages; different shoes.

It was never going to be good news, was it, this letter he'd written? Never going to be a nice hand-written note saying how very well dear Amanda was doing and could she possibly begin clarinet lessons next term or have Friday afternoon off for an optician's appointment?

'He's very worried about you.' O'Brien fumbled the reading glasses back on to her densely powdered nose in order to remind herself of one of the more affecting passages. 'Very worried.'

No he bloody wasn't. He was very worried about *him*, about the mess he was making of Project Amanda, about his failure to meet targets, reach the bonus threshold.

Bob Baker usually got his wife to type up his letters to the school, but he had written this one himself in his spidery scrawl. Pam was losing interest. She'd started volunteering to stay late at work: a report to type; a leaving drinks to go to, 'training' – for what? She'd arrive home barely in time to get supper on the table, after which his skinny, gymslipped little madam of a daughter would idle away the rest of the evening playing darts with herself or lying in front of the telly, homework untouched, while he and his wife exchanged whispered screams of frustration over the washing up.

Once a month his mother-in-law – also called Pamela, funnily enough – would ring from the Falkland Islands and he could always tell from his wife's wary replies whenever she was asking about the wicked stepdaughter: didn't interfere, get involved, stick oars in – or give a twopenny damn? He did wonder sometimes.

She used to be interested (or pretend to be?). Early on, anyway. But then all of the women who ran across him after Patsy cleared out seemed keen to show what lovely stepmothers they'd make, made a point of buying presents for darling Amanda: pyjama cases; manicure sets; dressing table sets; wickerwork sewing baskets; hankies with As and roses on, but you could tell that the presents were for his benefit – might just as well have been a bottle of Scotch. Pam had been different. Pam took the young Amanda to museums, taught her an easy way to draw a horse, read to her at bedtime. The rot set in when she started reading from her old book of Bible stories. Little Amanda had told Grandma all about loaves and fishes and bloody Patsy had got wind of it. Managed to get Pam on the phone (reversing the charges) and gave her an earful about patriarchal mumbo jumbo and how bloody well dare she, and it hadn't really been the same after that: '*Your* daughter', 'Bob's daughter' not 'Amanda' any more.

But it wasn't Pam's fault that Amanda had turned out like this. It was the school's bloody fault at bottom. They took delivery of a nice enough, no-nonsense eleven-year-old: head of house, keen on games, six badges in the Brownies and they handed you back what? *Amanda.* If someone did that much damage to your car or your dry cleaning you'd demand compensation. Or a replacement (*money refunded if not delighted*).

Not that they ever admitted liability. Three times a year he'd be made to queue for hours in the ritual humiliation that was parents' evening, being patronised by some blue-rinsed battle-axe with a voice like the Speaking Clock who said that your daughter paid no attention to her lessons and didn't do any of the work set. Like it was nothing to do with them. They were the ones standing at the front of a classroom, term in, term out, boring for Britain on Boyle's Law and then had the cheek to complain when no one took any notice.

He tried to imagine being taught by any of them and thought wistfully of his own schooldays: getting picked for the second eleven; oranges at half time; names engraved on cups or gilded onto scholarship walls or stitched onto cricket whites or stencilled onto tuck boxes. Kindly men in corduroy taking donnish delight in Grecian urns or Latin verse or Franco–Prussian wars (and their three main causes). All the things he had wanted for Jeremy (not Amanda). Mildred Fawcett was no comparison.

Hence the letter. No sense just waiting for yet another parents' evening. Monday night had definitely been an all time low. He had almost enjoyed the one before last – no thanks to Amanda, mind. Once in a bright blue moon, Miss Peters the Biology mistress had the pleasure of teaching a model pupil, one who had copied every diagram and taken every note so faithfully that Miss Peters simply hadn't the heart to part with her exercise book – *Excellent! This is exactly what you were asked to do*. A moment's work on the staples with a butter knife and a virgin yellow cover from one of the current batch of stationery, plus some deft dabbing at any tell-tale dates with her miniature bottle of ink eradicator and June Torrance was immortalised as a model pupil – *for any year*.

This handwritten vintage textbook was invariably left open on the front desk to be slobbered over by passing parents who would flick shamefacedly through its pages, silently comparing its copperplate perfection with their own daughters' efforts. The narrow feint's faint brownish tinge scarcely noticed beneath the fluorescent strip-lighting required for evening meetings. For nearly ten years Miss Peters had been wheeling out this reproachful paradigm until Bob Baker went and spoiled it all.

'A half crown?'

He had leafed through to one of the back pages of the Torrance testament where young June had drawn an exceptionally fine diagram of a sheep's heart, delicately shaded, scrupulously labelled ('always use a ruler') and in the bottom right hand corner, just below 'parietal pericardium', an unusually fine scale drawing of an obsolete silver coin.

'Amanda has a 50p piece on hers. All the others have 50p pieces.' Amanda's heart also had 'Volvo' and 'escape hatch' written very, very small where 'valve' and 'ventricle' ought to be but her labelling lines had been drawn with a ruler and Miss Peters had not registered the words themselves.

Miss Peters barely missed a beat: 'June is a numismatist.' The look on her face betrayed her. *Oik*, it said. *He won't know what it means*. But Bob Baker, who had always worn his public schooling very lightly (a safer bet on the building site), was one too many for her. 'I don't care three groats what she does with her leisure time. The half crown was demonetised in 1970. I think you've been rumbled, Miss Peters.' He'd arrived home much chirpier than usual that time.

He hadn't mentioned any of this in his note to Dr O. The letter, written in a miserable rage after his Monday night nightmare, was as brisk as a site report, expressing general disappointment at the school's failure to motivate Amanda and floating the idea that she might be happier 'elsewhere'. Any number of staff meetings had floated the exact same idea, of course, sighed Dr O'Brien as she re-read the sheet in her hand. A great many people would be a great deal happier if Amanda Baker were elsewhere but £1,200 a year was not to be sneezed at and besides, Dr O'Brien's stubborn streak was aroused by this talk of Elsewhere. What did Elsewhere have that Mildred Fawcett didn't? She was determined to use this meeting to see off all this defeatist talk. She settled back in her chair and beamed mildly in the girl's direction (Judith hacking away at Holofernes could be a huge help at such moments).

'Have you been happy here, Amanda?' (She'd toyed with 'Are you happy?' but the past tense kept up the tension, kept up that sense of axes about to fall.)

'All my friends are here.'

'Ah. Yes. *Friends*. Amanda Bunter-Byng? The older Stott girl?' the head topped up her smile with a refreshing glance at Moreau's *Salome*. 'Are you sure that you are all a good influence on each other? Amanda Stott could lose her scholarship if her grades were to slip. Have you thought about that? Would you want that on your conscience?' It sounded almost, well, like a *threat*.

Baker's shoulders curled forward and her attention strayed to the window behind the head's head, to the steel ash tray tucked almost out of sight on the sill outside. O'Brien watched as the girl's pupils shrivelled in the morning sunlight and two discs of almost yellowish green turned to face her, but Baker still didn't reply. Dr O'Brien looked down at her desk, pretending to gain inspiration from the papers on her blotter. 'Miss Gleet is very pleased with your novel. *Snapdragon* something? *Promise*? *Summer*?'

'Harvest.'

'*Harvest*? I'd no idea snapdragons were grown on that kind of scale.' She gave a slight shake of the head to stop the thought from landing there. 'Miss Gleet wants me to take a look at it. Very original style, she says.'

Original? Moron. Called herself an English graduate?

'And she was most encouraging about your plot summary: "A haunting tale of love and loss" she tells me. I very much look forward to reading the finished draft.'

Was that the answer? frowned O'Brien to herself. Legend had it that if you stumbled on something that one of your girls was good at, be it chess or the cello, it unlocked their confidence and other successes would follow. Worked every time for Enid Blyton. Perhaps the Baker girl's scribbling would keep her out of mischief. If that failed, she'd have to suspend her – she'd have a staff room coup on her hands otherwise.

'Mrs Horst tells me that you were reading this during her lesson.'

O'Brien produced the confiscated copy of *Ads and Admen* from an in-tray to the right of her telephone. It fell open at the spread on 'The Four Faces of Adman's Eve' (housewife; icon; instructress and something known as 'the self-touching nude'). O'Brien's glance batted between the bubble-bathing beauty savouring the softness of her own scented shoulder (*patchouli, bergamot and wild jasmine open up a world of sensuous secrets*) and St Agatha, stroking the proud curve of her disembodied breast. *Plus ça change.*

'Three Wishes ...?' The head's face had the same troubled, faraway, quiz contestant look that Bunty's had worn – as if there were a right answer and she had forgotten it. What would Salome's other two wishes have been? She dragged her thoughts back to the matter in hand.

'Have you perhaps been thinking of a career in Sales? Jennifer Osborne, Head of Stanhope, 1972 I think it was, is with some sort of market research outfit. Housewives, butter, margarine, washes whiter, that sort of thing. Very enjoyable apparently.'

'All the margarine you can eat? No, that wasn't why I was reading it.' Baker straightened slightly. 'More a case of knowing your enemy.'

'Ah. Sisterhood.' A pitying smile. 'Strange isn't it how women conspire in their own enslavement.' She glanced back at the magazine: *a radiant, lovelier you* – just a few petrochemicals in the bathwater. 'When I was a girl, the chemist's shop in Battle High Street sold two kinds of bath salts: cheap bath salts and expensive bath salts. In the war we used lavender.'

Baker felt confused by the sudden change of subject, the confiding tone. Whose side was she on?

'Rather an unusual letter.' O'Brien too had spotted that their little chat was heading off-syllabus 'He's clearly very angry, but there's a strange third person quality about it. Like a lawyer's letter, as if he wasn't personally involved. And he uses the past tense at times. Rather revealing. As if it were already over and done with. As if you ...'

She stopped short at the look on Baker's face and pulled another smile.

'I am taking trouble with you, Amanda,' she continued, 'because you are worth trouble and because your mind appeals to me. I want you to get the results we all know you are capable of, and we are all here to help you in any way we can. I know you find discipline frustrating, but I hope you're going to knuckle down and produce some decent results in this week's exams.'

Knuckling down. Everyone to dress the same, wear the same ponytail, draw the identical diagram, sing the same notes, want the same jobs, buy the same bubble bath, eat the same cheese.

'Get some good grades under your belt and Sixth Form will all feel very different. Fresh challenges. Far more *freedom*.'

The freedom to wear grey instead of blue.

Chapter 11

Thursday's first exam was being held in the assembly hall. All four Mandies bundled their bags into a corner under the grand piano and, while they were waiting, Queenie (the canasta player's daughter) reached down the pack of hymn numbers and shuffled them expertly, the cards fluttering within her hands like a trapped bird. She then replaced them neatly on the corner of the hymn number frame. 'Plough the fields and sca-tter,' hummed Stottie.

The Geography mock had been co-written by Combe and Mostyn and was an oil-and-water mix of urban planning and palm fibre. One third of it was missing-words-and-labelling, one third short essay questions, and the rest was multiple choice (*Which of the following is NOT a type of irrigation: a. Archimedes screw; b. noria, c. sakia or d. silage?*). Mrs Mostyn had been left in charge of producing the final result and the pages were, as always, run off on the school's ancient Banda apparatus. 'Bandered copies', Mrs Mostyn called them but it couldn't really be made to work as an English verb – or so Stottie said. Italian no problem: *bando* (I run off countless purple copies), *bandiamo* (let us run off countless purple copies).

Mrs Mostyn arrived a minute before kick-off to explain apologetically to Miss Combe (who was invigilating) that the extreme right-hand edge of the hand-written master had not *quite* copied as it ought. She then proceeded to delay the start, clocking up ten minutes in injury time while she made sure that each page was properly corrected. Miss Combe (whose own papers were always flawlessly typewritten) gave a small, superior smirk at the methanol-scented sheets.

Miss Combe relished invigilating and paced the room Colditz-style, occasionally ratcheting up the tension with the inevitable 'Thirty minutes have gone, you have sixty minutes left' lark.

Swivelling squeakily on her high-gloss crepe-soled brogues every time she was called from her station to dispense more paper, she would look obsessively over her shoulder, convinced their requests were merely a blind to allow notes to be passed, or for mad, map-related mimes to be enacted while her back was turned – like they were all playing a huge game of Grandmother's Footsteps. As she patrolled the rows she pulled aside blotters and parted the lips of pencil cases with bony, ink-stained fingers. Like a medical. Yuk.

The Mrs Mostyn half of the paper was all Ordnance Survey symbols, typical homes in Malawi and a map of Africa to label. Miss Combe was obviously responsible for the rest: rift valleys, pebble formation and (a special favourite) Brasilia. Bunty *hated* Brasilia, convinced that Miss Combe and all the little Combes back at headquarters had personally invented this paradise of plate glass and toy trees purely as a means of tormenting fifth form Geography students.

'Why would anyone want a *new* capital? I mean,' persisted Bunty after their first lesson on it, 'if someone tried to sell you the idea of ditching London and building a new one at astronomical expense in the middle of North Ants or somewhere, you'd have them sectioned.'

'It's *all* made up,' Queenie had drawled in reply. 'D'you think anyone really uses an Archimedes screw, for heaven's sake? Or that daft buckets-on-wheels thingy? You'd have a hose or a syphon or a watering can or something, like a normal person. It's all bollocks.'

Today's Geography questions were either far too easy or completely bloody unfathomable: *Account for the limited population of **either** the highlands of Scotland **or** those of Wales. Give a geographical account of the African savannah.* Not even a 'please'. Queenie, who kept a copy of *Mad* magazine inside her Geography textbook, was more familiar with her own virgin body than the continent of Africa and had little chance of passing the latest exam but the clean sheets of folio and the unnatural silence of the exam hall triggered a surreal flight of fancy when she got to the missing words section.

*During the Cretaceous Period, Africa's coastal areas were almost completely covered by **custard** and glacially derived **lemon curd**. These formed superficial deposits of **Marmite** which in places are so thick as to eradicate all visual clues as to the nature of the underlying **toast**. Much of the **Arctic roll** melted causing large amounts of **jam** to be released forming important **puddings** in the coastal areas. Today, **Ovaltine** and **Tizer** drilling is conducted both on land and offshore on the **sideboard**. The continent's considerable geological age has allowed more than enough time for widespread **despair** yielding soils leached of **marmalade**.*

The Mostyn's late start meant that there was hardly time for Bunty to wedge in a Mars bar before three of the Mandies were back in the hall for their Chemistry exam (Queenie was over in the annexe for her Domestic Science practical, making a pig's ear of a lamb's liver).

Miss Gray, invigilating, was quite a young woman but her suspicions gave her a tight-lipped, thwarted look, as though she were utterly certain that crimes were taking place and was only prevented by pettifogging notions of Fair Play and the rules of evidence from disqualifying the whole miserable lot of them. She was absolutely right of course: everybody cheated.

Baker's furry pencil case was a mess of chewed, unsharpened HBs and the lids of long-forgotten felt tips each of which contained the miniature crib-sheets she had made the previous evening – French irregular verbs, Boyle's Law, noble gases – each printed in tiny, exquisite lettering like doll's house shopping lists. At junior school there had been a girl, Wendy Somethington, who used to amuse herself by writing the Lord's Prayer on the back of fourpenny postage stamps with a very sharp pencil. Angels on the heads of pins would have been a piece of fucking cake in comparison.

Unfortunately, Baker's cribs did not contain the method for making carbon monoxide and so, when the watchful Miss Gray's back was turned, she passed a note to the girl in the seat behind her while scratching an imaginary itch between her shoulder blades. Barely two minutes later she felt a tap on her back and reached behind her to retrieve an exquisite diagram the size of a bus ticket detailing the flasks, retorts, marble chips and acid required. Baker copied it faithfully, using her ducky little chemistry stencil, then panicked as Miss Gray's chair scraped back from her desk and she began yet another brothel-creeping circuit of the room. The tiny scrap of white was thrown into dangerous relief by the dull green of the blotting sheet.

Miss Gray was already three-quarters of the way up the adjacent aisle, turning over each blotter as she went, unmoved by the snorts of outraged innocence. She reached the back of the room and, just as she made her turn, Baker wet her finger, dabbed at the diagram and posted it onto her tongue. Her mouth was instantly parched by the Quinky scrap of narrow feint and it took two goes before she could finally swallow the evidence.

'Is that *chewing gum*, Amanda?'

'No, Miss Gray.' The truth for once.

Baker had almost forgotten about Julia but the passed note reminded her of her lunchtime tryst and the worry of it pretty much turned her brain to mush. She shivered. The school heating system had been put on a timer thanks to some sort of oil crisis and the radiators were now off from ten thirty till afternoon Registration, thanks to energy saving by Dr O'Brien who had a handy slimline convection heater in the knee-hole of her desk but who maintained that warm teenage bodies would keep the school at a reasonable temperature once the morning chill had been taken off the classrooms. Baker nuzzled her face into the top of her sweater and *huurrred* unavailingly into the wool. Still bloody freezing. Her watch said quarter past one.

Baker dawdled her way to the bottom of the out-of-bounds staircase that led to the organ's innards, darting up the steps the instant a passing goon disappeared round the corner – first prefect she'd seen all break. Were the rest all holed up with Julia in the loft, ready to make threats? To pinch where it wouldn't show? She leaned against the wall when she reached the turn in the stairs, screened by a long row of filing cabinets, and listened: no voices above, no footsteps below, just the faraway slaughter-house screams from the playground. They called it butterflies, that horrible churning fear you got in your stomach before exams, fillings, meetings with Julias. Why butterflies? Butterflies wouldn't hurt.

Baker tiptoed up the last few steps, checked over her right shoulder, then opened the unmarked door, being careful not to disturb the padlock that still looped through the rings of the broken hasp.

Julia was entirely alone, sitting with her legs outstretched along one of the joists, blazered back propped against a palisade of organ pipes.

'Watch your feet, for God's sake. It's like paper in between.'

Baker looked suspiciously around the room, waiting for the trap to be sprung. She watched her footing as she negotiated the next solid stretch of timber then looked up to see Julia placing two long, thin American cigarettes between her lips. They were from a soft-sided duty-free packet with nothing about damaging anybody's health on the side. A handful of unsafe red-headed matches had been tucked into the top and she winkled one out and struck it – dead, dead casual – against the three-inch zip on her purse belt, releasing a bonfire night whiff. Baker reached automatically for the cigarette held out to her.

'Took your time.'

Julia began blowing smoke rings towards a skylight that had been pulled open by a dangling loop of grimy string.

'I've brushed up most of the dust – dead giveaway otherwise – but no one ever comes here, doesn't even feature on the prefects' lunchtime circuit. Just have to be sure to pull the latch thingy back in place when you close the door. *Relax*.'

She propped her lean, bare legs against the opposite wall: no red blotches on the thighs, no goosebumps on the milky skin.

'Don't you ever feel cold?'

'Nope. Anywhere's warm after double hockey.'

'Says you.' Baker unknotted the belt of her gym slip and tented the pleats over her raised knees. 'The radiators in our form room don't come on again till half two. They'll be too hot to touch, let alone sit on, but the room's still like ice. Quite a trick.'

'Fuckface ought to set it as a physics problem: heat capacity and whatnot. Like filling baths full of holes.'

Julia held out a tube of caramel sweets. 'Wanna choc?' Baker shook her head and Julia gave a mirthless laugh.

'I don't think I've ever seen you eat.'

Baker flashed a tight smile. 'So why am I here?'

Julia checked the time on her wrist, the kind of butch watch that probably told you what depth it was or measured background radiation or fired poison darts.

'Relax, for Christ's sake. Eat something. Smoke something. Don't be so paranoid. Should have seen your face on the train yesterday – talk about condemned man. I just felt ...' Sorry for you? Was that what came next? If it was she had more tact than to say it, but Baker reached across and pincered a sweet from the packet.

'I thought you were on their side. If O'Brien writes home ...' Baker broke off. 'My dad hasn't spoken a word to me in three days.'

'You and your little lot are practically all they talk about at the staff's prefect meetings: vandalism, persistent rudeness, failure to hand in work, unhealthy influence, cigarette smoking. *Unschool*, basically. You wanna watch it. They're *dying* to expel somebody. How many pink slips have you had this term?'

'Dunno. Four?' Baker nibbled at her finger. 'But O'Brien didn't seem too fussed when I saw her this morning.'

'Means nothing. O'Brien likes to think she's in charge but she's taken her eye off the ball lately: letting Mrs Mostyn do all the assemblies, bunking off staff meetings. The staff hate the whole fireside chat thing: undermines discipline they reckon. There they all are, doing their best to crack the whip and then O'Brien goes and tells you everything's fine and what kind of career were you planning. You watch: they'll force her to expel somebody, *anybody*, and she's such a weasel. Mind you, they'd probably rather sack one of their "charity pupils", snobby old cows – don't lose any fees that way.'

They each lit another fag. Baker, annoyed by Bunty's flowery smokes, had switched to a high tar brand with a picture of a bearded sailor on the packet (not actually very nice but she was damned if she'd say so).

Julia left the cigarette burning on her lower lip and began mocking up a wedding ring with the foil from the roll of sweets. 'You remind me of me.' She brushed a few atoms of ash from among the pleats of her skirt. 'O'Brien say anything of interest?'

'Told me to bide my time, get some decent grades, then try for "a nice little job in market research".'

'She's big on that lately. Last year it was Punch Card Operators.' 'And you?'

'Fuck knows. They want me to be a PE teacher.'

'And?'

'I hate PE. Hate all games. Hate them, hate them, hate them.'

'Could have fooled me.' Baker jerked her head at the pick 'n' mix sports kit. 'If you hate them, why the hell do you play so many?'

'*Because they leave you alone*. You can wear what you like, go anywhere in the building, slope in and out at strange times, use the staff room phone. And the extra-curricular bollocks takes up so much time they let me off prep. I don't even *play* very often any more: just pick teams and referee – "A shining example to the younger gels." Beating them at their own stupid games. Talking of which, I got you a little present.' She reached into her bag and produced a tiny tube. 'Superglue. A thousand uses. Miles better than bleach. More subtle. And I've had a brilliant idea for Founder's Day: fun for all the family.'

Julia stretched herself back along the joist and sucked on the last millimetres of her cigarette (*Leave a longer stub*).

'Nice legs.'

'So Miss Drumlin keeps saying.' Julia twisted her knees in and out, admiring the lean curves. 'Show us yours.'

Baker unbent her knees and hitched up the gymslip, gazing forlornly at her bulging thighs. *Sausage.*

'Lovely and thin. You should get yourself a shorter skirt. Wear games kit. I'll say you're doing shooting practice with me if you like. Under my wing. O'Brien'll like that: likes wings.'

'Why me?'

'I told you, doll: you remind me of me. Besides, there's no one nice to play with in the sixth form. Bunch of swots and goody-goodies. They don't even smoke unless there's a bloody boy watching.'

'Are you actually doing A levels? You seem to get a lot of free periods.'

'Naah. Maths re-take and elementary bloody Book-keeping. My dad made me. I was supposed to be doing Spanish O level as well, but sod that: French was bad enough. One more term and you won't see me for dust.'

The bell sounded for afternoon Registration.

'Same again tomorrow? We could have a picnic.'

Julia slipped her chewing gum under the hasp of the latch as she closed the loft door behind them, even had the presence of mind to start shouting at Baker when they reached the bottom of the staircase. The corridor was out of bounds to Shells and the bell had gone and where was her room and get a move on and do me a hundred lines by Friday ('I will not be late for Registration'). Spoken like a native.

Chapter 12

There was just time to pop to the loo before the Latin mock. The secret graffiti patch was almost completely filled in ('I live in hope; I sleep in Sydenham'), plus a fresh string of increasingly nutty attacks on the Snog Monster and various students ('Davina Booth is an evil cock-sucking whore' being the mildest). Some joker had added a new one under the loo roll holder really low down where only someone sitting on the loo could see it: 'Domestic Science O levels: please take one'. 'Beware of lesbian limbo dancers' was also new, probably written by one of the Brians.

Bryony and Co had a bit of a thing about lesbians. Any close friendships were immediately suspect and best friends were frowned upon. Gangs were more 'School'. They were pretty vague about what lesbianism consisted of, and an approach to the Biology mistress (via the anonymous question box she used for the muckier parts of the syllabus) met with a bare-faced 'I can't read the writing on this one'. The Mandies were little better informed.

'What do they *do* exactly?' wondered Queenie.

'Fuck knows.'

'Fuck nose?' (much sniggering).

'Tri-bad-ism,' said Bunty.

'Eh? Wossat?'

'Haven't the foggiest. Read it somewhere. Nothing about it in the *Reader's Digest Family Dic*, but then the *Reader's Digest* people don't have cunnilingus either, or orgasms. I checked. *Tri-bad-ism* . . . probbly rather enjoyable. Maybe it's tribad as in *tribe*: feathers and tattoos in a special hut made of palm fibre . . .'

Baker left the loo and hurried down to the exam hall where Miss Hurd was invigilating her own exam and handed out the two-hour paper the instant they sat down.

The Latin mistress had spent the last two terms chipping away at her group's encyclopaedic ignorance of participles and datives and gerunds (what did the English department *do* all day, for pity's sake?), and line by painful line she had helped them thrash out a close, literal translation of Book Four of the *Aeneid* and Livy's account of Hannibal crossing the Alps. Pacing the room like a tigress in tweeds, she was surprised to see that today's examinees were all getting through their Livy translations at an *extraordinary* speed.

Miss Hurd was fairly new to teaching, but any seasoned classicist could have told her what was happening. Despairing (rightly) of ever being able to crack that fiendish Patavinian code from a standing start, the entire class of thirty had quite simply learned the whole lot by heart. All of it. Unfortunately one bit of Livy XXI looked much like another and quite a few of them had plumped for entirely the wrong passage. Thus, having learned their translation with much loss of evening hours and with considerable effort, the Upper Fifth, notwithstanding a fine and dedicated teacher, made a complete bloody shambles of the Latin literature paper.

Baker, translation done, had drawn five neat rows of cassocked martyrs tied to stakes on a fresh sheet of exam paper and, as the minutes ticked by, built up a heap of faggots beneath them, sketched in the flames, crossed them through and pinged a halo above their bowed heads: six down, thirty-nine to go. Across the aisle Stottie, bored with martyrs, had drawn a matching set of caped vampires who were finished off with an encircling coffin shape and the all-important stake, working away happily until she looked up at the clock: five to four. Only five more to go.

'Ensure that your name and candidate number are entered on each sheet and make sure your handwriting is legible,' droned Miss Hurd.

Stottie looked back over her handiwork, tidying up the fangs and widow's peaks here and there until the papers were finally collected.

Baker and Stott emerged from their exam room to find Queenie and Bunty leaning against a wall outside the neighbouring Biology lab, staring glumly at the open exercise book in Bunty's hand.

'I give up. I really give up. Really, really, *really* give up.'

'Wossup?'

'*Look* at it.' She held the book out at arm's length.

The double page spread was taken up with a gorgeous orangey-red octopus that Bunty had copied from her brother's *Junior Britannica*. Bunty could really draw. Bunty could make colour pencil shading look as good as the examples on the lid of the tin (a Technicolor study of an African elephant running amok in a municipal flower bed). The body of the octopus was faithfully tinted with feathery strokes, every sucker coloured and shaded to create a glorious creature of Naples yellow, raw sienna, burnt sienna, Venetian red, Van Dyke brown, basking in a sunny cerulean sea, every feature fully and correctly labelled in neat black ink. But Miss Peters' Biro had spoken, a red line looping spitefully across both pages, deliberately spoiling the picture: 'This is not what you were asked to do.'

Baker, steaming with rage on Bunty's behalf, moved her friend away from the open lab door and, taking the new thumb-sized tube of glue from her blazer pocket, jammed the nozzle into the keyhole and squeezed hard while the rest of the form shoved its way out of the room.

'We will take our revenge.'

'Where d'you get that?' asked Queenie, suspiciously.

'A friend,' teased Baker.

There was a fifteen-minute break before the next exam and all four Mandies sprinted up to the bicycle shed to discuss plans for Founder's Day, less than a week away.

'Can we un-tune the piano?'

'Nah. Probbly need special tools.'

'And very dark glasses. And a labrador,' said Queenie. 'Skilled work, piano tuning.'

'We could have a *go*,' persisted Baker.

Stottie, who'd been playing since she was three, said they'd be better off just knackering a couple of strings so that the show would be in full swing before anyone noticed.

'Who are they wheeling on for the speeches this year? Bob Hope? Katie Boyle?'

'Lady Henry Clyde. Busy little bee, Lady Henry. She doesn't just do schools,' said Bunty. 'Daddy caught her at some Rotary Club thing. "Depresses the parts other bores cannot reach," Daddy says. Talks hind legs off donkeys, apparently.'

'Talented.'

'Shame none of us is getting a badge,' said Bunty.

'I'm getting my Grade Six piano,' said Stott.

'But your piano lessons aren't here,' protested Queenie.

'Mum sent O'Brien the certificate for prize day porpoises and O'Brien'll take credit for anything. Miracle she doesn't do Brownie and *Blue Peter* badges.'

'Excellent,' grinned Baker. 'I have devised a dastardly little plan. It calls for a small, syrupy polythene bag in one blazer pocket and a damp hankie in the other. I'll supply the necessary.'

Miss Revie's Maths exam was considerably easier than advertised. Lousy test results played very badly in the staff room and she was keen to crank up her average – particularly with young Miss Bonetti snapping at her heels. Miss Bonetti had worked wonders with the gamma group, most of whom normally turned spastic at the mere sight of a sheet of graph paper. 'Let's hope you can have a similar impact on *your* girls,' Dr O'Brien had said to Miss Revie in that nasty, no-pressure way of hers.

Then again, Miss Revie had been pleasantly surprised by the consistently high standards achieved in the beta group's spring term homework (their matrix sheets were particularly pleasing). She hadn't wanted to risk them all forgetting everything they ever knew under 'exam conditions', so this afternoon's paper was two thirds multiple choice. Statistically, in a group that size they should score a minimum of 22 per cent, even if they ticked the answers at random. Given the shameless eccentricity of the all-important rogue responses she had dreamed up (some of which were in degrees Fahrenheit), they should all score quite a bit higher than that. What's more, a study in a recent issue of *Mathematics Teaching Today* had established that the weaker multiple choice candidates tended not to opt for answer A (ours not to reason why), and Miss Revie had adjusted the distribution of correct answers accordingly. All in all, Miss Revie was fairly confident that the results could be skewed in her favour; a fee-paying chimpanzee would stand a sporting chance.

'No matrices in this one,' she said as she handed round her papers. 'Didn't want to make it too easy peasy.' *Peasy.* The perky expression sat on Miss Revie's face like a party hat on a bust of Beethoven. Miss Bonetti was very chummy, apparently. They liked chummy.

The Mandies had an easy-to-master deaf-and-dumb system for relaying multiple choice answers round an exam room, so the papers were finished even more quickly than the Maths mistress had anticipated, once Queenie got into her stride. More martyrs surrendered to the flames.

'Be sure and check through your answers.'

Chapter 13

The Upper Shells were officially unexcited by a rubbishy boys' school dance that coming Saturday, but had still talked of almost nothing else for a fortnight. In the cloakroom next morning, Brian and the lads were all fretting about what to wear, which was complicated to the power of six and then some because they insisted on buying identical clothes. Not that they necessarily minded dressing the same ('Are you two sisters?' always broke a lot of ice), but more than three of you and you risked looking like the Nolans. They were still at the French-length-skirt-or-trousers stage and trying to decide whether they should all wear their bowling shirts.

Bunty meanwhile was offering the usual prizes for the worst chat-up line.

'Oh God, remember last year?' groaned Queenie.

'What?'

'Some twerp comes over and actually says, "If I said you had a beautiful body would you hold it against me" – must have been doing it for a bet.'

'And you said?' Bunty had heard it before but Bunty didn't mind, never minded – Wise to her Morecambe.

'And I take a drag on my Black Russian, puff a whiff in his face and say, "If I said piss off would you piss off?"'

Funny how it was funny the first time.

Queenie liked being asked, liked telling you about being asked but actual dates frightened her. What were you supposed to talk about? What did they expect you to do? Where did you draw the line? The other big turn-off was Mr McQueen, who insisted that boys collect Amanda from the house so that he could take a good look at them and could then spend the next fortnight pouring scorn on their shoes and referring to them as 'the son-in-law' until Queenie eventually brought home the glad tidings that she'd given whoever-it-was the push while Dad said he wasn't good enough for his princess and Ma revealed she'd never liked him anyway. This was why people left home: mental cruelty.

Brian and Tash had the right idea really, reckoned Baker, because getting dolled up was the only seriously good bit: all mustering at Samantha's house, crowding round her light-up make-up mirror, lips glossed like glacé cherries, smearing concealer on their spots, dabbing scent onto 'pressure points'. Downhill after that. Shuffling rhythmically around a school assembly hall or a pub function room in near darkness, fending off approaches until you'd effected some kind of compromise between Dream Boy and Available Boy who would then join you in a pointless conversation that was the preliminary to a gropy slow dance. Which school did they go to? Did they like Lou Reed? Like talking to the Germans on the Baden Baden trip. *Haben sie Brüdern oder Schwestern?* Only you had to shout hard in their ears to be heard over Harold Melvin and his Bluenotes. Deaf Germans.

And then lover boy might buy you a paper cup of warm cola and tell you of his passion for canoeing or carpentry or Cream.

'D'you really think there's a single, solitary girl in the world who likes Cream?' said Bunty. 'Or Hank Zappa? Or Erich Von Daniken? Or motor racing?'

'Davina Booth goes motor racing.'

'Yeah, but only for pulling porpoises. Davina Booth is an evil cock-sucking whore. Well-known fact.'

Bunty wasn't going to the dance. Bunty was busy.

'Stottie, swee-tee?' Bunty on the scrounge.

'Yup?'

'I'm staying at your house Saturday, OK?'

'I'll air the west wing, milady.'

'Where you off to, Bunts?' asked Queenie.

'Ma and Pa have to go to a wedding in Shwop-sha some-where, and I'm supposed to sleep over with a *chum*.' A dirty cackle. 'All will be revealed.'

Only it wouldn't, would it? thought Baker. More secrets, more half-arsed fibs and apologies.

When the Mandies filed back in for Registration they found the beta Maths group in a huddle and Hilary Osgood in a frenzy of mental arithmetic.

Miss Revie, much to the disgust of the rest of the staff room, refused to list her results in order of merit, or to go to the bother of calculating a mean mark. For Hilary Osgood, who had twice won the class prize for Effort and whose reports were a master class in faint praise ('Works steadily', 'Has done everything that could be expected of her'), that red Biro line drawn across the marks list was as good as a winning tape and she was lost without it. She was frantically making a list of all of the percentages on the noticeboard, trying (and failing) to divide 1352 by 26.

'What are you doing, Hills?'

'Five twenty-sixes are one hundred and thirty-two carry three ... Oh *sugar*' ('strewth' was reserved for major emergencies), 'I need to find the average. Dad'll kill me if I'm below average. What's 1352 divided by 26?'

'44,' said Bunty, trusting to luck that even Hilary Osgood would have scraped a higher mark than that.

'Honestly?' A disbelieving look from Hilary. Could anyone, anywhere compute that fast?

'Bunty can do sums,' Baker reminded her, 'does gin rummy scores without a pencil, remember: Bunty knows best.'

Bunty beamed. Friends again.

'Wanna go shopping Saturday?'

'Thought you were having your dirty weekend.'

'Not *completely* filthy. It's clean as a whistle till lunchtime. He plays five-a-side every Saturday morning. All weathers. Bee-*zarre*.'

'Five-a-side what?'

'Fuck knows.'

Funny how they did that. Even the keenest goal attack never netted a ball again after leaving school (apart from nutters like the Drumlin, ob-viously), but men carried on running about in shorts well into middle age. Dad was the same, some old school thing. He'd drive off before breakfast every Saturday and do Old Boyish things at a special clubhouse place out beyond the ring road, wisteria hanging gladly from the red brick façade like crocheted purple bunting. Wives were welcome (after a fashion) but they were only allowed into the licensed lounge (tables only) between six and seven. Spam and Baker had been once: Spam in bar, Baker in car, while Bob and the other old boys played on in a steady drizzle, tapping the ball a few feet, barking and grunting about the relative positions of legs and wickets. He was clearly having the time of his life.

He was much nicer that day. The other old boys were all peculiarly pleased to see him and he kept laughing and then making them laugh and then laughing again. A completely different man. Baker joined them in the bar and looked at Spam's proud, puzzled smile at the man she married, back for the afternoon, like an access visit.

'Nick goes to the pub with the lads afterwards, so chances are I won't see him till gone three. Plenty of shopping time,' urged Bunty.

Whenever Spam went shopping she came home with whatever rubbish she had bought, poured herself a gin and sat in the front room surrounded by carrier bags, taking out the things and looking at them and putting them back. If by any horrible chance they hadn't had her size or didn't have the matching oven gloves and she came home empty-handed, then her outing would be deemed a failure but the Mandies didn't shop that way. Once in a while one of them would actually shell out for a lip gloss or a paperback or make a note of possible birthday presents to hint for, but most of the time 'shopping' meant drooling over the empty album sleeves in the record shop, cadging squirts of scent from disbelieving cosmetic consultants (*Diorella* for Bunty; *Rive Gauche* for Baker), striping the backs of their hands with lipsticks, or choosing their top three posters in the trendy stationery boutique. Bunty had wanted a Toulouse Lautrec and Dustin Hoffman last time they looked.

Then Bunty suddenly remembered that she couldn't go shopping on Saturday after all.

'Got to wash the car and mow the lawn.' But those were Dominic's jobs, weren't they? More secrets. But Bunty wasn't the only one with secrets.

The breaktime prefect patrol was considerably relaxed during exams, with most of the sixth form off revising the subjunctive or memorising Keats (or whatever bits of Keats had made it to *Cole's Notes* – no sense knocking yourself out) and so Baker had no trouble sneaking up to the organ loft at lunchtime, leaving

Bunty to a solitary fag behind the bike sheds – serve her jolly well right.

Baker hadn't contributed much to the picnic (two apples and some chocolate biscuits from the tuck shop) and she nibbled on a Golden Delicious while Julia scoffed a pork pie and a packet of chocolate Swiss rolls.

'You free all afternoon? Me too. '*Study periods*,' she giggled.

Julia had trebled the available floor space in the tiny room by dragging two gigantic hardboard playing cards left over from a production of *Alice in Wonderland* all the way from the Drama cupboard so that both girls could stretch out in comfort. The new flat surface was a perfect place to lay out the papers and piece together a large, wonky joint.

Baker's heart began a drum roll of panic, partly fear of getting caught but mostly fear of making a tit of herself. She watched Julia, noting how her fingers gripped the roach, how long she held the smoke, and then copied the older girl exactly, fighting to stay cool as the groovy gases seeped into her blood: a lovely, fuzzy-wuzzy tingly feeling. She drew the relevant diagram in her head (extra marks awarded for clear labelling): an alveolus and a passing capillary with little dots and arrows showing the dopey doings plunging into the bloodstream. She began mentally colouring it: blue for the oxygen, yellow for the dope.

It occurred to Baker that she ought to say something about the joint. It was traditional – like Sunday lunch: this is delicious, darling. Did you bake these yourself?

'Nice.' (Seemed safe enough.) 'Where did you get the stuff?'

'Boyfriend got it for me.'

Julia had a real boyfriend with a motorbike. Bunty had seen them at a pub on the river: helmets on the bench beside them, his 'n' hers leather jackets. It never featured in the Tampax ads, funnily enough, but it was what everyone truly wanted. You'd think market research could have told them that. Ask bloody anybody: blue-eyed bloke with bike. Sod *snorkels*.

'Baz knows a guy.'

Baker let out a tiny silent moan of envy. *Baz*. Trust Julia to have a *Baz*, or a *Zak*, or a *Jed*. Hairy, scary, heavy metal names. Fifth form boyfriends had wimpy names: Tim, Mark, Robert. Or Jeremy. Then she remembered Baz was short for Barry – or just possibly Basil – and felt better. Then she tried to picture herself on the back of a bike – not knowing where to put her hands and trying to put on a brave face for the view in the wing mirror – and felt worse again.

Julia puffed away expertly, her other hand retrieving a (confiscated) mag from the bundle in her bag: *For women who know where they're going*. She flicked through it and let the pages flutter to a halt between her fingers.

'Got this one off a first former. She hasn't dared do the quiz: "How to tell if you're good in bed". Good in bed?' she scoffed. 'Chance would be a fine thing, doesn't even wear a bra.'

Other girls had to answer their questions with the aid of a dream boyfriend: how you'd like him to respond. Or had to improvise – what would Donny Osmond do? Not Julia. Julia had Baz. And now Bunty had Nick.

'"*If your boyfriend asks you to try a new position do you a. agree reluctantly? b. suggest some of your own?*"'

'*Or c: Archimedes screw*,' interrupted Baker, giggling uncontrollably. 'Always godda have a silly answer.' She pecked guiltily at one of the Jaffa Cakes. She had forgotten how nice they were. Gingham tablecloths again.

Julia frisbee'd the mag across the room. It skimmed over Baker's head, alighted briefly on a rank of pipes then slithered down the back while Julia moved on to the next title in the pile.

'Do you think *anyone* over twenty-one actually reads this rubbish?'

'Sometimes.' Baker thought of Spam and her code books. 'But I know what you mean. You'd think they'd get over it. I mean if you want lipstick you can just go to the shops, see what there is, buy lipstick. Don't need a map. Switch to *New Statesman* or *Popular Mechanics* or something.'

'Popular Statesman,' puffed Julia. Giggles.

'Or, or, or,' Baker rummaged tipsily in her own bag, '*Spare Rib*. Supposed to work like an antidote to women's mags – still all about willies mind you.'

'Yeah, but you've got to look at all the normal mags as well, got to know your enemy,' said Julia. 'It's just like the whole Fawcett thing,' another scorching puff on the tissue paper firework in her hand, 'no good starting a fight about it. It's just about looking the part. A bit of lipstick won't hurt. Camouflage. Then once you're inside you can do what you like.'

'Yeah, but suppose the wind changes and you stay like it?'

'Oh gawd. D'you reckon? Is that what happens? Get married, have *babies*, forget what it was you came in for? Oh gawd.'

Both of them sad suddenly. Like the end of the tea party on the ceiling in *Mary Poppins*.

Julia began sticking some more fag papers together, a toddler in craft corner, tongue between teeth.

'My mother had a baby.'

It was the first time Julia had mentioned parents. Baker had imagined her home alone like Pippi Longstocking, living on pancakes and peppermints.

'Just now? How old is she?'

'She's forty-fucking-two. That's dis-*gust*-ing. And it smells and makes a noisy noisy noise. *I* don't smell and I hardly make any noise, but nobody decorates *my* bedroom or buys *me* a mobile with little sodding rabbits on it.' The trace of a tear in the corner of those pretty blue eyes.

'Bastards,' said Baker, consolingly, patting her leg. No hairs on it. *I look better in trousers: my legs are so rough and hairy* moaned the woman in the ad.

'Read me from your magazine,' said Julia.

'My friend Bunty hates me reading things out.'

'Silly moo.'

Baker grinned gratefully at Julia who began reading the ads from her own magazine – *Over 21* – while Baker rummaged through her *Spare Rib* for the antidote.

'"Be sure of total personal freshness with *Fresh 'n' Dainty* feminine deodorant, available as spray, sachets or gelée,"' said Julia. 'Gel-lee? G-ross.'

'Oh yeah? Says here: "Women are mobilising to overcome the ravages of thrush and allied vaginal disease."'

'Mobilising? Like tanks?' More giggles bubbled up from beneath the cricket jersey. 'Wonder what the uniform's like? Expect it's all in Miss Batty's drawer: "Join the WIFFs".'

This turned out to be the funniest joke ever told but then each joke was more hilarious than the last.

'"Dress up to the nines, even if you're only going to the pub – a flash of pretty knicker won't go astray."' Then on the next page: '"What your knickers say about you."'

Julia had her knees up, showing the usual glimpse of ageing blue gusset.

'I'd pay mine hush money if I were you,' said Baker.

She flicked past the 'Spotlight on Eating Disorders' to the *Spare Rib* small ads.

'"Neurotic ex institutional psychologist would very much like to contact fellow sufferers." Woffor?'

Julia was putting the finishing touches to the new, slightly smaller joint. 'Netball. Or hockey if she gets enough replies. Where did you get that thing?'

'My mum – my real mum – got me a subscription. It comes addressed to "Manda Baker", that's what she used to call me.'

'Manda . . . mandibles,' mused Julia. 'D'you ever see her?'

'Lives in the Bahamas now, but she gets a friend of hers in Basingstoke to send me stuff. Awful stuff. It's like having a really-really-really *terrible* pen friend. Ran away when I was three. This was "not what she wanted her life to be like" apparently. What she told Dad, anyway.'

'So you got a stepmother?'

'Yup. *She's* over twenty-one but *she* still gets magazines and buys what they say. All sorts of rubbish. She likes scenting things: the insides of drawers; shoes; *carpet*. And she likes *hiding* things under other things. Even the toaster has a cosy; it's shaped like a lickle thatched cottage. We make toast every single bloody day but we have to hide the doings for some reason. Or keep the dust off. Keep it safe from the toast monster.'

Spam's Valentine from Dad that year had been a large, brightly coloured, quilted chicken to put over the food processor. 'Talk about the way to a woman's heart.'

'She sounds bored to me: bored, bored, bored. Does she have any friends?'

'Not that I know of.'

'Must have. Be miserable otherwise. Do you do stuff together? Shopping?'

'She likes being on her own.'

'Bet she bloody doesn't. Ask her.'

Baker wriggled guiltily and looked back at her magazine, desperate for a change of subject.

'"Isolated Aberystwyth feminist would like to meet others."'

Julia winced. 'Oooh, don't hold your breath, Gwyneth love. Have you *been* to Aberystwyth? I have. On holiday.'

'Don't be silly,' slurred Baker. 'You can't go on holiday to Aberystwyth. Be like going on holiday to Croydon.'

'Except Croydon has better pubs. The actual holiday was in *Llann* something. In a caravan. Llancaravan.'

A caravan? Baker frowned uncomfortably at the thought. The Bakers went on smart package holidays to hotels where you had your own stretch of beach with banks of tip-up deckchairs and stripy parasols and waiters bringing Spam another Cuba Libre. She tried to visualise Julia and the Smiths all eating, sleeping and farting in a blue and white box slightly smaller than Bob Baker's garden shed. Sounded crap.

'Nice.'

'Nice? It rained every bleeding day.'

'Any feminists?'

'Nah. Not a sniff. Not even for ready money.'

Baker went back to her *Spare Rib*. '"Dear Holly of sw11. Re Semen Allergy. Please write to us again as several readers have written with the same complaint and would like to contact you." Told you. All about willies. Wonder what Holly's knickers say about her.'

'Their lips are sealed.'

Baker thought her lungs would burst from the effort to contain the volume of laughter.

Julia took another exaggerated, super-groupie puff on the joint then stood unsteadily on the nine of hearts and began a great swirling, looping scribble on the only pipeless patch of wall with a giant red felt tip she had stolen from under the whiteboard in the Maths Room.

I hate Mrs Mostyn.

She was wiggling her bum as she wrote.

Mrs Mostyn is an evil, cock-sucking Snog Monster.

She had beautiful, flowery, very arty writing – the kind you got from practising a lot in the back of your rough book – with curly Ws and a great waggly tail on the g. The indelible scribble completely covered the wall and Baker felt the laughter die inside her. The fear was back. She felt sick, a weird fizzing sensation in her hands as if the magazine in her fingers were wired up to the mains.

'Your face!' a stuttering yodel of a laugh, like a cartoon character: 'It's okay. Got a poster.' and Julia began to unfold a giant picture of a tall, skinny black man wielding a guitar which she stuck over the scarlet ink with four scrunches of sellotape. 'Don't worr-ee!' A drunk's delivery, like Spam on the sherry. 'We'll be long gone by the time they get the organ donations together. *Long*-gone. Over twenty-one, Well Housekept.'

Baker truffled around in her bag some more and dug out a paperback called *No Gentle Possession* (another jumble sale find).

'My mum reads those. Load of rubbish. What do you want with it?'

'Research,' said Baker.

'Research? Research for what?'

'Miss Gleet has got us all writing novels. She's quite keen on mine, so Dr O'Brien says.'

'You want to watch that.'

'Watch what?'

'All that *unlocking* crap, "releasing your potential" like you were a dry cell battery or something. You know: success in the school play and before you know it she's top in Maths and captain of lacrosse. It's all bollocks. S'not about you, s'not about unlocking your gifts. It's just about making you spend more time doing the stuff they like. Trust me: I've studied their habits.'

Baker was asleep on one of the sitting room sofas when Stottie rang on Friday night suggesting a mooch round the high street on Saturday, or a trip to the pictures, or maybe even the boys' school disco thingy? A female voice was shouting in the background about homework and the size of the last phone bill. Stottie sounded really disappointed when Baker said Spam wasn't letting her out. Could she tell she was lying? She'd hung up almost at once: poor old Stottie.

The phone began ringing again the instant she replaced the receiver: Bunty's voice wanting to know where had Baker disappeared to all afternoon and saying that she was excused lawn-mowing and what time should they meet tomorrow. 'It'll have to be quite early. Meeting Nick outside the Wheatsheaf at three.'

Just what Baker had wanted, only now she didn't want it after all, just someone to kill time with till the pubs closed? No thanks.

'Can't. Sorry. Spam's taking me shopping.' (Always a first time.)

Baker spent the rest of the weekend alone in her bedroom making a poster to pin up in the hideout, cutting up Spam's magazine archive and teaming the scraps with random headlines. Spam popped by with mugs of tea and plates of biscuits and sandwiches every few hours or so, in between dashing off to the shops or running back down to the kitchen to get something out of the oven. Baker stuck *The bust you've always wanted is probably your own* over a picture of Burt Reynolds showing off his chest hair. And the shark from *Blue Water, White Death* was nuzzling up to a half-naked blonde stroking herself in happy anticipation: *Things happen after a Badedas bath.*

'That's nice.' Spam back again. Cheese on toast this time: horrible cheese – men's cheese. Her stepmother's hair was in curlers and her bare feet were snared in a sponge thingy that was supposed to make painting your toenails easier. Maybe Julia was right: bored bored bored.

'Very nice,' she said again. 'Clever. What's it for?'

'It's a *project*.' You could say that about anything. Baker could have been sat there on her corduroy bean bag stripping down a Kalashnikov and Spam wouldn't have batted an eyelid if she'd said the magic word. Dad, back from an old boy meeting planning the cricket season, was less convinced.

'Haven't you got any revision to do?' droned Captain Black, just for a fucking change.

Chapter 14

Baker arrived at school unusually early on Monday. Dad was en route to a business meeting in Ipswich (or possibly Droitwich) and was up and about, knotting his tie and huffily buffing his shoes. Spam had an equally early start every Monday for staff training or, just possibly, coffee and Danish pastries in a cosy Italian café with her mate Sandra. (Bob didn't like Sandra.) Spam always laid out her toothbrush, cleansing lotion, make-up bag and styling comb by the kitchen sink and was up and out before you knew it. Her husband's (far rarer) early starts would rouse the whole house at six with his very vocal search for a Thermos flask, a book of road maps and some kind of recognition that he, the main breadwinner, had had to get up at the crack of bloody dawn (win more bread).

The general upheaval meant that Baker was in early enough to hide her poster behind the filing cabinets in the organ corridor before nipping up to the Shells cloakroom where she found Bunty in a twisted heap in the corner. Her face was swollen with old tears and she was crying still.

'God, I am *so* stupid.'

And yes, she was a bit as it turned out.

After a Saturday night and Sunday morning of mad passionate love in the monster bedroom suite, Bunty and the mysterious

Nick had removed all the evidence, changed all the bedding, then gone off to the pictures for a goodbye grope in the cheap seats. The car was in the drive when she got back and her red leather, day-to-a-page, gilt-edged diary was on the tea table in place of the usual fruit cake.

As ill luck would have it, the conversation at the Shropshire wedding breakfast had turned to childhood diaries and Bunty's mother had remembered that the one she had given Amanda last Christmas had never been seen since and she had thought about it all the way back down the M1. The toy lock on a battered old briefcase was never going to be proof against Gloria Bunter-Byng once her curiosity was roused. A quick twist with a nail file had seen off the catch and she found herself in a sordid teenage world of French letters and back seat couplings and unnatural acts with chocolate bars. She raced through the three-month confession in a fever of blushing, watched over by Bunty's father wearing weekend corduroys and a look of furious anticipation.

'What is it, Gloria? What has she written?' demanded Roy. 'What has she said about *me*?'

'Everything was in it,' wept Bunty. '*Everything*. Oh God. I am such a silly cow.'

The missing Mandies arrived and were swiftly brought up to speed.

'Oh you poor dozy mare. At least mine's in code,' said Queenie, smugly.

'Bully for you,' snapped Bunty. Oh. The sour note in her friend's voice distressed Baker more than tears. Bunty was never bitter.

'Sorry. Stupid thing to say.' Queenie squeezed her hand, almost in tears herself.

'Don't you start,' sniffed Bunty. 'Didn't even know you kept a diary. What kind of code?'

'Made it up: hearts, diamonds, squares and circles and plus signs. They'd never crack it.'

'Might try.'

'You kidding? Mummy has enough trouble with the new washing machine instructions. Got "Do not bleach" confused with "Do not wash". She was taking everything to the dry cleaners when we first got it: pyjamas, rugby shirts, everything.'

The cloakroom had filled and the Upper Shells were undressing and dressing again, ready for the Monday dose of Drumlin.

'Sod that,' said Baker. 'Let's go and have a fag.'

'Bring plenty of matches,' said Bunty, reaching into her tote bag, 'we need to burn this.'

Queenie managed to smuggle out the cloakroom waste paper bin by folding the thin metal almost in half and ramming it under her coat. The four of them tramped up past the netball courts to the bicycle shed where Bunty opened the handsome little book and began tearing out page after page after page, shredding each sheet with her fingernails and scattering the scraps into the blazing bin. The other three joined in, but made a special point of not watching their hands at work, each wanting Bunty to see that they weren't seeing, weren't trying to steal her secrets, but you couldn't help yourself reading the shreds of charred paper as they floated into view with the updraught: *days late*, *bi-lingual!*, secrets shared with Bunty's gilt-edged confidante. Not with Baker.

'God! Yesterday evening was a *night*-mare,' wailed Bunty. 'She insisted on setting up shop in the spare room and Daddy's now on the sofa bed in the study because their bed is now unusable – "soiled" was one of the words she used, like sanitary towels. Gross. And "polluted", that was the other one. *Polluted*! Like oily puffins. I wouldn't mind, but we always did it on a towel.'

'Gross.' Queenie made a gagging gesture.

'And darling Daddy is doing his darnedest to mind as much as she does, but after a couple of hours of carrying on he starts mooching around the drawing room, poking the fire and winding the clock and bashing the barometer in a kind of "Where's my bloody supper? Am I master here or not?" sort of way. Didn't get any supper in the end – had to make himself hoops. I feel a bit sorry for him to be honest.

'Then *she* gets hold of the upstairs extension and shuts herself in the spare bedroom to phone Aunt Marcia in Shwop-sha. I caught the odd word.' Bunty puffed ruefully on her fag. 'I'm a *"perverted, depraved little tart"* apparently. That must have been the you-know-what.' Bunty made a pout with her lips, like she was daring them to ask what she meant. 'And never leaving off about the bed: "The bed we bought when we got married ..."' Bunty tightened her larynx to match her mother's county contralto. '"My *bridal* bed."'

There was an awkward silence while the other Mandies mentally beat off thoughts of Ma and Pa Bunter-Byng finding a legitimate use for a queen-sized, pocket-sprung Slumberland mattress. *Gross.*

Bunty's mother had put the sheets and pillowcases in the dustbin (which was a bit of a joke as her daughter had only just changed them all), and the silver satin eiderdown was hanging on the line in the vegetable garden where it was given a vicarious thwacking with a Celtic knot of wicker every time Mrs Bunter-Byng passed it on her way back from dead-heading live daffodils.

Bunty's diary was almost completely consumed.

'You might have known she'd read it, you twazzock,' said Stottie. 'They can't help themselves. My mum reads mine. I always know when she's been at it. I do that thing with a hair.'

'What thing with a hair?'

'That thing where you stick a hair over the cover so you can tell if anyone's opened it. I knew she would. I only write it for her to read: worry about homework, worry about marks, must try harder, that kind of thing. And what a pain Stephanie is and how all the teachers hate her and how I wanted to kill myself when I didn't get distinction. All that. Definitely does the trick. She got me some chocolate yesterday.'

Stottie seemed genuinely taken aback by their silence.

'What?'

All four girls were so busy looking for a stick to stir the ashes with that they didn't hear the Drumlin tiptoeing up to the shed in her green flash Dunlops.

'And what the Devil do you think you're doing?'

The games mistress hadn't been able to keep the thrill out of her voice. *All four of them*. Smoking. Out of bounds. *Arson*, practically. Wilful damage. It was like a dream come true until Amanda Bunter-Byng turned her bloated, tear-stained face towards the games mistress and you could see wind visibly leaving the Drumlin sails.

'Bunty's mum read her diary.'

Baker's toneless voice robbed the scene of all its drama. Miss Drumlin stared down at the leafless leather cover, the charred fragments of excited girlish scribble: *cock*, *packet*.

'How rotten. Gosh. Gosh that is rotten. Still,' she brightened, 'no excuse for being out of bounds. You can all report for detention to Mrs Mostyn this lunchtime: "Idling away an entire Games lesson". And clear this mess up, Amanda, Amanda.'

'Wossat word?' said Bunty as they dawdled back to the main building.

'What's what word?'

'That word.'

'Brick?'

'Thassit.'

They weren't alone in that lunchtime's detention. Natasha and Bryony, of all people, had written the name of some pop star all over their white canvas shoes in Biro (a fashion the Drumlin was determined to stamp out) and had also been made to report to the Geography Room for a summary punishment. Bryony had never been in detention before. Bryony's dad had promised her a colour portable for her sixteenth birthday if she kept a clean sheet. Bryony had been crying.

'I need hardly say how disappointed I am, Bryony,' said the Snog Monster, already mentally composing the stiff letter home. 'You have always been so ... so *School*.'

Mrs Mostyn was actually rather pleased to see them all as she had a bit of a rush job on. The three daughters of a South Asian diplomat were starting at Fawcett Upper after Easter and it was finally time to address the sad fact that Ceylon was no more.

'We did *mean* to do the updating at the time,' she smarmed, 'but it's never really been on the syllabus and Africa was so much more *pressing*.'

The mistress carted the huge stacks of atlases to the glueing tables. She was wearing the violet Crimplene again. It looked even nastier up close. Like Artex, thought Stottie, like it would graze your skin if your mum pushed you into it after a pint of Cinzano.

'Amanda?' Four heads failed to look up. 'Bunter-Byng? Perhaps one of you could colour and label this final batch of Africas while the others get on with –' a cross little pause '"*Sri Lanka*".'

She left them alone and sloped off to scrounge fresh supplies of glue from the Art Room.

Bunty pursed her lips and began shading the maps and inking in the names of countries with furious concentration, while the other five cut out and stuck down two hundred Sri Lankas under maps of India and Southern India and ruled through the Ceylons on a hundred world maps.

'I can't believe I'm doing this. I feel like a medieval monk. Has she never heard of Xerox?'

'This what you were doing last week?' asked Queenie, casually pasting another maplet into place.

Baker nodded. 'There are worse jobs, much worse. The Drumlin made me blanco her tennis shoes once.'

The Mandies raced to keep up with each other, but the mountain of atlases in front of Brian and Tash was slower to melt because the pair of them, unseen by the Geography mistress, were passing a long note backwards and forwards, half in blue, half in the prattish turquoise ink that Natasha thought expressed her personality ('What does your pencil case say about you?').

'Bryony Cotter! Hand me that paper!'

The terrified Brian tried desperately to post the note through the hinge in the desk but the Snog Monster snatched it from her sticky fingers just as the bell sounded for lunch.

'Stack the atlases on the shelves and put the rest in the glueing tray. Look lively! I'll deal with you later, Bryony.'

All six ravenous fifth formers dashed from the room, leaving Mrs Mostyn squinting crossly at the note. The new girl – Natasha? – was apparently asking the other one about a member of staff. A very unpopular member of staff it would seem.

Why do they call her the Snog Monster? The note began. How coarse. *Got off with a forest ranger on a field trip*, Bryony had replied. *Name three people who haven't*, quipped the other one.

Mrs Mostyn realised with a not altogether unpleasant ripple of shock that they must be discussing Miss Combe. How cruel girls could be. *She is such a stupid fat ugly old cow.* Old? The poor woman was barely thirty. *Dad says she smells of wee. No wonder everyone gives up Geography. She is so fucking boring.*

Mrs Mostyn felt a warm wave of vindication despite the revolting language. The girls' opinion of Miss Combe's brand of Geography was manifestly as low as her own. Should poor Miss Combe be shown the note? The temptation was all but irresistible. That would wipe the smile off her face, if she were to learn what the girls thought of her precious pebble formation: *fucking boring*. There was more muck on the other side but a tardy twinge of Christian charity prompted Mrs Mostyn to tear the note in two without another glance. She screwed the scraps into a tight ball and lobbed it into the corner bin. *A goal for Mostyn minor!* (One never really lost the knack.)

Chapter 15

Bunty's eyes were dry the next morning but she had been crying almost all night and no amount of cold water or witch hazel seemed to soothe her swollen and sausagey eyelids. The black rings underneath didn't look real – old lady make-up: Lady Bracknell, Miss Havisham, Mrs Mostyn.

'Christ, doll. Look at the state of you,' said Baker. A rare hug and the tears started again.

'She spent yesterday morning up in town choosing a new bed. Got to the Tottenham Court Road before the showrooms were even open and tipped the salesman twenty quid to get it delivered today because no-power-human-or-divine was going to make her spend another night in her old bed after *this*.'

'Is your old man still on the sofa?' wondered Queenie, who had just arrived with Stott.

'He's away on business all this week. Sorting everything out before we *g-go*.' The last word, a great gasping sob, only quietened when she stuffed a man's hankie into her mouth.

'Go?' Baker's mouth had dried so suddenly that she almost barked the word.

'Australia. Mummy didn't really want to go when they first offered him the transfer, but now I've given her no choice, apparently.'

'*Australia*?' It didn't sound any more real when Baker said it out loud, and when she tried to picture it she only saw koalas and eucalyptus leaves. An orange and yellow map showing concentric circles of rainfall (or lack of it).

'Blimey. She didn't waste much time.'

'She was on the phone half the night in floods. "Transported" she called it. All my fault obviously. Dad turned the posting down a couple of months back,' gabbled Bunty, 'but they still want him so she made him ring and say he's changed his mind and yes please can he have a zillion ozzie dollars and house with pool after all please and they said yes so we're g-going.' More tears.

When would they go? Where would they live? What would they take? Who would they know? What were the men like? On and bloody on went Stottie and Queenie, like it was just chat.

'A swimming pool . . .' drooled Stott.

Baker kept her head down, scrabbling under the bench for her tennis shoes. She ripped out the broken lace and began threading it back in a different pattern, awkwardly pinching the frayed ends of tape through the eyelets with the ragged pads of her nail-less fingertips. She breathed deeply, concentrating hard on reabsorbing the tears gathering in the back of her nose, but her eyes were wet when she met Bunty's bloodshot glance and it was all she could do not to howl out loud.

As they marched off to assembly Bunty filled Baker in on further details. Big brother Dominic was furious at his parents' plan to leave the country and Bunty had a bruise on her cheek to prove it.

'All my fault, he says. I tried telling him that I can't be the *only* reason we're going – I can't be, can I? I'm sure Dad's got a floozy somewhere, some other reason Ma wants out. Anyway, Dominic insists he wants to stay behind and be a boarder and just doss down with Aunt Marcia in the holidays. Australian schools would be full of *grockles*, Dominic says.'

Dominic had unveiled this plan over supper the previous evening and, although his father was sure he'd see sense eventually, Mrs Bunter-Byng had a horrible feeling he was serious. He could be very stubborn. Once the plates were cleared the two children could hear her screaming and carrying on: that Roy had to *do something* and that she couldn't go to Australia without her baby. Brother and sister, listening from their usual spot at the top of the stairs, retreated, embarrassed, to their rooms.

Bunty's mother had spent her life dabbing a sort of conversational concealer over the ugly fact that she preferred one of her children to the other. She had never hidden it particularly well. Yes, true, she was always scrupulously fair when filling stockings or slicing chocolate cakes or deciding bedtimes or smacking anybody but you only had to look at her, only had to watch her brush back his curly golden fringe with the tenderest possible touch of her pearlised coral manicure, to see that Bunty had only scraped silver in this particular race.

It infuriated Baker. Mummies were supposed to be above all that. Weren't supposed to go off in search of themselves, weren't supposed to have favourites like a silly little child laying out its foreign doll collection in order of preference. Couldn't the stupid woman have kept it to herself? It would all have blown over eventually, that creepy crush on her baby boy. Love didn't stay the same. Give it five years – ghastly girlfriends, debts, in-laws, babies – and love could flood in or leak out, curdle, boil dry, evaporate. It wasn't for ever – whatever the songs said. Any more than you could decide for ever and always which was your very favourite dress or which was the most comfortable chair in the drawing room. Ask yourself again in ten years' time. Twenty. Ask when your knees didn't bend any more. Bunty wouldn't always have come second.

Founder's Day preparations meant that Tuesday morning games was cancelled (no sense getting them all sweaty) and school assembly was taken at an unusual lick. There was a rather terse prayer (the shortest in the book) followed by two verses of 'The King of Love My Shepherd Is' played *allegro moderato* by the versatile Miss Batty (the Prizegiving service would be starting at eleven and there was no sense giving them all hymn fatigue) followed by the news headlines. The Upper Third hockey squad had disgraced itself again, and could girls please note that the Biology Lab corridor was out of bounds until the locksmith and the insurance people had made their report (a happy snigger from Baker).

The hall was dressed to look its best. Every girl wore a blazer. There were explosions of iris and pussy willow in two of the four urns and a strong smell of Traffic Wax rising up from the now slightly slippery parquet. Mrs Mostyn had swapped the familiar purple passion-killer for a very tight dress and jacket in a hideous hymn book green.

Baker lived through assembly in a trance of misery at Bunty's news. When she eventually looked up and scanned the stage she saw that the head girl's rosewood throne was empty – not like her to miss a speech day. Whispers were being passed down the long rows of canvas chairs. By the time the chain of hisses reached Baker's end it sounded like 'knicker wiping' but was, in fact, 'nicked a white pin'. The surplus chair left vacant by Alison Hutchinson, the light-fingered head of Nightingale House, was under a cloth in the green room and would now be joined by another from the set because Mrs Mostyn had finally spotted the unearned badge on Linda Sprake's blazer lapel. Nothing was said, the girl's name wasn't even mentioned: just a brief announcement that Heidi Dobrowski had been appointed head girl (and head of Fry House) with immediate effect. Mrs Mostyn cut short the puzzled applause and launched into some heart-warming yawn from *Gladsome Minds*, her delivery unusually impressive. She seemed almost *aroused* by the gravity of the offence.

Baker managed to dodge the others after assembly and hid herself in one of the loos in the junior cloakroom, smoking her way through a new pack of JPS, trying to conceive of a world without Bunty. The imagined future stretched ahead of her, a photograph album with captions but no pictures: Bunty and Baker go flatsharing; Bunty and Baker get jobs; Bunty and Baker get married . . . So much of their future was bundled up together in Baker's head that Bunty emigrating was like a fiancé dying, or being gazumped or having a miscarriage or failing the eleven plus: a whole chunk of your future cancelled. *And what will you be when you grow up?* People didn't ask you that any more but, whichever of Miss Batty's pink folders she ended up in, Baker had never been in any doubt of the only answer that truly mattered.

Things had to change, Baker knew that. School would stop, parents would die, the man of your dreams might turn out to be a nightmare, an ex-husband, a *late* husband even (more room in the bed; less mess on the floor). But Bunty would have been a *Diorella*-scented shoulder to cry on when he dumped you for a dolly bird, been around for a long boozy lunch after the divorce came through, been there to squeeze your hand and pass the hip flask in the first car at the funeral, rung you up when another old girl dropped dead or had twins.

But not from *Sydney*. Nobody ever just rang from Sydney. And even if they did, it was only ever thrifty, three-minute hellos, like Spam and Old Mother Spam: fine-thank-you-how-are-you-I-never-interfere.

The tightness in her chest as she sat curled up on the loo felt like a great big blood pressure cuff, binding her ribs, making it harder and harder to breathe. The sobs gave her away.

'*There* you are.'

Baker could hardly see Stottie for tears as the other girl sidled into the cubicle and wedged herself into the ledge of the narrow window below the cistern.

'Bunty's been looking everywhere for you.'

'I'll never see her again.'

'Of course you will. *Course* we'll see her again. She won't have *died*. She'll just be living somewhere else.'

'In Australia. Might as well be dead.'

Talking made it much worse. She glared up at Stottie, snotty strings gumming her mouth together as she wailed.

'I don't want to *grow old* without her.'

Anyone but Stottie would have sniggered, but Stottie wasn't sniggering and Baker was too tear-blind to see the stricken look that opened and closed on her friend's face the millisecond before she patted Baker's hand and settled for silver.

'She might come back.'

'Don't be daft. They're *emigrating*.'

'No, I mean once she's left school. Come back here, get a job. We'll all see her again. She won't stay there for ever, she can't do . . .' Stottie's certainty shaken by the thought of a swimming pool.

She made Baker wash her face and comb her hair. Stottie herself was all tidied away in readiness for Founder's Day and her Lady Henry handshake. She produced the all-important polythene bag from her inside pocket, then did the necessary with the contents of a twist of cling film.

'Hope to God my mum never finds out.'

'Nothing in the diary.' said Baker, tartly.

Lady Henry had been planting a tree, a crab apple, and had had to change her shoes in the back of the car. Lady Henry was much in demand. She had few obvious qualifications but she arrived in a Bentley, wore pearls and a hat and her name looked well in school magazines and local papers whenever she presented a cup or cut a ribbon or let tiny crumbs of mortar trickle from the blades of gilded ceremonial trowels.

The headmistress took the floor, her gown flowing impressively over her tweeds, her blue-black hair held in tight, cartoonish waves by the best part of a can of lacquer, the gas cabinet pong cut with a few dabs of long-fermented *Blue Grass*. Applause was the life-blood of any Founder's Day. Dr O'Brien, like Julia (and unlike Mrs Mostyn), had learned precisely how best to harness the energies of four hundred bored but excitable adolescent girls: noise and plenty of it. Like a music hall barker, she began to talk up the delights of their guest – distinguished, tireless charity work, active on many committees, a true Fawcettian and so on – and cranked up a fairly respectable ovation as Lady Henry's clean navy courts made their way to the platform where she was installed behind a refectory table, its lino hidden by a length of red plush from the drama cupboard and dotted with a burglar's wet dream of silver plate.

Lady Henry ran her eye along the table of silvery empties and let off a small chirrup of pleasure as she spotted the largest of the trophies. She simpered nostalgically at the Drama Prize, thoughtfully swivelled round so that her own maiden name faced her. Her smile grew wider at the memory of the handsome corduroy doublet she had worn ... buskins dyed to match and the spiffy gown Mama had had made for the first act before Rosalind went into the forest. And the applause! Wonderful waves of sound breaking over her. The Lower Fourth had gone quite potty (no second-former had ever taken the lead in the school play before – or since, as far as Lady Henry was aware).

She idly scanned Dr O'Brien's list: funny how the same girls tended to win everything. Always had. Games of all kinds were monopolised this year by a Lower Sixth former called Smith who had also won 'Girl who best embodies the Ethos of the school'. In Lady Henry's day the Ethos cup invariably went to one of the swots, ideally someone with grade eight bassoon who'd won a place at Girton. The Smith girl was not that type. Lady Henry, who had been introduced to her on arrival, spotted her sitting alongside the dais with the other sixth formers and shuddered with distaste. Julia's ensemble was slightly less *sportif* than usual but she still wore a divided skirt. Lady Henry glanced crossly at the veinless teenage thighs, at the tiny blazer plated with enamel pins – they'd give a deportment badge to anyone with a comb these days.

Miss Kopje (Elocution and Drama) felt her heart sink as Lady Henry placed herself before the lectern. Once in a while you got a speaker who really knew what they were about: who came in under five minutes with an address as dry and bracing as a double gin and tonic, but there was a collective sigh from the whole SCR as those queen motherly peep-toed shoes took up their ten-to-two, viola solo stance. They were clearly in for a marathon.

Lady Henry, one-time winner of the Mabel Sledge verse-speaking competition, liked nothing better than a few well-chosen words. The previous year, Miss Kopje had asked Lady Henry for her secret at the sherry gathering traditionally held in the head's study afterwards and Lady Henry (who had a tin ear for irony) confided that her models were her father and 'dear Winston'. Churchill had very likely given her that irritating habit of emphasising stray words, and Miss Kopje could hear him in those cheesy periods, in that fatal weakness for the triple construction, ('Aspiration, Application, Dedication' – you could practically see the capital letters, smell the fibre tip underlining them). One presumably had her papa to blame for the mania for internal rhymes: 'Deny oneself; apply oneself; rely on oneself' was a favourite (she'd used it last time she came). Every cliché was her friend. Miss Kopje and Miss 'Fuckface' Dempsey (Physics, Applied Maths and emergency Chemistry) pressed knees as the hoary old soldiers limped past: *nine parts perspiration* forsooth.

Mrs Mostyn slotted the base of her spine more securely against the back of her chair, consciously pressing each vertebra into the veneered wood, unfolding her shoulders to mirror the square curve of the high back. She tilted her chin to listening mode, her gaze stretching above the speaker to the raised top of Miss Batty's baby grand. Like everything else in the hall, the pocket Bechstein had been given a brisk seeing-to with furniture polish and a fluffy duster but you could see the print of the great spanking hand that had pulled the instrument from its usual corner, a matt mess on the gleaming black surface.

Miss Batty, seated at her instrument in readiness for the first hymn, was meanwhile building a mental A–Z of symphonies (with a point deducted for every Haydn): Archduke, Baba Yar, Choral. She was already stuck at K when the speech finally got started.

'It has *orphan* been said,' Miss Kopje swallowed a smirk: what a tight, regal larynx the woman had, 'that making a speech is like giving birth: easy to conceive, but difficult to deliver.'

Oh dear. You couldn't call it silence, not with all those farts of mirth escaping from red-faced fourth formers. Their visitor saw at once that she had struck the wrong note. She had culled her opening remarks from the keynote address at a recent masonic ladies' night, but it played very badly with the Fawcett staff and those parents (mothers mostly) whose girls had won a prize and who were gathered in the back of the hall (only one of them in a hat but that was South London for you). Happily the rest of her speech left the labour ward behind and stuck to old favourites.

One did best to start with the prizes for dull things like chess and music and the Duke of Edinburgh, Dr O'Brien had found. The chess prize (the glum glance at the book's cover made it clear that the girl had it already) was followed by the Lady Jane Scott prize for needlecraft, then it was straight into the music certificates. These were so numerous that they were seen off in batches: piano; strings; woodwind.

Grade Six piano came fairly early in the running order and Baker felt Queenie pinch her arm as they watched Stottie gingerly extract her right hand from the bag concealed in her pocket, then join the queue for her Lady Henry handshake. They held their breath as the prizegiver's face congealed with shock. The production line – nod, handshake, certificate – stalled for a long moment before she got nervously back into step like a schoolgirl timing her jump into a playground skipping rope. As Stottie clumped down the steps, she looked at the palm of her hand in a pantomime of disgusted disbelief then made an elaborate show of wiping it on her (pre-dampened) handker-chief. Behind her, sundry seventh- and eighth-grade pianists clumped off stage, ineffectually stroking their sticky hands against their skirts. Baker saw Stottie fish the tacky placky bag from her pocket and slip it unnoticed into one of the empty urns beside the steps. She caught Julia's eye and both managed not to smile.

Dr O'Brien, who was still reciting the endless list of achievements, frowned slightly as one prize-winner after another had the same bizarre reaction. It looked to be some kind of mass prank. Exasperating. The whole stunt had evidently been undertaken on far too large a scale for any meaningful punishment. The thing was to establish the ringleaders: make an example.

The head's hands carried on passing the squares of card to Lady Henry while her trained eye scoured the hall for abnormal levels of mirth, like a Post Office proof-reader scanning a sheet of stamps for a missing perforation. Nothing as yet ... tubby little Prudence Compton had just picked up her grade three clarinet. She'd be back later for Most Improved Girl and yet even she, *even she* was rubbing her palm against the front of her jumper. Most peculiar.

The prize-passing lark was traditionally broken up by a musical interlude during which the choir sang the 'Skye Boat Song' and two thirds of the school anthem (the final verse about 'mothers of England to be' had been dropped over a decade ago). It was set, rather cheekily, to 'Jerusalem' and the piano had been primed by Stottie to go haywire when the melody climbed to its top note ('Give thanks for *all* our school has done') thanks to the velvety bulk of a long-lost board rubber bunged under the hammer of top E.

Baker and the Mandies were almost shaking with excitement as Miss Batty made her last-minute adjustments to the stool and shuffled showily with her sheet music. The head, anxious to shave vital seconds from the running time, always cut Parry's hopelessly florid introduction and so the school song went straight into the first verse: 'Shine Fawcett Shine' etc. (The founder was a remarkable woman in many ways, Miss Batty conceded, but she was a lamentable lyricist.)

The Mandies held their breath . . . Worked like a charm. Miss Batty took an unscheduled bar's rest to allow the muffled laughter to subside before they got to the second verse but a good half of the hall was still stifling uproarious coughs.

Lady Henry was scraping ineffectually at her sticky palm with a paper tissue and running through her deep breathing exercises ready for the second part of her address. She had already vowed to give the Fawcett prizes a miss in future.

The second set of prizes passed off without incident. Finally Lady Henry came to the Fawcett Cup, won this year by Nightingale, whose captain strode smugly forward as the guest of honour placed a still sticky paw on each handle of the solid silver rose bowl and presented it to the sixth-former, drenching the girl's skirt, flooding the prize table and filling her own snakeskin shoes with cold water as she did so.

Teachers' eyes instantly criss-crossed the room, a web of infra-red beams, ready to trap anyone whose reaction was more (or less) than the normal range of giggling. Dr O'Brien, with the presence of mind that distinguished a headmistress from a mere deputy, rose to her feet and, with the merest glance of command, jerked Miss Batty into gear and led the astonished hall in a rousing rendition of the closing hymn (*we shall not suffer loss*).

Mrs Mostyn smiled grimly as the youngest girl in the school presented Lady Henry with a bunch of jonquils, while O'Brien chuckled through some cock and bull story about having kept the bouquet in water but no amount of hearty business-as-usual could deflate the happy hall. The traditional epilogue (nine cheers in all for head, staff and school) broke all previous records for volume. Word had already spread about Lady Henry's syrupy grip, and the ceremony's watery finale was like the climax of a television comedy programme: a boss to dinner, a custard pie lying in wait on a table, a tray of drinks, a soda syphon. The piano played them out with the school song (a skilful switch from D Major to E Flat Major made the right hand safe once more) and Mrs Mostyn almost expected to see the credits roll: 'Based on an idea by –' whom? Probably one of the Amandas in Upper Shell. Amanda Baker? Surely not after last week. Or Amanda Bunter-Byng? Emigrating, apparently. Nothing to lose . . .

The rest of the staff instinctively manned the swing doors as the girls filed out, listening for clues, watching for any signs of triumphalism. A few minutes later, as the hilarity cleared and the first lunch sitting gathered into a rough queue for the dining hall, Mrs Mostyn skilfully picked off one of the more callow and feeble Lower Fourths: huge, lashless eyes blinking rapidly behind heavy convex lenses. The wily Geography mistress framed her question with care:

'Was anyone *with* Amanda Baker when she filled the trophy with water?'

Resistance was useless. Every foe is vanquished. We will take our revenge.

Baker had headed back to the Shell cloakroom for a quick fag. Two of the cleaners were putting away their mops and buckets. They had just been paid and the older one was checking the notes and coins in her mini manila envelope. The other, younger woman was off down the shops with hers (something nice for his tea), but the old crone managed things differently. Her cleaning hours were nine till one which meant that her old man was out at work and none the wiser.

'Finks I only work Fridays. Keep the rest in the Post Office. Don't need him to sign nothing like you do with the bank.'

'Rainy day?'

The woman scoffed.

'Raining now.'

Sitting on the loo in her usual sideways pose Baker noticed with surprise that the scribbled gag about Cookery O levels had been wiped from beneath the loo roll holder. She pushed gently at the enamel notice on the back of the door with her foot. The missing screw still let the plaque swing freely but the graffiti beneath had disappeared. Gone. All of it. In its place a freshly painted oblong in a slightly whiter shade of pale grey. The extra coat fitted the sign to the millimetre.

Chapter 16

Julia was already two thirds of the way down the first joint when Baker arrived.

'Excellent work with the treacle yesterday, Mandibles.' She picked a baby Swiss roll from the pack she'd brought and posted the entire thing into her mouth, a factory chimney of sponge collapsing into her waiting face.

'Did you hear about what happened to the head girl?' You could hardly make out the words for cake and butter cream. 'Indefinite suspension from duties pending investigation. What *swines*, eh? Wonder where she got the badge from? Can't have pinched it from the office, not Linda.'

Baker's whole body was suddenly paralysed with guilt, so that the smoke she had just inhaled remained trapped inside her by the held breath. It had only been a cautious puff but now every particle of dope was maximised, fizzing under her skin, scrambling her brain. All at once she was too afraid to speak, convinced that she would blurt out the truth and Julia would hate her for ever and tell everyone and make her spend the rest of her life in Coventry.

'Why Coventry?' she demanded, out loud.

'What about Coventry?'

'*Coventry* Coventry. You know. When nobody speaks to you.'

'Maybe that's what Coventry's like: *very very quiet*,' whispered Julia, 'one big grudge ... Anyway. None of the sixth are sending Linda to Coventry. Everyone likes old Lindy-Loo and they can't put the head girl in detention so it'll all just blow over. Bloody hope so. Bloody boring. S'all they talk about in the common room. It dies down for a bit then Heidi Doodah starts it up again. Well she would, wouldn't she? Being deputy. Suppose she thought her luck had changed. Maybe it was her with the badge? Those creeps will do anything for promotion. It'll be *murder* next: a compass point between the sixth and seventh vertebrae, a cyanide capsule in her third of milk. The head girl is dead; long live the head girl.'

'Hip-hip,' hiccupped Baker. The organ pipes were starting to curve and taper like a really, really big stick of celery. She handed back the joint and took a few deep, dopeless breaths.

'Cow.'

'Who?'

'Heidi Doodah. Pathetic – that badge business.'

Baker felt very clever, very cunning, a master criminal, as she persisted that yes, that would explain everything: Heidi and the white pin: motive, means, wossname. Heidi. Not Baker. Not Baker at all.

'You've been crying.'

Baker tried to explain about Bunty but Julia didn't seem to understand somehow, didn't see that a great chunk of Baker's future had been torn away, but then of course Julia didn't have a best friend. No one to play with. Unless it was Baker? She tried pasting Julia's face into the gap: Julia at the wedding, Julia at the christenings, a different twosome in the lovely white flat then remembered that Baz or similar would be there to spoil it, then remembered Nick.

Julia was licking the chocolate off a chocolate Garibaldi now.

'I love this room. Lovely lovely room. No *sofa*, though.' She looked about her crossly, rolled up her blazer and tucked it behind her head. 'Weed me a stor-wee.'

Baker turned the pages of her *Spare Rib*, frowning.

'I was thinking about what you said. All that "beat them at their own game" cobblers. *Baaaad* idea. Mustn't pretend. You'd *turn*. Turn into one of them. Has to be another way. I mean,' words were sliding away from her, 'look at Spam.'

'S*pam* Spam? As in tins of?'

'Noooo, silly, Spam-my-stepmother-Spam. Pamela Dawn Baker Spam. Got a proper job, Spam has. Proper, good-as-a-bloke job, but there she is painting her face, depilating her armpits and lining her drawers and putting cosies on the toaster. I mean you don't catch blokes monkeying about with toasters.'

'Or lining her drawers, I hope.'

Baker pulled a face and turned back to the personal column.

'"SE London man would like to meet some liberated women socially."'

'I bet he would,' snorted Julia. 'Dirty bugger.'

Baker turned back to a centre spread on communal living. The *Rib* women might not depilate their armpits but they'd all end up with the same rash by the look of it, making themselves freely available to anything with a beard. Very liberating.

'Nice for them and all that but it isn't exactly *helping*, is it? I mean *who cares* if some bird in dungarees swears off lipstick and then shags her entire kibbutz? Won't change anything. Not while there's a single Spam left pairing socks and pining for an infra-red grill.'

But Julia was looking bored, the way Bunty did whenever Baker got into her stride, and so Baker hastily read out another small ad.

'"Jo Hollins would like to hear from other women who have had vaginismus about their experience."'

'Would she? Would she really? God almighty. You'd pay money not to, wouldn't you? I bloody would. Is it all sex, that magazine?'

'Pretty much.'

Julia basked in her big, beautiful sunbeam, hair spurting across the blue cushion of blazer in a messy stream of golden syrup. The catty stretch of her body and the never-ending warm, white legs seemed to grow longer than the room: Alice in Wonderland with a foot up the chimney. Reaching blindly behind her she dragged a nylon make-up purse from the side pocket of her bag and began squeezing ointment-coloured goo from a tube and systematically concealing her freckled face with expert fingers before coating her lashes in blue mascara and dusting coloured powder on and around her cheeks, sucking them in as she brushed. She finished off with a jammy smear of lipstick from a tiny white pot with a daisy on it before snapping the mirror shut and cramming the whole grubby little kit back in its pocket.

'Seeing Baz later.'

The snotty, sucked-in look stayed in place even after she had finished – had the wind changed? Didn't look like Julia any more as she flicked her hair behind her shoulder with a fillyish toss of the head, just looked like the girl on the back of Baz's bike.

'Got to look my best.'

Bunty would never have said that. The old Bunty wouldn't anyway.

Baker took her last lovely drag on the joint while Julia scoffed the remaining Swiss roll.

'If we had enough cake – which is a pretty big "if", I admit – we could stay here indefinitely. A cake machine, that's what this needs, or *helicopters*; helicopters could deliver it through the roof hole. Food parcels.'

The heedless trill of a bird was pouring in through the open skylight. Baker didn't know what kind. Dad would probably have known (but he wasn't telling). Jeremy would have known . . . The fuzzy buzz of dope and the sunshine and the sweet tastes on her tongue all joined forces to lift Baker's arm and place her hand in Julia's warm, strong, hockey forward fingers.

'Me tooooo, babe,' crooned Julia huskily (though Baker hadn't spoken). 'Me too me too me toomee toomy toomy.'

The birdsong shut off as the door to the loft was flung open.

'So this is where you eat your lunch, is it?'

Mrs Mostyn was standing in the doorway, flanked by the lunchtime duty prefect and the school caretaker (who was holding a large wrench behind his back like a surprise bouquet). The Snog Monster's spectacles winked unnervingly in the sunlight, as if her eyes had caught fire.

Chapter 17

The duty prefect (who was a tiny bit of a party animal on the quiet) had caught a whiff of spliff on the draught coming down the forbidden staircase and was just about to nip up and investigate when she'd been spotted by the deputy head who was giving Mr Dingle a guided tour of things that wanted sanding down or waxing or repairing or painting over with dove grey non-drip gloss.

'Where are you going? What is it?' and moments later she was wheezing up the stairs behind the sixth-former, nostrils twitching at the familiar smell of tobacco, shoulders squaring with pleasure in anticipation of the coming scene.

The Snog Monster had pulled the door towards her so hard and fast that it sucked a sharp breeze in through the skylight, ripping Julia's poster from the wall and exposing the graffiti-fest beneath. The horror on the evil, fat cock-sucking Snog Monster's face as she stared at the vandalised wall was partially veiled by the cambric handkerchief that she had pressed over her mouth and nose to avoid breathing the drug-drenched air, but you could still see her upper face which wore a bewildered, almost child-like expression behind the blue sweep of her glasses. *Snog Monster?* But that was Miss Combe, surely? Wasn't it?

Her map-reader's eye surveyed the tiny room, noting the pub ashtray with its load of cinders and charred cardboard. The Snog

Monster's corseted torso, the hairsprayed helmet on her head, the plucked arches of her brow all seemed to swell in size and importance as the gravity of the impending arrest came home to them all. Her whole manner had altered. She wasn't the nutty, gladsome-minded, atlas-fixing old Geography mistress any more. Narrowing her mouth somehow contrived to pull up the slack in her jowls and tighten her face like there were wires inside, backstage, changing the scenery. *Drugs.*

'See that nothing is touched.' A TV policeman sealing off a crime scene. Her next move was to separate the two suspects: Julia was to remain under guard in the organ loft while Baker was marched off to the headmistress. 'It's off to Dr O'Brien for you, young lady.' Her pearly claw made to pinch Baker's elbow and guide her from the room but Baker twitched her arm free.

Girls were log-jamming the corridors on their way from afternoon Registration, but the blue stream of serge meandered either side of Baker and the Geography mistress, sneaking glances to gauge the fifth-former's state of mind. Defiant? Defeated?

Baker instinctively kept her guard up, composing her face into a weary scowl and somehow bullying her legs into walking in a straight line.

The Mostyn hadn't spoken since they left the scene of the crime but you could tell her mind was struggling with the enormity of the offence and the hideous dilemma now facing the head. Expulsion was traditional but that could be a two-edged sword. Expulsions got into local newspapers and, while the headlines might make it plain that the school stood for no nonsense, the publicity inevitably let slip the fact that nonsense was taking place.

It *had* happened before (under a previous administration) and the then head had very cunningly finessed the offence into 'smoking on school premises' (even the *Advertiser* had bigger stories than that to run with).

The handkerchief that had covered the Snog Monster's face when she first smelled smoke was now rolled round the remains of the last joint which she held cupped in her hand so that passing girls shouldn't spot it. When they reached the main lobby she fished a brown envelope from the tin bin beside the staff pigeonholes and carefully placed the cambric bundle inside it. You could almost see the thought of fingerprints crossing her mind before it trotted back to the corner where her wildest dreams resided. Hard to imagine the head wanting to go as far as fingerprints – or involve the police at all (more's the pity).

And was Dr O'Brien even in her study? Mrs Mostyn gave a tut of vexation when the coloured lights stayed unlit. Typical.

'Wait here.'

There was an ache in Baker's head. Her forefinger tracked the pain to a pulsing line on her temple which stopped when you pressed it and surged back whenever you let go. She blinked dozily around her. Her eyesight was still playing tricks with perspective and the wall of dead heads seemed to be nosing out at her disappointedly through their parcel gilt windows, whispering to each other. She breathed deeply, trying to clear the weirdness from her blood, trying to picture those blue blobs of oxygen climbing aboard passing rafts of haemoglobin, pushing the dopey particles overboard. Could they do tests? She lurched to her feet and began pacing the lobby. It was what they did in films. That and coffee. And hot towels? Or was that something else?

She stopped pacing and stood unsteadily in front of one of the notice cupboards on her way back to the bench. For a split second she thought that the list of school governors was the same one that Queenie had pinned there – same position in the box, same flimsy yellow paper – but she looked in vain for Magda Goebbels or Dr Crippen. The next frame still sported the newspaper cutting about the victorious skating team. It looked almost exactly as it had looked before, just slightly narrower where happy little Bunty had been razored away. Even the caption had been doctored so that her name, conveniently at the end of a line, had been filleted out. Bunty. Unbunty. Remembering the loss of her best friend took the edge off Baker's terror – briefly, anyway – gave her a choice of scabs to pick.

She half opened her eyes. Spam was saying her name over and over and shaking her awake. The alarm clock was much much louder than usual. Spam didn't use to wear glasses . . . horrid, old-lady glasses with blue upswept frames . . .

'Pull yourself together and come with me.' Dr O'Brien had gone AWOL and Mrs Mostyn, damp with perspiration from trotting back and forth between the staff lobby and the organ loft in her least sensible shoes, was taking out her frustration on Baker who now had to be moved so that the Smith girl could be brought in for interrogation. She grabbed Baker's elbow and bustled her along the corridor and into the Drama cupboard. 'Sit there,' said the Snog Monster, gesturing uncertainly at a papier mâché toadstool. 'Dr O'Brien will be back at any moment.'

Baker sat heavily on the red spotted seat, hoping hard that it would crumble beneath her, but its novelty outline had been modelled over a genuine stool and the structure held her weight. She heard the key turn in the lock and the tarty tap of the Mostyn's sling-backs on the linoleum as she winced off in search of the errant headmistress.

The Drama 'cupboard' was in fact a fair-sized box room, sister hutch to Careers and nosebleeds and filled with scenery and props from dramatic productions. There was a wicker skip filled with jerkins and buskins and a great wardrobe rail holding everything from Mephistopheles to the March Hare. The shelves too were lined with theatrical bric-a-brac: a gramophone horn for *Pygmalion*, a cracked and mended tea set for *The Importance of Being Earnest*, a huge paper pulp teapot for the Dormouse in *Alice* with a prompt sheet still glued to its back ('I breathe when I sleep,' said the Dormouse).

Baker was very very sleepy and the wicker skip was almost the size of a single bed. People escaped from prison camps in laundry baskets – on the telly they did anyway: forged papers, uniforms made from army blankets and dyed with boot polish ... She lifted the lid of the basket, releasing a home-to-a-strange-house-for-tea smell of mothballs and stale scent. The chest was filled with costumes that had been pieced thriftily together from old curtains and scraps of mumsy finery, moth magnets that had been sulking unworn in the backs of wardrobes: waists too small, rags too glad for the spammy mummies who had once worn them so prettily. Baker hoicked her leg over the side and climbed in, the wicker lid slamming with a scratchy squeal behind her.

Hours later, days later? – with no clocks and no daylight it was hard to gauge the time – angry incredulous voices joined her in her Shakespearean nest: the girl could not possibly have escaped, the door was locked. Then one of the speakers noticed the open window (the Mostyn's voice this time), refusing to believe that anyone could get through an opening so small. The other voice, O'Brien, gave a doubtful hum, noting that the child was unusually slender.

Baker froze every muscle, hoping they'd wander out into the quad below, looking for evidence: footprints, a scrap of torn blue serge on a rose bush. But the mere act of clenching her muscles unsettled the squeaky equilibrium of her giant hamper.

'Amanda! Come out of that basket!' The Snog Monster delivered her instruction in 'Prism! Where is that baby!' tones.

The head and her deputy each seized an arm and hauled Baker from her hiding place. She could feel the catastrophic catch of her stockings against the basketwork as she tumbled over the side.

'Come along. You've got some explaining to do.'

Chapter 18

Salt? Vinegar. Narrow? Wide. Rich? Poor. Long? Short. Big? Ugly. Bugger.

Miss Carson liked to begin with the word association wossname. Should have been so easy to fake but, six sessions in, a week after Mrs Mostyn caught her in the organ loft, Baker was still letting herself get tripped up, partly because the Carson woman would start firing words at her faster than she could dredge up a smart answer (or a safe answer, or a silly answer), but chiefly because she couldn't bloody well think straight.

Funny really, that being caught taking drugs should result in being given lots more: a contradictory cocktail of tranquillisers, anti-depressants and sleeping tablets. *Mandies* – would have been funny if there had been anyone to share the joke with, but jokes didn't work if you were on your own, like trees falling silently in empty forests. Julia would have laughed: no Julia, so not funny.

'One normally waits *months* for an appointment with Delia Carson,' O'Brien had gushed to Bob Baker, 'but I spoke to her yesterday evening and she has agreed to see Amanda out of hours. Miss Carson is an old student of mine, scholarship to St Hilda's.' The head's attention had wandered fondly to her own undergraduate photograph (hanging behind the study door where departing parents would be sure to see it – like having your karate medals in the downstairs loo). 'And we have Delia to thank for getting us the appointment with Dr Sexton,' oozed Dr O'Brien in don't-thank-me mode. 'Dr Sexton's list has been closed for quite a while now, but Delia has persuaded him to find you a cancellation. That man can do more good in fifteen minutes than anyone else in his field.'

As it turned out, Dr O'Brien's pet psychiatrist had had larger, more exciting fish to fry than Baker (a ten-year-old boy due to stand trial for the attempted poisoning of his stepfather – fascinating case) and so the consultation had lasted only eight of his magic minutes, three of which were spent looking for his prescription pad. He had barely glanced at Baker, who sat curled up on the big leather chair with her knees folded inside her gym slip, sucking annoyingly at the knitted cuff of her outsize school cardigan while he ran through his usual check-list: anxiety? any depression at all? problems sleeping? Each response earning a fresh line of inky hieroglyphs on the illegible drug list at his elbow (*tab t.d.s. Ut dict.*) and a scrawled sentence or two on the pale green notebook on his knee. His writing was not quite as illegible as he liked to think: 'Bitten fingernails' said the pad. 'Sullen little hussy'.

Dr Sexton's three-way prescription, was supposed to keep Baker's behaviour tidy: alert but calm until you were ready for bed then 250 mg of methaqualone in lieu of sleep. Dad and Spam had begun handing out the pills at the six-hourly intervals written in neat block capitals on the side of the bottles and within a week the effects all smudged into each other like the backwash on one of Dora Hardcastle's cloud studies.

There had been no mention of any of the psycho stuff at the first awful meeting after O'Brien and the Mostyn had dragged Baker out of the Drama cupboard.

'I don't need to tell you that you are in very, *very* serious trouble,' the head had announced when Baker first sat down. 'Your father will be here to collect you shortly and he and your stepmother are coming back tomorrow morning for an emergency meeting. Do you have anything to say for yourself?'

Baker, still woozy from the last joint, had screwed up her face in an effort to moisten her eyes. Mrs Mostyn had left the evidence on the desk before leaving the room and O'Brien was poking the white cylinder out of its hankie wrapping with the paper knife from her desk set.

'And where exactly did you get this?'

Mandies never told tales. In fact, bless 'em and all that, none of the fifth form did. You kept your mouth shut, and even the staff played nicely because they'd been girls too (before all this happened) and they appeared to respect your silence so that when they said, 'Who was it, who stole it, who painted it green, put glue in it, stuffed herring into it?' you could deny all knowledge, even though you knew they knew you knew . . . But O'Brien wasn't playing by those rules. This offence was (as Amanda well knew) grounds for immediate expulsion, she said, and any reference supplied to another school would include full disclosure of today's events. It might easily prevent Baker sitting her O levels that summer.

'Your entire future as . . .' O'Brien had tailed off, peering through her glasses at the file in her tray and pulling an exasperated face: *Query actress* said Miss Batty's most recent careers note *Further meeting arranged. Leaflets given. Query shorthand/typing.*

'And you had always had such a bright future . . .'

Baker frowned harder at this grammatical S-bend. Did they have a special tense for that?

'Do you want one thoughtless episode to ruin your life?' persisted O'Brien. 'Because you are most certainly going the right way about it. *Where* did you get this?'

And then, quite unexpectedly, O'Brien's voice had changed its tune, like strings taking over from brass and woodwind. It wasn't Baker's fault. A sixth former? she had cooed. It happened sometimes; it wasn't uncommon. Julia Smith: such a powerful influence on younger girls . . . she could quite see how the glamour of the playing fields might also be a force for evil if the older girl were herself to make a false step . . . *Glamour of the playing fields?* Could she hear herself?

O'Brien had paused for a few seconds, waiting for Baker to play the joker she had been dealt and say that yes, Dr O'Brien, sir, she had been led astray and yes it was all Julia's fault, sir.

It shouldn't take long, thought Dr O'Brien to herself, they usually caved in quite quickly. She refreshed herself with a long-sighted gaze at *Salome* while she waited for Baker to ask for Julia's head on a plate, but the girl sat mumchance, pulling the old Fawcettian fifth amendment as if those *Philippa of the Fourth* luxuries could possibly hold good in a situation as grave as this one.

'Talk it over with your parents this evening. I'm sure you will come to your senses when you've spoken to them. Your father has agreed to collect you at five o'clock. The last time I was required to telephone a father at his place of work it was to break the news of his daughter's death,' said O'Brien, remembering how Bob Baker's voice had stiffened when she gave her name. She had heard him swallow, preparing himself for the worst – drowning? a hideous accident with the Art Room kiln? a fall from the four-inch beam? – although death or dismemberment was possibly only second worst, given the look on the man's face when his car pulled up at the school gate.

Coventry was no place for talking things over. Dad hadn't said a word in the car during the ride home. Spam, back early in honour of the crisis, was already in the kitchen when they arrived. Bob Baker joined her once he'd tucked the car in for the night and the pair of them remained holed up in their Formica-lined jury room till suppertime, loud voices intermittently drowned by the sound of one of the minor electrical appliances. Spam (having the extra hour to play with) was catering to weekend levels: liquidising soup, whipping cream and fumbling together the strange set of cogs and prongs that made up the cooker's rotisserie attachment.

'You don't cook sausages on a rotisserie, woman!' Bob Baker had screamed above the din of the mixer.

'Watch me.'

The meal was eaten in silence, just the occasional rueful half-smile from Spam, Dad forking up his food Yankee-style and pretending to be absorbed in the quick crossword in his evening paper.

'*Fruit*. Five letters.'

'Apple?'

'Second letter e.'

'Lemon?' said Spam.

'Melon?' suggested Baker 'Peach? Berry? Pears?'

Ignoring her, Bob Baker plunged the top of his Biro with his thumb and carved LEMON in the grid's bottom left-hand corner in his angry-note-to-the-milkman capitals and turned his attention back to the across clues.

'*Relation*. Six letters.'

'Mother? Father? Sister? Cousin? Auntie? Granny?'

'Starts with an O.'

'Oh.'

Baker left most of her dinner. The soup was too spicy, she'd had chips for lunch, she hated whipped cream. She saw Spam controlling the escape of a sigh as she scraped the scraps together.

'I'll give you a hand.'

That would make a change, growled her father who had begun overwriting the L of LEMON with the P of PEACH.

You didn't 'I'll-wash-you-wipe' with Spam. She was too fast to take half the job, using near-boiling water and wearing industrial rubber gauntlets to get the whole Forth Bridge-y business over as fast as she could. The steaming plates dried almost as soon as she slotted them into the rack and Baker had only to put them away.

As they stood at the sink Spam relayed her husband's thoughts, a UN translator trying to defuse a diplomatic *problème*. He was very disappointed, he was very upset, he only wanted what was best for her, he'd set his heart on a school-switch at sixth form and now Baker had gone and spoiled everything and it was starting to look like he wouldn't have the choice ...

'Unless ...' Spam had hesitated uncomfortably. 'Unless there was *something* that would explain it all. Something he could tell your headmistress when we see her tomorrow, something that might have upset you?'

Spam rubbed so hard at the wine glass she was polishing that the bowl snapped from the stem, slicing right through her blue rubber glove. She teased it off with her teeth and, one-handed, fiddled a sticking plaster from the tin on the shelf and looped the plastic strip round her bleeding finger. She tried to sound casual: had Amanda's mother written lately?

So *that* was it. Baker felt sorrier still for poor Spam asking Bob Baker's questions for him, checking to see if Patsy had provided all three of them with an escape hatch.

'Had a card a couple of weeks ago. She sent me a badge with "Wild Child" on it.'

'Wild? Last Bob heard she was working as a receptionist for an estate agent.'

Spam jabbed at the electric kettle with her bandaged finger, more cheerful suddenly, and Baker realised that her mother's last missive – the first since Christmas – would probably be enough for Bob Baker to let himself off the hook. His ex-wife's raised consciousness, her fruitless search for herself, the unfit motherliness that had earned him custody in the first place would all count in his favour with O'Brien and the goons. They liked all that broken home business. Poor old Spam would take a back seat and he'd present himself as a lone father doing his best. No mother to guide her.

When the three of them set off for school the next morning, Baker saw Spam raise her eyebrows and lower her eyelids in a mime of despair when she registered the back-of-the-wardrobe suit and shirt and the ugly, sale bargain tie her husband had sorted out for his helpless bachelor disguise. Spam, naturally natty for any sort of meeting with strangers, was wearing a dark brown trouser suit with an orangey shirt collar folded neatly over its lapels. She looked smart but not attractive (six out of ten from Brian, probably). Dapper. Like a nancy hairdresser. What would it take to make her fanciable, wondered Baker: lip-gloss? A few more buttons undone? A 'wild child' badge?

Baker had come down to breakfast in mufti but Dad had made her change back into gym slip and blazer – they hadn't chucked her out yet, he said. He didn't even notice the newly acquired lacrosse colours.

'Have you washed your face?'

Could he hear himself? How would he like it? Are your socks clean, Bob? Have you flushed?

None of O'Brien's coloured lights came on when they knocked, so Baker and Spam sat down on the bench while Dad pretended to be interested in the list of school governors (the real ones). The only one of the doctored notices that hadn't been replaced was the one about what to do in the event of fire ('Do panic. Remain hysterical until everyone has fried.') which had its own blonde wood frame over by the sand and water buckets together with the various extinguishers which were for use on some fires but not others. What happened when you sprayed the wrong one on a blazing staff room toaster or a raging fume cupboard? Would it feed the flames or just fail to quench them? Nothing on the label. Didn't say *why*, just said *don't*. Typical.

There was a muffled *drrring* from behind one of the doors and the school secretary, a knitted fifty-something woman who seldom surfaced, crept from her cell to say that Dr O'Brien was now free and that the head would be grateful if she could have a few preliminary words with Amanda before the meeting proper. Again? What could she say that she hadn't said the previous afternoon? Bob Baker gave a sort of house-trained snarl as his daughter rose from the bench and followed the secretary's moss-stitched backside into the headmistress's lair. Standing up had made her see stars and she stumbled against the door frame as she entered the room. Three chairs were lined up on the head-less side of the desk and Baker collapsed groggily into the middle one.

O'Brien replaced her telephone receiver then began tweaking at the pens and pencils aligned around her blotter. The papery blue and white skin of her hands was foxed unpleasantly with large brown freckles. She began making the familiar combing action with her fingers down the smocked folds of her bachelor's gown – did French schoolmistresses have bachelors' gowns? wondered Baker. Or were they spinsters' gowns?

The original Fawcettians had been in two minds about academic dress. The blessed Mildred's bluestocking band had rejoiced in their gownlessness, even after the less enlightened universities had caved in, but the sight of her own photograph in the illustrated papers had convinced the founder that subfusc was a sine qua non of academe. Tweeds alone and one looked like a minor lady novelist – not a happy thought.

Dr O'Brien's gown normally resided on a quilted coat-hanger on the bentwood hat stand. She didn't generally teach in it but it brought a dash of theatre to the morning assembly and it worked like a charm on the parents: intimidating the self-made sort and acting like a masonic handshake on the doctors and lawyers.

She looked back at Baker, expectant. Was she still waiting for a confession? marvelled Baker. An apology? She'd have a bloody long wait.

'Now then. This morning's staff meeting has voted unanimously in favour of immediate expulsion. They all feel – and I have to say they have a point – that you are *a flaw in the pattern*, Amanda, and that any leniency would set a very dangerous precedent.'

She leaned back in her chair and tested its swivel slightly.

'In the terms of the Fawcett charter, I, as head, have veto over any vote cast, but it is also my duty to listen to the senior common room's concerns. If this sort of behaviour is not a matter for expulsion then one would need to condone any number of lesser transgressions. As one member of staff rather pithily put it: are we waiting for grievous bodily harm?'

The laugh was obviously false but Baker did feel her own face brighten slightly at the thought of grievously harming somebody. Mrs Mostyn most probably, tarring and feathering her with the gummy white glue and the tray of new, improved Africas.

'As I say, I, as head, have that right of veto, but without your full cooperation I will be disinclined to exercise it. Will you please remember, throughout the coming conversation, that I have it in my power to expel you at any moment.'

The head dabbed vaguely at the green button on her traffic light gadget, like a Bond villain launching a missile, and seconds later the Bakers peeped apologetically round the door. Spam's trouser suit and shiny eye shadow trio looked far too trend-set for the self-consciously brainy room.

What does your decor say about you? O'Brien's screamed 'recovering academic' with its vertical parquet of leather-bound volumes (books laid so tightly into their alphabetical mosaic that the spines tore away if you made the mistake of trying to tweeze one out and read it). Baker saw Spam squinting at the arty gloom of the head's chosen prints, at the side table with its batch of uninteresting curiosities: an ammonite (acquired during the field trip that had given the Snog Monster her nickname), a flint arrowhead, a beetle-shaped thing carved from a hardstone pebble (sold to Mildred Fawcett as a scarab of the eighth dynasty) and a glass paperweight with a piece of coral trapped inside.

Her father recovered first. Slipping into his make-that-sale persona, he strode across the carpet, hand primed for shaking.

'Dr O'Brien? Bob Baker. Howjadoo?'

O'Brien sized them both up with a look and stuck out a hand.

'Mr Baker. Good of you to come so promptly. Mrs Baker? I don't believe we've met. Do sit down.'

Baker hurriedly shoved one place on like the Hatter in *Alice* so that her father ended up sandwiched in the middle of the threesome.

O'Brien resumed her seat, placed her elbows on the blotter and paired off her wrinkly fingers to form a lobster pot of skin and bone.

Her voice took on that chant-y tone she used for Bible readings. The school, she purred, had a dilemma. While they undeniably had a duty of care to any student in difficulties, they also had a duty to students who weren't – and to their parents. It was a matter of balance – her fingers parted and did a stupid hand-jivey thing like a pair of wonky scales. They wanted to help, she said, but yesterday's incident was a very serious matter, a matter which, in the opinion of many colleagues, ought to be taken further. Strictly speaking it was a criminal offence, after all.

Baker heard her father catch his breath and then the whimper of his chair as he sighed deeper into it.

'And?' It was Spam who spoke. O'Brien gave her The Look over her glasses, but Baker saw her stepmother stare right back. She had assumed a no-nonsense, professional, further-to-my-letter demeanour that Baker had never seen, that *Bob* Baker had never seen (not much call for it at home).

'And?' frowned O'Brien.

'*Have* you decided to involve the police? If it's your duty and all that.'

'The police?' O'Brien smoothed her tweeds. When she spoke again it was like an invisible conductor had stopped the proceedings and started again from the top in an entirely different time signature.

'Cigarette smoking is something we take very seriously at Fawcett.'

At no point had she referred to the content of Baker's roll-up and her manner now was strange and she spoke in a peculiar, very deliberate way as if she had just winked at them or as if the room were wired for sound.

'*Have* the police been called?' persisted Spam, craning her neck and giving a theatrical look over her shoulder like she was wondering when the rozzers would arrive. 'If that's what your staff room want . . .'

O'Brien began to back-pedal and admitted that no, the SCR had opted to deal with the matter in-house – up to a point. The teaching body had long been of the opinion that Amanda was – a tiny pause – *disturbed*. Dad's breathing made it plain how badly he took this: *disturbed*. Out of the corner of her eye Baker could see Spam shrivelling in sympathy for her husband as the head-mistress pressed on with her proposal. Dr O'Brien explained that she had only had time for one, relatively brief meeting with senior colleagues, but it had been decided that, whatever the eventual verdict, professional help and advice should be sought without delay – for Amanda's sake.

Her plan, designed to keep the staff room sweet without involving the authorities, was that Baker would be assessed by Delia Carson. Miss Carson had a great deal of relevant experience and was always a huge help in cases of this kind. Always? Bob Baker had recovered enough to ask just how Dr O'Brien came to be so clued up on all this exactly: did the school get a lot of this sort of thing?

Dr O'Brien didn't actually say 'Don't take that tone with me' but her voice grew steelier as she spelled out the terms of the deal.

'Remind me, what is it you *do*, Mr Baker?'

She didn't really need reminding. The file was on her blotter and she had the speech ready before he'd uttered his reply.

'So you'll understand that we need to get the professionals to take a few measurements before we blunder in.'

She was speaking far more quickly than usual – as if to imply that valuable time was being wasted and to render further interruption almost impossible. She delivered her ultimatum in a series of tetchy telegrams. Extremely serious matter. Very important not to act precipitately, but there was no time to be lost. These things could easily drag on for weeks, even months, but, given the seriousness of the case, Miss Carson had persuaded Gerald Sexton – she'd paused here the way she did in assembly when she expected laughter or applause, as if the name must surely be known to all fathers of delinquent teenagers – *Doctor* Gerald Sexton, to squeeze Amanda in for a preliminary assessment that very afternoon, then Delia would take over the reins on Friday morning. She did the tweaky thing with the desk furniture again, then looked up in a 'You still here?' sort of way.

'Six sessions ought to give some indication of how the land lies.'

Bob Baker's unhappiness was now complete and he sat crumpled in his chair, mentally kicking himself for not switching schools while he still had the chance.

'Couldn't you ... ? Is it really ... ?' He could barely speak for shame. 'I mean ... *psychiatrists*?'

Dr O'Brien was quick to correct him: Miss Carson was a *psychologist*. Baker's daily sessions were to start the very next morning at 8.30. Probably best if she didn't return to school for the rest of the week and she should be denied all use of the telephone.

'I appreciate that as you are *both* out at work,' (weird the way full-time teachers – even married ones – always had it in for mothers who 'went out to work'), 'a traditional suspension would create difficulties.'

Baker would be allowed back in to school after her Monday morning appointment, but only under strict supervision.

'Miss Bonetti has kindly agreed that Amanda can spend the day doing private study at the back of her Mathematics class. If you could supply a packed lunch?' She nodded bossily at Spam. 'Breaks and mealtimes to be spent in the sick bay and no contact with classmates until further notice. A return to normal lessons is out of the question until Dr Sexton and Miss Carson have made their reports and the staff have had the chance to review the case. I suggest we all meet again on Friday afternoon next week? My secretary can arrange a convenient time.'

Bob Baker had driven off to work, leaving his wife to chaperone Amanda to the clinic where the psychiatrist had his Thursday surgeries. Spam settled down in the waiting room with a lapful of *Country Lives*, but had hardly chosen her first dream house (paddocks, trout stream, all mod cons £32,000) before Amanda reappeared.

'That was quick.'

'Famous for it.'

'What did he say?'

'Not much. Was I depressed and did I have any anxieties, and take this lot three times a day.' Baker brandished her prescription. 'Not even "call me in the morning".'

They went home via the chemist's in the high street. Baker wandered around the aisles, painting random stripes of varnish on the stubs of her nails while Spam played at reading the contents on a box of cough lozenges and the man in the white coat wrote the dosage instructions on the three brown bottles. Spam was mortified: he must think she was mental, all those pills. 'It's not for me!' she felt like screaming as he bagged up the drugs, but he would already know that because she had ticked the 'Under 16' box on the back of the prescription. 'She's my stepdaughter,' she blurted. But that only made it worse. A broken home? Poor mite.

Dad phoned to say that he was working late to make up for his wasted morning, so Spam made a lazy supper for herself and Baker.

'Brown or white?'

'Hovis?'

'Can do.'

When Bob Baker finally got home his solitary supper had been grilled sirloin and mashed potatoes and, as always, his wife had watched him slice the meat clean in two with his teak-handled steak knife before tilting a cut side into view, to check that it was done to his liking and complain (or demand further grilling) if it wasn't. It was perfect (but he didn't say so).

The dining room table was slippery with prospectuses. Spam said they should wait and see how it went with the psychiatry lady, next week but Dad said they should have Plan B in place in case. Spam said Baker should maybe help choose and he harumphed so hard that he squirted whisky and soda out of his nose.

Baker spent the rest of the night in her room crying, not even surfacing for *Top of the Pops*. She broke Spam's sandwiches into bird food for her window sill and fed the beaker of chocolate milk to her spider plant. Spam stood over her while she swallowed her Mandrax, but after she'd gone back downstairs Baker went to her stepmother's bedside drawer and sneaked another three sleeping tablets from the bottle at the back, next to a sunglasses case with foil packets of contraceptive pills hidden inside. Four Mandies.

She fell asleep almost at once and immediately tuned in to eight hours of demented dreams, like an all-night Marx Brothers screening. Lady Henry had been made headmistress and was conducting a whole school pencil case inspection and suspending any girl who didn't have a speculum. And there were to be new portraits of past headmistresses all done by Dora Hardcastle and showing them as Salome and Judith and St Agatha. Julia and Baker were discovered by Mrs Mostyn in the organ loft again, but this time Julia stepped away from Baker and Mrs Mostyn gave her a white pin and when Baker reached out for it she fell through the thin plaster floor, down into the assembly hall where Lady Henry was handing out chocolate biscuits dipped in golden syrup. Bob Baker had finally been asked to redecorate the school: William Morris, shag pile, white piano:

the works. The fluffy new carpet caught on the crepe soles of the Upper Thirds' indoor shoes and was already peppered with ink stains and pencil shavings. Then the dream camera dollied into the refectory kitchen where Spam was making hundreds and hundreds of butterfly cakes on the rotisserie and lots and lots and lots of plates of party sandwiches with flags telling you what was inside: palm fibre, bauxite, yam, Spam. And then Miss Gatsby put a winner's medal round Baker's neck and gave her a big fragrant hug.

There was loads more. Baker had meant to write it all down when she stirred briefly in the small hours, but told herself as the thought occurred that she would be sure to remember it all: so outrageous, so vivid. She had forgotten most of it by morning.

Chapter 19

There was a bus stop just round the corner from Delia Carson's consulting room but it had been decided that Dad should drive Amanda to her early bird appointments (to make sure she kept them). She was then trusted to make her own way to school in time for the ten thirty bell.

When they had left the house the next morning for Baker's first appointment Dad had done what he always did, putting his hand inside the letterbox, pushing and pulling at the door even after he had double-locked it. Did he expect the hinges to give way? As he unlocked the passenger side of the Rover he spotted lumps of fresh bird shit on the windscreen and wouldn't get in the car till he'd scraped them off with a tetchy twig.

He even drove angrily, bullying the gear stick, pushing in front of other cars, hooting at pedestrians even when they weren't trying to cross the road, constantly looking at his watch to remind Baker that the detour was wasting his valuable time.

The car radio was on loud, making speech safely impossible, but the only station with a decent reception played pop music which made his mood even worse, like he suspected Baker of sending postcards personally requesting each record. Dad despised pop music and, as with anything that wasn't to his taste – curry, flares, Campari, David Frost – assumed that other people only pretended to like it because it would make them seem 'different'. All just one big hoax to annoy him. If Baker was listening to the kitchen radio when he came home from work he would walk into the room, still in his hat and coat, and push the 'off' button without a word. As if it had merely been left on by mistake, like a light.

Unable to bear another pop song, he began micro-rotating the dial with the safe-breaker fingers of his left hand until he found the ghost of Radio 2. The disc jockey was giving the turntable a rest and cajoling his listeners through a keep-fit routine, like Miss Drumlin with an Irish accent. Baker mimed doing star jumps in her seat. Not a flicker.

Miss Carson's office was the front room of her flat in a four-storey modern block up beyond the Common. There were weeds growing in the gravel and through the street doormat which looked like a giant version of the thing Spam used to slice boiled eggs with. The voice on the entry phone told Baker to take the lift to the second floor where the door was opened by a middle-aged woman in a bobbly brown cardigan wearing a long string of wooden beads that looped even-handedly over each armour-plated D-cup in turn.

The consulting room had the look of a very small school library, filled with yellow wooden bookshelves and uncomfortable modern armchairs made of stringy springs and slabs of foam rubber covered with hairy stripes. The tiled surround of the coal-effect electric fire provided a sort of makeshift mantelshelf on which were ranged a collection of china cats and kittens. It seemed a weirdly cutesy hobby for Miss Carson with her tweedy togs and Swede-y furniture, but it turned out that the first of these ornaments had been a present from a grateful patient (or its mother). A second patient had assumed she liked cats (which she didn't) and bought another, and subsequent under-achieving, hyper-sexual, introverted, anti-social teenagers had all added to the herd.

The few unshelved spots of wall bore framed maps of English counties and a few certificates proving that Delia Mary Carson had all the qualifications necessary to nod a lot and ask you why you felt what you felt.

Not that there had been much of that in the first session. Her opening gambit was 'Do you know why you're here?', followed by a spot of word association with Miss Carson firing the triggers at Baker with a sinister part-smile on her face as if every answer were giving the game away. Black: white, house: plant, fruit: five letters.

Spam had produced grilled grapefruit for supper that Friday evening served in stainless steel hemispheres like the cups from a great big robot bra. The fruit was cruelly bitter, barely edible at all unless you shovelled sugar onto it, and the two tastes – Tate and Lyle and sulphuric acid – made Baker's teeth scream in agony but she didn't dare say as much in case Spam remembered how long it had been since her last check-up. The pain unlocked another fragment of Thursday night's epic dream: trying to bite the chocolate off a Mars bar and leaving her front teeth behind in the caramel.

Bob Baker was happy growling over his idiot crossword and refused to join them when Spam suggested a family round of Scrabble. It was the only board game he could be made to tolerate – *educational* – but it was always a relief when he didn't play. He huffed and puffed when they didn't put their words down straight away but would then take ages over his own turn, flicking through the dictionary or consulting a dog-eared list of two-letter words he'd once cut out of the *Daily Express* and which he kept under the plastic insert in the Scrabble box.

'*Za*? What in blazes is *Za*?'

'It's on the list.'

But he never liked it when Baker played him at his own game. 'That's never a word.'

'It's in the dictionary at school.' Baker had held her face in place perfectly (the way you always could when the lie *really* mattered) but Spam had tumbled immediately.

'What the 'eck is *ek*?'

'*Ek*?' Not the ghost of a smile. 'It's a disease of sheep.'

It was over a month until the cricket season got going, so mowing the lawn and stabbing it repeatedly with a garden fork took most of Dad's Saturday. Spam thought it might be fun to go for a drive somewhere on Sunday. Hampton Court? Whipsnade? But there was a great deal to do in the greenhouse, apparently, and Bob Baker spent the whole of Sunday tickling his double fuchsias with a squirrel hair paintbrush, making Winston Churchill mate with Dollar Princesses in hopes of bigger blooms or longer stamens.

Baker wasted the morning in an oily bath of Three Wishes (she hadn't yet made any) and when she came downstairs she found Spam sitting at the kitchen table surrounded by a nest of straw and about half a dozen steel discs perforated with a swirl of sharp holes which, if correctly assembled, became a device for mincing meat and grating vegetables. Spam – who could replace the vacuum cleaner bag blindfold – had been completely unable to engage the wingnut as shown in diagram A and was left with just the base unit clamped uselessly to the Formica table top, waiting in vain for something to mince. The near-hysterical Spam was wheezing quite nastily and her cheeks were streaked with mascara. She held a finger to her lips, picked up one of the steel discs, aligned it with the flange (*diagram B*), and pointed, magician's assistant-style, as it rattled straight through and clanged against its friends in the little heap on the table.

Baker picked up the box which was decorated with a noughts and crosses layout of drawings of finely minced foods. She put her hand in and rummaged down the sides, lifted the flap in the base, assuming the missing component was hiding inside. Spam, still weeping with laughter, had now turned her attention to the recipe booklet.

'What kind of person serves grated carrot as an hors d'oeuvre?'

Dad returned to his half-hardies after lunch and stepmother and daughter stayed indoors with the Scrabble board. Spam sent Baker out with a cup of tea and a plate of butterfly cakes at three o'clock and she found her father cutting Lady Boothby into dozens of tiny pieces with a razor blade.

He grunted and nodded his head at a space on the bench when he saw the tray, then carried on slitting each cutting down the middle before dipping the twigs into a jar of fungicide and poking them into one of the compartments in a vast egg-box-like tray. Forty-eight? Ninety-six?

'What will you do with them all? You've only got four hanging baskets.'

'What? Just put the tray down, can't you?'

And she went back inside to find Spam slotting 'banjaxed' across two triple word scores.

'Did you cheat?'

'Course I cheated. I *hate* this game,' and with varnished finger and thumb she flicked hard at the edge of the board and sent the tiles flying across the shag pile (X and J were never seen again: bye-bye *banjaxed*).

'Maybe there's a film on?'

And the pair of them took a sofa each and Spam poured two large amontillados and they watched Bette Davis playing identical twins (identical-looking anyway; their personalities weren't a bit alike).

Spam had poured the sherries without a word. On the rare Christmasy occasions when Dad included Amanda in a round of drinks the doling out of the stingy half glass would always be accompanied by a significant look and his idea of a joke ('Don't go getting drunk') and his eyes would follow every sip, but Spam glugged out equal measures using white wine glasses rather than the skinny cranberry-coloured schooners that came with the decanter (a wedding present from the firm). Dr Sexton had said nothing about abstaining from alcohol or operating heavy machinery but both were contraindicated in the small print on the 'dos and don'ts' leaflet that came with Baker's tablets. Didn't say *why*. Just said don't.

Spam topped up both glasses the instant they were empty, and returned the sherry to its hiding place. Bob Baker had built a louvre-doored cocktail cabinet in one of the alcoves, but Spam always kept her sherry bottle in the cupboard under the sink. At one time she used to write 'window vinegar' on the label in magic marker, but soon realised that it was not one of the cupboards her husband ever went to.

'I'd better put the kettle on again.'

Evil Bette Davis was out in a rowing boat with nice Bette Davis.

'Oh dear,' giggled Spam, pouring herself another drink. 'This'll end in tears.'

She placed her glass on the undershelf of the coffee table between sips and Baker instinctively did the same: not *hidden* exactly, but you wouldn't necessarily spot them from the sitting room door. She lay back on her sofa and looked at the one wall-papered wall through half-closed eyes, a psychedelic explosion of acanthus, hibiscus and palm fibre. Trippy.

Bette Davis was in Glenn Ford's forgiving arms and Baker and Spam were fast asleep by the time bad light stopped play in the greenhouse. Bob Baker wore the same hard-done-by air he wore on weekday evenings, like fuchsia-fucking was a full-time job.

'Any danger of a cup of tea?'

Spam stumbled down the dusky garden path in her bedroom slippers to retrieve the teapot, tray and untouched cup that he had left in the shed, then shut herself in the kitchen with the Cliff Adams Singers.

'Bit loud,' he said, before striding in and turning the harmonies down to a barely audible whisper.

Baker wandered woozily into the room after him, her arms at her sides, her middle fingers inside the sherry glasses. Spam was standing at the sink, washing-up brush in her blue-gloved hands as her husband neutralised the offending broadcast. She gave him a fixed, three-large-sherries stare, picked up the teak-sided wireless by its handle, dunked it in the boiling bowl of suds and scrubbed at it before leaning the stuttering appliance against the plate rack.

Bob Baker glared coldly at his daughter.

'This is your fault.'

Three Wishes? I wish I was dead; I wish I was dead; I wish I was dead.

Chapter 20

'Dr O'Brien left instructions that you are to wait in here. Miss Bonetti was expecting you at ten thirty but she will be back directly.' The school secretary ushered Baker into her office and closed the door behind her just as the bell went for the next period.

Baker had caught the empty train from Miss Carson's flat after her session on Monday morning and then spent a naughty forty minutes nursing a cup of black coffee in the station café, watching workmen attacking great platters of bacon and beans and sunny sided eggs while she read a discarded copy of the *Daily Mirror*: 'John and Yoko step out again'.

'Was your train delayed?' asked the secretary, suspiciously, as Baker sat down.

'I just missed one. I got lost looking for the station.'

The secretary wasn't even listening but was busy with a box of newly printed prospectuses, opening the back cover of each one and using a ballpoint to add a neat zero to the fees.

'I was on leave when the proofs were sent,' she explained. 'I doubt anyone will imagine you can get a term's education for the price of a box of cigars, but I'm not sure I could bear all the jokes from the fathers.'

'I was expecting you at ten thirty,' said Miss Bonetti as they dashed up the stairs to the Maths Room.

'I just missed a train. I couldn't find the station.'

They stopped outside the classroom door.

'A word to the wise,' said the Maths teacher. '*Never* give more than one excuse: dead giveaway. I'll expect you at ten thirty sharp tomorrow.' Almost human.

The chatty room fell silent as Baker entered it and thirty thirteen-year-old stares followed the prodigal fifth former as Miss Bonetti directed her to a desk in the far corner of the room.

'Can you all turn to page seventy-three please: matrices.' She then handed Baker a bundle of bandered worksheets: French vocab, laws of motion problems, trigonometry problems, a précis to make, a human ear to label. 'That should keep you busy.'

Baker began labelling her ear with a pencil that had her surname embossed in gold on one of its faces. Spam had given her twelve of them as a stocking filler and she'd assumed at the time that 'Baker' had been chosen so that the whole family could use them, but sometimes she wasn't so sure – no one else wrote in pencil. As she worked, she listened to Miss Bonetti explaining what matrices were and what they were used for and why they had to be inverted.

Miss Kopje's blundering had not been confined to the English timetable and Miss Bonetti was forced to teach an almost identical Maths lesson three classes in a row, the exact same words over and over and over. And then again for revision. Then next year for the next lot of gamma mathematicians. What a life. By midafternoon Baker felt she could probably have given the lesson herself but, just as she was getting the hang of it, she was co-opted by Mrs Mostyn for yet more urgent work on the atlas mountain.

'Didn't we finish them all last Monday lunchtime?'

The Snog Monster, puffing along the corridor, didn't even look round.

'Not altogether.' Very tight-lipped. 'A *slight* problem.'

Mrs Mostyn barged into the Geography Room and over to the glueing table and the final batch of Africas. The new countries had been meticulously coloured then neatly labelled in black ink: French West Ivory, Tarzania, Upper Cheetah, Tangoland, Democratic Republic of Mambo, Rumbaba. Bunty's tell-tale Greek **a** was unmistakable and the shading was, as always, exquisite, but this was not what she had been asked to do.

Slap? Tickle. Village? Idiot. Finger? Painting. Mountain? Molehill. Brother? Big. A whole week of trying to second guess what a nutter might say. Quite a strain. On the day of the final psycho session Dad was going to wait outside and then drive Baker on to school for their meeting with O'Brien. Spam said she was in the middle of an audit and they both pretended to believe her. Another audit? Bob Baker had never involved himself in the finance side of his firm – birds and nerds, he reckoned – but she was ready with an answer as always. A takeover this time: due diligence (whatever that meant). Any more questions and he'd have felt a fool.

The car turned into the rainy cul de sac five minutes early and he pulled over some two hundred yards from Miss Carson's building and lit a cigarette. His hand shook as he struck the match. When Baker climbed in he uttered his first words in four days (a new personal best).

'So,' he began, for all the world as though they were on speaking terms, 'what sort of thing has she been asking you, this Carson woman? All *my* fault I suppose? That's the way now, isn't it? Blame the parents.'

Baker squeezed at the uneaten breakfast sandwich jammed into her pocket, feeling the soft white bread between her fingers.

'Doesn't say much. Just keeps asking how I feel about things.'

'Is that it? How *you* feel? How *you*—'

There was a piece of string tied around his finger, like a pinkie ring and he stopped shouting when he caught sight of it. An old trick of Pam's mother's (or so she said).

'Patsy – your mother – she saw a psychiatrist. Months and months it went on. "Depressed". *She* was depressed?' He turned wildly to Baker. 'Disappeared for six weeks. Didn't even telephone. And you in your carrycot in the back of the car when I was out on site inspections. Nappies. Depressed? She was never right after.'

He threw the remains of his fag out of the window into a puddle. His face was wet when he turned back. He restarted the car and drove Baker closer to the front door, sparing her a run through the rain. But he did it automatically, Baker told herself, just as he automatically switched off lights and closed gates, just as he automatically left the table without thinking to clear it.

The music started as he turned the key in the ignition *Something inside has died and I can't hide and I just can't fake it*. He punched the radio off.

Cat? Mouse. Blue? Sky. Cold? Hot. Sad? Happy. Needle? Haystack.

Miss Carson had begun their sixth and final session by whizzing through the usual preliminaries, like Miss Drumlin touching her toes, but after the word association warm-up she began probing more deeply than usual, conscious that she had had little of substance to put in her report to dear Dr O'Brien.

'Just try to *relax*, Amanda. I want you to think back again to when you were a very little girl, to when you first found out that your mother wouldn't be coming back.' She left a five-second pause, as if that were the time it usually took to look up a memory.

'Think right back to that and try to think how that made you feel. How did you feel?'

Were there right answers to questions like these? If there were, Baker hadn't revised them, couldn't even manage an intelligent guess. How did four-year-olds feel? Multiple choice would have been much easier but Miss Carson liked you to show your working. 'Fine' would definitely be the wrong answer – nothing could possibly be fine, you wouldn't be there talking to Miss Carson if anything was fine. The model answer was almost certainly 'I thought it was my fault.' Classic guilt trip material, meat enough on that for a whole symposium.

'I don't know,' said Baker, keeping her voice nice and flat, talking slowly so Miss Carson could get it all down and so that she herself would have time to monitor whatever nonsense she was saying while, backstage in her own head, she could wonder away at whatever she liked, like having a book in your lap while Mrs Horst handed out Xeroxes on Xerxes.

'Confused,' Baker said finally. The psychologist licked her lips. 'But Pam's my mother now.'

Miss Carson's face fell and a nervous finger hooked part of her blonde bead curtain of hair behind her ear.

'Were you very angry?'

Almost against her will, Baker thought back to that peculiar afternoon. Spam in the white trouser suit drinking white wine from a glass cross-hatched with cuts, like the pattern on a slab of gammon, a glass so new it still had a gold sticky label on it. Bob Baker in his favourite chair – were the other chairs jealous? – and Spam's white bell-bottomed bottom perched on the arm. The first Mrs Baker, the real one, had had a trouser suit in a jazzy green and orange check, and it went with a small orange-coloured suitcase, and she would wear it all together whenever they went on holiday or when she and 'Manda' went to stay with Grandma.

Grandma had a photo of her in it – probably why Baker could remember it so clearly. Patsy had never worn trouser suits at other times and so, when the four-year-old Amanda had seen 'Auntie Pam' in the same sort of get-up, she immediately assumed Daddy's friend must be off somewhere, *leaving* in her going-away outfit – only she never went away.

Baker tried to remember back to the day Spam actually moved in, tried to remember if anyone had made a speech. Something must have been said: 'Pam is going to be living here from now on', something like that, something plain, nothing about a new mother or loving each other very much – not Dad's style. And there must have been a decision made about who called who what, because Pam had definitely never tried to force the whole 'Mummy' nonsense. She never actually said as much, obviously, but she wasn't really the maternal type. She'd memorised all the words and could mime along fairly convincingly – baked cakes, embroidered initials, all that – but she was really *spastic* about the physical side. She gave strange, dry, loveless hugs like whole-body handshakes. She used sometimes to kiss the top of Baker's head when Baker was about five, but then she didn't kiss Dad much either – *ever*, that Baker could remember. Baker used to think they must be kissing passionately in secret and went through a phase of bursting into rooms in the hope (or fear) of catching them *in flag*, but they never were.

'Amanda?'

The psychologist always went very quiet after posing one of her questions (not that she said much when you replied, just a grunting coo and slow nods of her long, blonde head). It wasn't like a normal conversation. She never seemed to feel the least bit awkward about awkward silences, and so you found yourself prattling on to fill the gaps she left, talking bollocks and listening out for the worrying hiss of the pencil when you said anything she considered significant – when you gave yourself away.

A change of subject. Why did Amanda think that Dr O'Brien had arranged these meetings?

Because she was a silly bitch? Because she was a silly bitch and she had to be seen to do something? Because it was the ultimate punishment. Because she knew that Dad would never forgive her now.

'Forgive you?' prompted Miss Carson.

Baker realised far, far too late that she had said all of this out loud.

'Forgive you? For what happened at school?'

And Baker was so angry she almost spat at her. Was she really that thick?

'For all *this*. All this psycho-whatsit. He *hates* it and O'Brien knew he would hate it. The next-door neighbour saw us getting in the car this morning and he told her I had a dentist's appointment. He'd never live it down if she found out I was *mental*.' It was fun watching Delia pretend not to react to that one.

Miss Carson tried a different tack.

'What was the name of your friend?' She appeared to have had another chat with Dr O'Brien.

'What friend?'

'The older girl. The one you were found with,' said Miss Carson, pretending to truffle through her notes for the name. She made it sound kinky the way she said it: *found with*.

'Julia, I think you mean.' It came out much quieter than Baker intended.

'*Ju-lia*, that's right. Tell me about Julia. What was she like?'

A trick question, like those first-form English lessons where they got you to write about your family, knowing full well that there's no neutral way of describing people. Baker imagined herself filling out a passport application or giving the police a description of a missing person as she answered but even filling in a form could be revealing.

'About seventeen. Auburn hair.'

Another tickle from Miss Carson's pencil.

Baker looked round the room. The antique map business was bloody strange, like she was frightened her choice of pictures might say something about her. The print for the place names was incredibly tiny. Too small for the Snog Monster to put right if Surrey went to war with Kent or if Croydon demanded direct rule.

'Yes, but what was she *like*?'

'Was?'

'Is. What *is* she like? What *does* she like?'

'Likes sport.'

Only she didn't, did she? Not really. All just a front. A licence to wear the shortest skirt in the school, to show off those long golden thighs, that hot shower of hair, the dirty laugh, the clever fingers as they re-laced a pair of plimsolls or rolled a joint. Baker thought again of the groping glance that Julia had got from the pinstriped ponce on the train. And Baz. Baz with his motorbike and his heavy metal records and his 'dealer' – a man in a pub with little polythene bags in a little polythene bag.

'Did Julia ever introduce you to him?'

Shit. Baker's empty stomach rolled over. She had been thinking aloud again. What else had she said? The pencil was still scribbling hard. She must have said something.

'Do you often make friends with older girls?'

'Her birthday's in August. Only two months older. Are all your friends forty?' Made her smart, that one. Serve her right.

But *friends* meant something else here, didn't it? Like *found with*. She was a prefect, explained Baker. First smart thing she'd said, she could see the woman absorbing the new information, could practically have coloured in the picture it had evoked, the cosy Angela Brazil-ian idea of how prefects and younger girls might co-exist: good examples, hairstyles copied, racquets borrowed, advice given. All Baker had to do now was stay awake. One of her teeth was slightly loose – bit weird. Did you still have first teeth at fifteen? It was sore when you bit down on it or pushed hard at it with your tongue. No sleep while that was happening.

Next topic on the list: was Amanda good friends with her stepmother? What planet was this woman on? *Good friends?* Were Stottie and her mother – her real, actual Cinzano-drinking mother – 'good friends', *chums*? Or Bunty and Gloria? And Spam wasn't even a relation.

'Pam's very kind,' said Baker. Keep it simple, translated-from-the-German: last Christmas she has me a typewriter bought.

Did Baker write stories? Did she perhaps keep a diary? Must be gravy for Miss Carson when they said 'yes' to that one – unless it wasn't. Unless your patient had Stottied the whole thing and penned it purely for prying eyes to read: Dear Diary, I wish I had long apricot hair and long skinny legs and a long skinny boyfriend with a motorbike. I wish men creamed their pinstripes at the sight of my thighs.

'Is that really what you want, Amanda?' Scratch, scratch, scratch. Shit, shit, shit.

Miss Carson had made a farewell plate of sandwiches filled with 2,000 calories worth of salad cream and sliced egg (had she used the doormat?) held together with toothpicks. There were square, old ladylike tea plates with rudimentary hollyhocks drawn on them and weeny embroidered napkins on the tray. Baker explained that she'd had an enormous breakfast and just pecked at a miniature Swiss roll, remembering Julia jamming them in two at a time. Should have been disgusting, but it wasn't somehow. Not like she was fat.

Miss Carson looked at her watch. She had promised Dr O'Brien that she'd telephone with a further report as soon as the final session was over, but they'd made scant progress so far. A little more word association? Baker grunted, biting hard to keep herself vaguely alert. Flower? Power. Yellow? Submarine. Long? Short. Fur? Coat. Nice? Biscuit. Lamb? Slaughter.

When was Baker happiest? Ruddy cheek, honestly. When was Miss Carson happiest? Baker turned her head from the couch to look at the psychologist, at her tired-looking face, at the mousey pink ears poking through the rats tails of beige hair: lifeless, greasy, even a dusting of dandruff on the shoulder of her cardie. Three bathside bottles, three wishes gone. Miss Carson didn't look like she'd ever been happy. Had she ever had a dopey love-in with a beautiful sixth-former? Telling secrets and eating choco-late and laughing at the funniest jokes ever told. Had she ever sat under a Christmas tree expecting a facial sauna only to unwrap a typewriter and a ream of typing paper. ('I could have got paper from the office,' Dad had said: baffled; resentful. 'Janice has loads of paper – all colours.')

Miss Carson's face had gone very pink.

'You're the one answering the questions, Amanda.'

What had Baker just asked her? This was getting really weird, like she was talking in her sleep.

Were they doing all this to Julia too? And was Miss Carson getting both bookings? Did she already know what Julia was like? Baker tried to visualise Julia stretched out on the couch, Julia scoffing a whole plate of egg sandwiches, Julia thinking of clever answers for the word association: telling them what they wanted to hear, beating them at their own games. When had Julia been happiest? Was it up against a wall behind the Wheatsheaf with

Baz, or was it last Wednesday in the organ loft? Baker sighed softly at the memory of the dusty sunlit space, of the sweet taste of dope and tobacco and Jaffa Cakes on her tongue, and the sudden chocolatey thought shoved the more recent memory aside and all at once she was ankle deep in the rough cut grass of her infants school playing field, sucking on Cadbury's fingers. She could smell the starch on her sun-baked gingham frock, hear the shrill cries of the watching classmates, feel the scratch of the funny old straw hat and the chilly flap of the silky old kimono as she staggered triumphantly up to the finishing line in the dressing-up race and into Miss Gatsby's arms.

Miss Carson was hunting in her cupboard for a new spiral notebook and didn't see Baker rub her cuffs across her face.

When they arrived at school for the promised meeting Baker was once again called in first, leaving her father fretting on the bench in the lobby.

Dr O'Brien's voice was doing that mooing thing again and the musical tones were making it hard to stay awake. Baker stared at the hands in her lap. There was a numb hum in the fingers' ends and she noticed that the skin on the sides of some of the nails was bleeding where someone had been gnawing at it with their front teeth. Mid-morning sun broke open the showery clouds and raced through O'Brien's study window, unnecessarily bright. She tried closing her eyes against it but it made no difference.

O'Brien was still talking. Trouble sleeping? How had all the meetings gone? Miss Carson was a remarkable young woman. *Young*? She was thirty-five if she was a day, thought Baker. And Dr Sexton. A very eminent man. Baker was lucky to have been seen at such short notice, very lucky indeed.

The head glanced down at the typewritten pages on her desk and at the notes made that morning on her telephone pad.

Her mouth tightened into a smile, which was directed first at Baker, then into the middle distance: Saint Agatha. The smile warmed and widened a fraction.

'I may yet give you another chance, Amanda, but I have to be sure that you aren't going to let me down. You have to tell me exactly what happened last Wednesday, exactly who was responsible. As I told you last week, this isn't a matter of telling tales; that sort of schoolgirl loyalty has no place here.'

Baker frowned back up at O'Brien who seemed to be waiting for her to say something but the sunlight was starting to really hurt her eyes now, boring into her head as if a geographer with a magnifying glass on a field trip were trying to light a fire in her skull.

There was a loud knock at the study door, but before Dr O'Brien could pick a button to press Bob Baker's head appeared. Was this going to be much longer? He had a client waiting. He always called them clients – made him sound professional, he thought, like a lawyer (or a prostitute).

He had slipped his friendly, normal face on uncomfortably over the impatient, unhappy look it was wearing underneath: head on one side, an almost pleasant expression. A face only ever seen outside the home, like the hearty laugh for pubs and party porpoises. He cast the briefest glance at Baker, but his pained gaze flinched away from the sight of her.

'We shan't be a moment. Amanda is going to cooperate, aren't you Amanda?'

Which of course meant that he had to look at her again out of politeness, turning his head dead pan, like a TV puppet.

'Is she? Good,' he said as he ducked back out of the door.

Even Dr O'Brien must have been taken aback by the sheer dislike he packed into the three syllables but she showed no sign of it. Baker bent right forward in her chair, wiping her eyes on her knees as she pretended to fiddle with her shoe, then came back up too quickly, bringing on the sick, giddy feeling she'd had when she first crawled out of bed.

The black plastic minute hand of the wall clock gave the faintest possible quiver as it surreptitiously mapped the minutes. Was it even moving? She thought of Dad back on his bench outside, the obsessive twitch 'n' twist of his wrist as he looked yet again at his watch. O'Brien was silent now. The TV Gestapo didn't do silence. They strode about, airing the skirts of their kinky leather overcoats, slapping desks, hands, other people with the gauntlets of their snazzy black gloves. Ultimatums? Ultimata (*Please remember every day: neuter plurals end in A*). Threats. Promises. There wasn't a word for that was there? For a terrible thing you were definitely going to do. Not in English. German probably had one, Italian definitely would. A whole mood: the vindictive.

'Well?'

Baker hadn't moved from her sulky slump in the chair, but some kind of telepathic shrug must have escaped her because O'Brien bridled at once and leaned across the desk which seemed to narrow as the powdered face grew nearer. Her voice lowered: if Baker didn't jolly well snap out of it and pay proper attention, then Things would become very Unpleasant, very Unpleasant indeed. Serious offences must be brought to the attention of the Fawcett board of governors, and the ultimate decision would lie with them. She paused while Baker chuckled to herself at the thought of Dr Crippen and Magda Goebbels debating her imperfect future.

'There is nothing to snigger at, Amanda. I have only to pick up that telephone and your time here is at an end. The governors may even wish to take things further. This is not a moment for leniency. An example needs to be made – of someone. A fitting punishment.'

'It won't happen again.'

O'Brien steamed ahead as though Baker hadn't spoken.

'This could still very easily become a police matter. Very easily, whatever Mrs Baker may like to think. And if that happens, it won't just be your place here that's put at risk. Your whole future life will be changed for the worse. And don't console yourself with delusions' (surely she was the only woman on earth who pronounced the 'you' in 'delusions'?) 'of that "fresh start" elsewhere. No other decent school would take you, unless I were to perjure myself with a very partial and generous reference. Everything will depend on my report and what I say when that telephone rings – *off* the record.' She leaned back in her chair and her voice when she spoke again was both softer and harder. 'When I spoke to your father on the telephone yesterday afternoon, he seemed to think you might benefit from a change of scene, as if it were merely a matter of paying a deposit, buying a new uniform, learning a new song. He seemed very distressed when I indicated that it was unlikely to be as easy as that. He mentioned that your mother – your natural mother – had had quite a few problems. A residential home was mentioned? He didn't elaborate. All very painful, I'm sure. Does he ever speak to her?'

Baker thought miserably of the box of butchered snapshots.

'No.'

'No. A very single-minded man in that regard, I should imagine. He's going to be *very disappointed* if all his plans are scuppered by your refusal to cooperate. Very disappointed indeed.'

Baker bit hard on her tooth again, but the pain seemed very far away and didn't even hurt any more, not really.

Dr O'Brien stared steadily at Baker, giving the girl time to grasp the seriousness of her situation, time to decide whether this silly little pash was worth the sacrifice, worth invoking her father's perpetual displeasure.

There was a metal bin in the corner beneath the window and Baker eyed it fixedly, calculating how many steps it would take to stagger across and be sick into it, but instead she finally retched out the confession that O'Brien was waiting for. It was Julia. Julia Smith. Tell him Julia did it all. It was all Julia's idea. Not me: Julia. And she burst into tears.

O'Brien removed her spectacles and put them in the leather caddy of her desk set.

'Sit up straight and blow your nose. Daddy is waiting.'

Chapter 21

Bob Baker was quite pleased with the hotel in the end. He hadn't planned to go away at Easter time (they had Corfu booked for August), but he felt a bit better about it when his firm chalked it up as compassionate leave. Dr O'Brien said they should get Amanda away from her little gang and a two-line chit signed by Dr Sexton, upgrading Baker's joint in the organ loft to the status of 'Nervous Breakdown', meant that the three weeks weren't going to eat up his annual holiday after all. Spam's friend Sandra the travel agent had found them a late cancellation in a five-star full-board package in the Canary Islands and he was pleasantly surprised: linen changed daily, lavish buffet lunch, silver service, crazy golf, English newspapers and a separate swimming pool next to the car park for all the screaming kids.

Baker had devoted the first two days to mooching on her balcony getting hideously sunburned and now spent the daylight hours sweltering under an orange umbrella, fastidiously lifting the edges of the burned patches and peeling off the skin in the largest possible sheets before laying them over the arm of the sun lounger. The towel under her was permanently damp – with sweat, not pool water – 'Come all this way and you won't even swim,' moaned Dad, staring crossly in his daughter's general direction as she lay dozing in a saffron-coloured kaftan (he didn't actually make eye contact any more, hadn't for weeks). 'There's English girls your age over there. Why don't you go and see if they want a game of table tennis?'

The girls, about six of them, all seemed to know each other already and passed the time painting their bitten toenails, monitoring the poolside and giggling about passers-by – marking them out of ten most likely. There was a German boy they all fancied and the level of chat dipped whenever he was within ogling distance. They stared at Baker; she could see them through the mesh of her straw hat and they were obviously talking about her. One of them had just wrapped herself in a towelling changing poncho then curled up under her umbrella, grabbing a book and sucking in her cheeks while the others all miaowed with laughter.

Baker was supposed to be revising and there was a George Orwell novel lying impressively (she hoped) on the table beside her, but she preferred writing postcards and drawing 'my room here' crosses in the middle of the swimming pool or on the tops of palm trees. The messages on the other side were all coded in aigy paigy although it was absurdly easy to decipher when you saw it written down: daygad haygates maygee naygow.

The first card had been for Bunty. Bunty was already in Sydney with her mother, staying in a company flat while househunting. Baker had the address but the postcard she wrote had not been sent because the hotel shop didn't have stamps for Australia.

'Can't I just use a load of the six peseta ones?'

'We'll find some,' said Dad, thriftily (they didn't).

Spam, born and bred in a cold climate, could never get used to holiday heat. As usual, she had pushed her beach umbrella up to the pool's edge and sat beneath it on a moored lilo, her legs dangling in the water, water so blue you expected her feet to come out covered in newly grown copper sulphate crystals. Every hour or so she would hail a passing waiter and order another rum and coke, *por favor*.

She had bought herself a Spanish phrasebook at the airport but German would have done just as well. The hotel was so Kraut-friendly they actually served bockwurst at the breakfast buffet (for the first half hour anyway; early German birds stripped the hotplates clean by eight o'clock). They began queuing long before the dining room opened, just as soon as they had secured the best sunbeds with bath towels and copies of *Brigitte* (*Wass junge männer von den mädchen wollen*). Everyone said that was what they did and that really really was what they did. Maybe it was *all* true, maybe Queenie had it all wrong and Africans irrigated their fields with an Archimedes screw, ate yam. The fraus and frauleins would lie on their baggsied beds, systematically basting and roasting every inch of visible flesh, hands behind their blonde heads to tan their armpits while husbands and teenage sons played a murderously hearty variant of water polo that put the grown-up swimming pool out of bounds for hours at a time.

'We will fight them on the beaches,' growled Bob Baker.

He did try boycotting the pool entirely on the second morning, but the nearest seaside had black volcanic dust instead of sand which dirtied your feet and left a sooty mess in the seams of your beach bag – 'like putting up deckchairs on a slag heap' said Bob – and so it was back to the pool after lunch where the only three remaining sunbeds were round behind the paddling pool.

The Germans had clearly devised some kind of rota for their daily colonisation of the poolside. Bob Baker didn't get up as early as they did (or was it stay up as late?), but after two further days of sitting in sunbed Siberia he simply nipped out of the dining room while they were still downing their breakfast brat-wurst, gathered up the artful litter of personal possessions, folded them neatly and put them in a pile by the spare beach umbrellas, before selecting a poolside lounger and stretching out on it.

'*Das ist mein platz.*'

A large red-faced blonde was pointing crossly at the trio of beds. Bob Baker, conscious of a group of watching English tourists on their way to crazy golf, pantomimed looking about him in search of a name tag.

'*Nein.*'

This refusal to play by German rules made him a huge hit with the other English families – with their dads anyway. They stood him drinks in the poolside cabana thingy (thatched, Malawi-style) where the cocktails were served in hollowed coconuts garnished with slices of uncertain fruits – *yam*, probably. He wasn't a great reader – give or take *Wisden* and the *Fuchsia Breeder's Handbook*. Other dads were wading through airport thrillers, but when Bob Baker wasn't infra-red grilling himself on a sunbed he preferred propping up the bar with his new friends, asking them which airline they came on and cadging cricket scores from their English newspapers.

'Ne-ver!' he was barking yet again.

Defeated Germans, thriftily downing alcohol brought from home, looked on disappointedly from their blue-glass balconies.

'You were very funny today being.' A blonde woman in a bikini had undulated by and begun making conversation. Spam was under her umbrella, reading, so self-contained, so detached from this good-looking, sunkissed Englishman in his tight blue briefs that the chatty fraulein hadn't made the connection and didn't trouble to lower her voice, so that both Baker and her stepmother were able to tune in.

'Only kidding,' Bob Baker suddenly fearing that his Churchill act would make him appear unsophisticated.

'Kiddink?' She made her blue eyes go comically wide.

'I make a leedle joke, yes?' Dad was saying in that silly sing-song English he always used for foreigners.

Her breasts were very large for someone so slim and Bob Baker was finding it hard not to gawp. They were the colour of hazelnuts apart from the tiny white triangles where her bikini top was out of line. Pam wore a one-piece. Pam preferred not to tan. He thought with distaste of his wife's pink and peeling chest and brilliant white belly.

'You make *ex-cellent* joke. Helga, my name is Helga.'

Helga leaned forward and Bob Baker suppressed a gasp as she put a brown hand on his thigh just as his daughter got up and walked past the bar to join Pam at the poolside, her scrawny teenage body encased in a long orange nightdress thing she'd been wearing since they arrived. He saw Helga sizing her up with a glance.

'Enklish girls. Zay do not like the sun.'

'Who's that woman Dad's talking to?'

'Where?' Spam put down her book (*War and Peace*? On holiday? Fooling nobody.) and raised the brim of her floppy hat to squint across to the bar. 'Dunno. Some kraut.'

'She had her hand *on his leg*.'

Spam raised one eyebrow and retrieved her book from the concrete lip of the deep end.

'In this heat? Rather her than me. Have you had your tablet?'

Baker had been on Dr Sexton's diet of tablets for nearly a fortnight now. The nightly mandies were having less and less impact on the daytime uppers and she was getting hardly any sleep. Her mind remained manically alert and the small hours were taken up with devising a bedroom farce written entirely in useful phrases gleaned from Spam's little book.

Do you speak English? I don't speak English. I am on holiday (I am on business). Is this seat taken? My wife is ill. I need a room with a large bed. I want more wine. The paella is very good. No thank you, I don't want any more paella. That is enough paella. Yes, it is very good. Just a small helping. My wife is in London. You have very beautiful hands/hair/eyes/buffet dishes. I don't understand. My wife doesn't understand. My room has a view of the sea. Please bring me an ice bucket and a bottle of your finest champagne. Yes, I slept very well.

Your husband is very nice. He speaks English very well. He is very tall. My wife has telephoned. I have spoken to the night porter. Can you direct me to a chemist? This woman is known to the police. What kind of a hotel is this?

Sleep, if and when it ever came, was kept busy with feverish dreams, most of them featuring Mrs Mostyn in a very small Fawcett-blue bikini.

There were still nearly two weeks to go of the holiday and the Bakers had got into a routine at the hotel: same table, same sunbeds, drinks poured before they'd even ordered them (local beer for Dad, rum and coke for Spam, coke for Amanda).

Spam, who'd helped herself to prawn cocktail and sauteed squid at the buffet, hastily scrambled off her lilo to make an emergency sprint for the powder room, leaving her untouched Cuba Libre on the pool's edge. Baker manoeuvred herself onto the vacant plastic mattress and picked up the abandoned glass (shame to waste it).

Dad's German bint had been dragged away to the ping-pong table by a rather proprietorial countryman (Bob Baker despised table tennis). She had pulled a zebra-print T-shirt over her tiny bikini in case of spillage and Baker saw both men's eyes home in on her breasts the instant her head disappeared. Bintless Bob grumbled over to check up on his daughter.

'You all right? Pam having a siesta?' He noticed the now empty glass and clicked his fingers at a passing barman: 'Same again over here, Paco, and a *cerveza, por favor.*' Like a native.

'Cheers,' said Baker when her highball arrived. You couldn't even taste the rum when you drank it through a straw.

Dad opened his throat to receive the contents of his beer glass, like a snake inhaling a rat, then wiped his mouth with the back of his hand as he looked around him to see if the coast was clear.

'Had your tabs?' Not a whisper exactly, but a sort of chuntering undertone like he was telling her that her flies were undone.

Spam finally returned from the loo and he ordered yet another round.

'I might take mine up with me, Bob. It's about time to get ready.'

They met again by the lift an hour later, Bob in a short-sleeved golf shirt, Spam in a khaki-coloured catsuit thingy with gold chains down the front. Baker was wearing a mortifyingly drippy cheesecloth dress Spam had probably bought for a joke but there hadn't been time to take back to the shop.

Before dinner, guests – guests who weren't downing thrifty tooth mugs of schnapps on their balconies – could sit in the piano bar overlooking the empty pool, drinking gins and tonics. The white artex-y walls of the terrace were all festooned with bougainvillea, the impossibly pink blossom looking like some primary school noticeboard display made out of scrunched-up tissue paper and thick dabs of map glue. 'They're *leaves*, not petals,' said Dad, in greenhouse mode.

Dad ordered 'the usual' and Paco winked at Baker as he placed her glass on its white paper daisy – her third rum in an hour. She thought again of the small print on the chemist's label. Did a piano count as machinery? Just as Baker was wondering whether to trip across to the white baby grand in her flowery flip-flops and vamp her way through 'Imagine' or 'The Entertainer' or the school song, the real entertainer arrived in his toothpaste-bright dinner jacket and began adjusting the stool and flicking through the handful of request cards that Paco had left on the lid underneath his water glass.

Baker sipped her drink as her parents chatted, uncomfortable to be eavesdropping on them being happy. A normal conversation because for once she was not the subject of it.

'"Moon River"?' suggested Mr Baker, eyeing the pianist.

'"Born Free"?' giggled Spam.

Both wrong: "Strangers in the Night" (what were the chances?).

'Lousy crisps,' said Dad, grinning, as he swiped a second bowl from the unoccupied next table. 'Want some?'

No sooner had he stolen the crisps than a guest took the table, an English doctor ('lady doctor' as Spam insisted on calling her) who was staying in the hotel by herself. She had ordered a whisky and soda. Very sophisticated, Baker thought, as she slurped up her Cuba Libre: a proper drink, a *bloke's* drink.

Dad kept looking towards the entrance to the bar – was he hoping for another sight of his German conquest? – Baker saw Spam checking over their neighbour, pricing her silk top and trousers.

'*Patatas fritas, por favor?*' Spanish accent and everything. Spam was cringing with embarrassment, hoping the woman hadn't spotted the two empty bowls on their table's glass top. Paco almost ran back with the crisps plus a sugar bowl full of olives and a saucer of diced cheese.

'Didn't bring us olives,' huffed Bob, then turned to his daughter in a show of conversation. Barbie's dad on holiday.

'So, Amanda, how's the revision coming along?'

Baker sucked up the last of her drink (as noisily as she could –
always drove him mad) then made to lean back against the cush-
ions, but the chair was deeper than she'd realised and she ended
up almost reclining, sugary ice cubes slithering over her cheesecloth smocking. The fan on the ceiling of the bar had a small
piece of paper streamer attached to it from the previous Saturday's
going home party and Baker watched, fascinated, as the long
purple shred fluttered in the artificial breeze.

'Amanda?'

Spam sounded very far away.

'Come on, sausage, let's get to the table.'

Evening meals were served by the open windows of the main
dining room where the tablecloths were made of damask so stiff
and starchy you could do origami with the matching napkins.
Sydney Opera House yesterday, water lilies today. The linen
changed colour every meal, same colours as the Mildred Fawcett
china: green, blue, lemon, ointment.

There was a bamboo dresser affair by the pillar in the middle
of the dining room where the waiters kept the re-corked bottles
of Banda Azul and the half-empty litres of Tre Naranjas and flat
Fanta, table numbers carved in Biro on the labels. The Bakers
always had a bottle of wine with their dinner and as usual
Amanda was given a glass, topped up with rubbish jokes about
not getting tiddly.

'Drop of beano tinto?'

Bob Baker nodded to the waiter who filled all three glasses
with the vinegary wine.

The hotel menu was full of disgusting things – especially the
starters which usually meant 'ensalata': parboiled vegetables
decanted from jars and doused in oil and lemon juice. Floppy
cocks of albino asparagus, palm hearts, tinned sweetcorn and
grated carrot. (What kind of person served grated carrot as an

hors d'oeuvre? Spam finally got her answer.) Even the carrots came in a bloody jar.

'Are you not eating that?' Her father's fork spearing a sweaty great heart of palm. What had they done with the rest of the tree?

Baker drank most of her wine in one gulp, staring in horror at her main course: something rectangular and grey with a side order of beans and yet more carrots: diced. Goody.

'Wossis?'

Dad tweaked the menu card from the swan-shaped gadget in the middle of the table and tilted his head back, narrowing his eyes so he could read the typed list.

'*Lemon sole in a girdle.*'

Would have been funny if Bunty had said it. Or Julia? Maybe.

The smell of fish was wafting up from the plate like the stink of the Upper Shell cloakroom at low tide. Baker lurched forward and as she reached to steady herself, sent the wine bottle flying, a great whoosh of red liquid shooting across Dad's yellow shirt. In the rush to limit the damage and hurl salt at the spreading purple stains no one spotted that Baker had lost consciousness.

When she came to, she was lying back in an armchair in the deserted piano bar, the cool, slim fingertips of the lady doctor clamped against the inside of her wrist.

'Lie still. You're going to be fine. My name's Jenny. I'm a doctor.'

'Lay-dee doc-tor,' drawled Baker.

The woman's superfine mousey eyebrows met for a kiss.

'Swot Spam always calls you,' explained Baker.

'Pam?'

'Spam-my-stepmother.'

'I've told your parents to carry on with their dinner, nothing to be alarmed about. I was watching you by the pool this afternoon: exactly how many of those drinks did you have?'

'Dunno. Dad kept saying "the usual" and Paki-whatsisface just kept bringing more rum and coke. Four?'

'And when did you last eat?'

'Lunch?' Baker couldn't meet those clever little brown eyes.

'Really? Could have fooled me.'

The fingers at Baker's wrist formed a ring with the tip of the thumb, a bony bangle round Baker's tiny forearm. Dr Jenny remained crouching by the armchair but raised her head and looked bossily behind her until a waiter appeared and let her show off in Spanish for a bit.

'He's bringing you a nice ham and cheese sandwich and some Coca-Cola – *plain* Coca-Cola.' Then she played doctors and nurses some more, pulling at Baker's eyelids and looking hard at her face.

'Your stepmother muttered something about tablets?'

'All sorts.' Baker sensed herself drifting off once more. 'Spam keeps them.'

When she woke up again Dr Jennifer was sitting next to her on an armchair she had moored alongside, reading the labels on the trio of medicine bottles kept in her parents' bathroom.

'And you've been taking this little lot every day for three weeks?'

'Probbly. Date's on the label.'

The doctor rolled her eyes but said nothing more, just handed Baker the glass of coke.

'Drink this and have a bit of your sandwich.'

'Aren't you a bit young for a doctor?'

'Nope.'

'How's the patient?' Bob Baker's hearty party voice, laid on for the new stranger.

'She'll be fine once she's had a bite to eat, but I think I should have a little chat with you and your wife if you don't mind.'

Little chat? Mr Baker winced at the familiar phrase. Never anything little about it.

'Goodnight, Amanda,' called Jennifer as she led him away. 'Try to eat up your sarnie. I'll pop by in the morning.' Pop. Doctor-y word 'pop': pop up onto the couch, pop your things off, pop this under your tongue, pop these pills.

Baker remained on the armchair, sipping at her coke, pretending not to notice the nosy glances of the other guests as they filed out of the dining salon and up in the lift to their schnapps bottles and backgammon boards. After about ten minutes Spam came back.

'Where's Dad?'

'Gone to bed.' A strained breath. 'Amanda? I was wondering . . .'

'What did she want?'

Spam abandoned whatever she had been planning to say and explained, almost apologetically, that Dr Cooke seemed to think that Amanda's tablets were too strong.

'Something about body mass – she did try explaining. She says you should only be taking about half the amount Dr Sexton prescribed because of your being so . . . petite. Says you'll feel much better – sleep better.' She unwrapped a smile and warmed it through. 'Might as well have an early night. Just half a tablet, Dr Cooke says.'

Baker struggled free of the spongy embrace of the chair and followed Spam to the lobby, leaving the mangled sandwich on the table, and assuring her that she felt fine, absolutely fine. She concentrated on taking deep breaths all the way up in the lift and managed a quick goodnight grimace before locking the door of her room and dashing to the bathroom. She was barely in time and some of it got down the front of her cheesecloth smock. She pulled the sodden cotton over her head, forgetting about the full-length mirror behind the door. As she dropped the dress on the floor and smeared it across the wet tiles with her sandalled foot she caught sight of her reflection. She ran a finger experimentally under the strap of her gaping brassiere, tracing the outline of each rib. She put a hand either side of her chest and pushed the whole lot together, remembering Helga's nutty cleavage. G-ross.

Baker spent the next day in her room writing unpostable post-cards to Bunty, reading *Sons and Lovers* and trying to finish her novel.

The dreaded Miriam's snapdragons had withered in the vase and the penultimate chapter found her crying over the news that Paul was about to be posted to a new job at an animal hospital in Melbourne. *A deep pain took hold of her and she knew that she must lose him and she lay on her bed like a beast awaiting the forgiving blade of slaughter. The memory of his loss came each time like a red-hot brand on her soul. It seemed that even her joy had been like the flame coming off of sadness. Her heavy head tilted at the sound of a taxi engine quivering on the darkling pavement below and she felt her whole soul coil into knots of flame.*

What she really wanted to do, Baker realised, was bump off all of her characters, but that would be copying Bunty, wouldn't it? ('I'm killing *everybody*.') And then she remembered that Miss Gleet would not be seeing *13 for Croquet* at all, now that Bunty was ten thousand miles away, and Baker curled up on her bed, the memory of Bunty's loss like a red-hot brand on her soul and cried as if she would never ever stop.

Spam, dial set to prison warder, brought up melon chunks and some rolls for breakfast (and half a tablet), then some scrambled eggs for lunch (with half another tablet), and Dad finally appeared with a ham roll and half a Mandrax on his way down to dinner and asked, almost shyly, if she wanted to go and look at some gardens tomorrow? *Gardens?* Not really, Dad, no. But the weird thing was that he and Spam went anyway: Baker flip-flopped down to breakfast at the usual time the next morning to find a note from Spam (two half tablets sellotaped under the signature) saying they'd hired a car and headed off and would see her at teatime.

Baker ordered tea and toast and was fiddling with the butter dish in grown-up solitary splendour when Dr Jenny Cooke skipped in, still in her girly white running shorts – like Julia, only thinner and without that gorgeous hair. Was Amanda on her tod? And, without waiting for an invitation, she had nipped over to the buffet, filled her plate with slices of fruit and sat down in Dad's chair. Pure chance? Baker didn't think so (there was no place laid at her usual table). Dr Jenny ate her banana with a knife and fork, cutting each slice into peculiarly small mouthfuls, and when she had finished she pushed back her chair, rolled back the bottoms of her Bermuda shorts and the capped sleeves of her blouse and began rubbing sun cream into her calves and fore-arms with a strange, unsensuous action, like Spam waxing the sideboard. Did Baker play much tennis? Baker began a muttered explanation about school tennis being a bit of a lottery with only three courts between thirty and the Drumlin only being inter-ested in girls who had learned to play elsewhere, and besides Baker loathed and despised games of any sort, but Jennifer Cooke cut her short.

'I could show you a few strokes if you like, but you're probably heaps better than I am.'

Baker once again felt as if she were watching her own body as it got up from the breakfast table and led this funny new tennis partner up to its room to change its shoes and then back down to the court where Dr Cooke proceeded to show Baker's body what it had been missing. It seemed that the secret was to carry on swinging the bat after it had made contact with the ball – a secret Miss Drumlin had never divulged.

They swam afterwards.

Baker's shirt billowed up around her as she stepped down into the warm water, like pyjama floats in a personal survival exam.

'You keeping that on?' More hard, rude, diagnostic looks at Baker's figure.

'I hate this bikini. Spam bought it.'

Dr Jenny dived straight in and swam two lengths under water (as Baker knew she bloody would). She was wearing a schoolgirl swimsuit with a racing back, a red one.

'What house were you in? Did you have houses?' said Baker's voice.

'Brontë.'

'No badges?'

'The old suit fell to bits. I just like them this shape – they stay on in the water.'

'Bet you did have badges though. You're the type: good prefect material.'

'Cheek. Race you to the end.'

She was out and on the side before Baker had gone ten yards.

'I'm useless.'

'You'll get faster, promise. I've got a stop watch upstairs. I could teach you the Australian crawl if you like.'

The rest of the morning was spent by the pool playing Travel Scrabble. And when lunchtime came the meal was actually edible for a change, because Jenny chatted up the hotel chef and got him to make special round omelettes with juicy bits of potato in, so they were spared the usual fight for the running buffet. The other guests were denied omelettes. Miffed or what.

'*Warum konnen wir nicht omeletten haben?*'

'*Sie muss ein spezielle diät befolgen,*' said Jenny, unanswerably, then turned to Baker to translate: 'I told them you were in training.'

And she was – in a way. The rest of the holiday carried on like that. Spam and Dad would go off to the other side of the island and look at a parrot sanctuary or some interesting rock formations ('oxymoron' Jenny said), and over the next fortnight Baker's swimming got quite fast. Even her German improved. The nightmares had stopped – she had no dreams at all now – but she couldn't lose the weird, out-of-body feeling, like it was all happening to someone else.

'It's a pity you weren't well and all that, but it's quite nice to have made some friends at last,' confided Dr Jenny. 'The other English families have got the idea that I'm stuck up. I requested a bit of Chopin on my first night – I was talking to the pianist in the bar and he's actually classically trained, would you believe it – but it didn't go down especially well. Silly of me, I suppose.'

Baker heard the click of a cigarette lighter and instinctively sniffed for the toasty aroma of the first pristine puff. They played a bit more Scrabble, Baker taught the doctor a few choice two-letter words until her opponent got *quixotic* across two triple word scores.

'So how come you're on so many drugs? And who is this Dr Sexton? Did he prescribe them over the phone? Jolly heavy doses.'

'Dunno. School made me go. It was that or get expelled. He's a psychiatrist, but I only saw him once for about half a minute.' Dr Cooke's bony face had that obsessive alert look Miss Carson used to get when she was taking notes in her head. 'Did my Dad put you up to all this?'

Dr Cooke took a last, filter-singeing drag of her fag (she smoked even harder than Julia).

'Nope. He's just worried about you that's all. Thought I might be able to help.' She tossed the fag end into the hibiscus bed. 'Time for lunch.'

Chapter 22

It was far too early for school – the gate wouldn't be open for a quarter of an hour – and the April breeze was whipping round the railway station and blowing a chill through Baker's hair, still wet from her early morning trip to the swimming baths. There was a smell of toast and fried bacon wafting from the Victory Café and she shoved open the glass door and made her way to a window table, studiously deaf to the mutterings of the breakfasting workmen – automatically on skirt alert, like dogs trained to bark every time a footstep crunched across the gravel driveway.

She'd ordered a twin pack of digestive biscuits with her tea and when they came she carefully snapped each one in half before jabbing it into the scalding liquid. She turned to the bag plonked on the seat beside her.

There were postcards from Dr Jenny in the side pocket. The latest was a picture from some Italian gallery of a woman sawing a man's head off. It looked familiar – or was it just something she dreamed? Jenny Cooke hoped she was well and eating properly and that her revision was all going to plan and that her backhand was getting plenty of practice.

Dr Cooke had sent her first postcard (Botticelli's Venus) in an envelope and Bob Baker had opened it (accidentally, he said) but then asked later how Dr Cooke was and was she enjoying her new job in paediatrics, which showed that he must have read to the end of it. Baker told Jenny what had happened in her reply which she had written on the topsheets of an invoice book she bought in Woolworths, leaving the carbon copies on the greenhouse bench under a jar of rooting hormone where Dad would be sure to find them. 'Wossis?' he sputtered, waving the pink flimsies at her over the breakfast table. She couldn't read the look on his face.

As he stormed off upstairs Spam had given Baker a funny smile, reached out an undecided hand and held it against her cheek for a moment. She probably meant it for a caress but she made contact like someone who had heard the whole icky business described but never actually seen it done, touching only with the back of her loose fist, like she was afraid to catch germs – or leave fingerprints.

'You sleeping any better, sausage?'

She did *ask*, at least. Dad hadn't asked. Dad was now up in the spare room taking the week's shirts from the cellophane bags the laundry put them in and steaming the folds from front, back and sleeves. Spam generally drew the line at pressing pressed shirts but hadn't been able to resist running a proud warm iron over Baker's school summer dresses. The brand-new fabric gave off the lovely old kindergarten smell and Baker had a happy flashback of hanging her tiny red blazer on her very own cloakroom peg. It had had a coloured picture of a teddy bear in place of a number, just as the sight chart at the annual medical showed outlines of a train, a house, an apple – like a page torn from a colouring book. A wonderful, friendly, wordless world.

There was a man in a suit at the café's corner table behind the workmen and he was gobbling up the monstrous 'breakfast special' as advertised on the blackboard outside – two eggs, bacon, mushrooms, sausage, beans and 'a slice' (didn't say what of). There was something wrong with the skin on his hand, a big, Ceylon-shaped patch that hadn't been coloured in properly. Baker had a sudden unwelcome vision of the rest of the uncorrected atlas on his chest, his thighs. She carried on watching as he made each million-calorie forkful of fried food before finally squeegee-ing up the egg yolk and tomato sauce with his last square of fried bread. G-ross.

Baker paid for her tea, feeling oddly daddyish (as she always did) at leaving her fourpence change for the waitress next to her uneaten second biscuit. She decided to take the bus the three stops up the hill (forty-four lengths of Australian crawl was enough exercise for anybody) but the next bus that came was full and an angry conductress – a slimline Snog Monster – was relishing her strict one-in-one-out policy. Baker leaned against the glass wall of the shelter, out of the wind, resisting the urge to light a cigarette. Someone would be bound to see, some beady-eyed prefect eager to pass on the news that Amanda Baker's latest copybook was now as blotted as all the others had been. And right at that very moment, when her head was so full of prefects and of cravings for the sweet rush of nicotine, she saw Julia.

She was with a group of girls from the school up the hill beyond Mildred Fawcett, and they were all slouched against the newsagent's window and pulling optimistically at the steel draw-ers of the fag machine. Julia had taken a tube of toffees from the pocket of her blazer and was handing them out with an auto-matic, Buntyish largesse that was sure to make the new girl very popular. The mismatched games kit was gone and, like Baker, she was kitted out in a new summer uniform, but the cheap-and-nasty striped fabric of the huge un-Fawcett frock, the chunky black purse-belt and heavy brogues made her look like an off-duty nurse. She hadn't been expelled, nothing so common, nothing the Fawcett governors need debate; she had been 'asked to leave' like a drunk in a pub.

The lovely auburn hair had been feather cut by a blind, one-legged hairdresser and the cornflower eyes, like those of everyone in her new gang, were crudely outlined with a ring of kohl pencil. Baker wondered how Baz felt about the new look.

Their spark of recognition was immediately spotted by a big scary girl with pierced ears and chipped burgundy nail varnish.

'D'you know each other?'

'My old school: year below.'

Julia handed the rest of her sweets to the girl and ambled across to the shelter.

'Still there then?'

'Just this term, Dad says. Wants me to go to St Ursula's next year.'

'Snobby.'

'What's yours like?'

Julia's mouth narrowed and widened: half leer, half sneer.

'Different.'

Funny how just a few smears of black wax, a few random snips of the scissors could defuse a person's loveliness.

The new pals would all like her so long as she was free with her sweets and fags. And dope? Might very well (it was a very Unschool school) but they wouldn't worship and adore, all the glamour had gone. The bloom. And it was all Baker's fault. If Baker hadn't caved in to O'Brien, if Baker had kept her mouth shut, told no tales, then Julia would still be at Fawcett Upper leading the cheers for the house tennis. Hip-hip?

'I told them it was you,' Baker said baldly.

Hard to say why it had to be said. She must have known.

'*I* told them it was *you*. Fat lot of good that did me; still got chucked out.'

Julia gave her another quick look of dislike then turned on her stacked heel and rejoined her mates as they jumped the queue for the bus and barged up the stairs past tutting passengers to blow smoke rings and swear and generally embody the ethos.

Old Dingle was unpadlocking the gate as Baker arrived and she was alone in the classroom: at least twenty minutes till Registration. Stottie was usually in early but there was no Stottie just now because Amanda Jane Stott had been suspended. Mrs Mostyn caught her consulting the equations of motion she had inscribed in Biro on the top of her thigh in readiness for a physics test and there was to be a governors' meeting to decide whether she would be allowed to keep her scholarship. No more scholarship would mean no more Stottie. 'She'll probably end up with Julia Smith. Her parents could never afford the fees.' (Or so Bryony had said.)

Baker felt in her tote bag for her homework and spotted the striped edges of Bunty's latest air letter. Warned off diary-keeping, Bunty wrote almost daily: long, rambling letters about beach barbecues in the balmy autumn sunshine and a man named Jason who drove a convertible but hadn't been circumcised and thought Bunty was twenty next birthday.

Mummy Gloria had picked out a house – heated pool, sun deck, walk-in closets and an 'open-plan conversation pit' – and she was coming back to London to mastermind the sale of the house and careful packing of her precious Imari dinner service. Mummy also had plans to throw cash at Dominic and somehow persuade him to give Australia a try. He could have his own car, jammy bugger. Dominic had been unimpressed. He could have a bloody car anyway, surely. All his friends were getting cars when they left school. What sort of car? demanded Mummy, who hadn't stopped fretting about it in case they bought the wrong sort and he turned his nose up. The Smeatons had bought their eldest a car so irredeemably naff it had yet to leave the garage.

Imp? Was that a car? Mummy had asked (she was clueless about cars). MGs were smart, weren't they? Perhaps Roy would run to an MG out of his relocation allowance? Did they have MGs in Australia?

Mummy Gloria had no plans to buy Bunty a car but they'd have to eventually. All her new friends could drive. She would be staying with one of them while her mother was back in London: Mimi, her new best friend. Mimi could drive; Mimi had her own phone in her bedroom; Mimi wore false eyelashes to parties. There seemed to be quite a lot of parties. Bunty's last letter had given a blowjob-by-blowjob account of the thrash held to celebrate the sixteenth birthday of a girl called Arlene who'd got a Swiss watch and a gold A on a chain and had worn a burnt orange halter-necked maxi-dress to blow out the candles on a cake shaped like a giant smiley badge. Bunty was getting the exact same maxi-dress in burgundy and what in Christ's name was she going to wear under it with her boobs and everything and Mimi's mum had cut her hair the same as Mimi's and some bloke called Garth (who *was* circumcised – like Baker was keeping score) thought they were twins and Bunty was saving up for a gold A like Arlene's because nobody had to call her Bunty any more thank God.

Baker frowned at the letter. It was definitely Bunty's writing. She tried picturing scruffy Bunty in false eyelashes and a convertible, tried picturing a Bunty who cared how her hair was cut. A feeling like pain seemed to hum through her but the sensation was muffled, as if the pain were happening next door, or next year. A lot of things felt like that. Even when Dad shouted something at her it wasn't loud any more: like a man two gardens away, like something upstairs she couldn't be bothered to fetch. No real urgency. Nothing to do with her. Not her problem.

Baker scrunched the blue sheet into a ball and volleyed it into the waste paper basket under Mrs Lorimer's desk.

The form room was gradually filling up. Almost last to arrive were Bryony, Victoria and Natasha who was arm in arm with Queenie. They all called her Mandy and she didn't even mind.

'Have you remembered your novel?'

It was Beverly Snell who had hurried in early for English monitoring porpoises. All the novels were due in today after their final Easter polishing. Miss Gleet had left her a cardboard box to put them all in. It had held forty-eight packets of smoky bacon flavour crisps and there was every chance it wouldn't hold the weight of thirty novels.

She was still hovering by Baker's desk.

'Amanda?'

Amanda. Nobody called Baker Baker any more.

Beverly beamed dimly down at her.

'I'd love to read yours. You can read mine if you like. Does yours have a happy ending?'

'No. Yes,' said Baker. 'No.'

'Is it finished?'

'I've just got one last bit to do,' said Baker. 'Shan't be a tick.'

Baker took *The Snapdragon Harvest* from her desk and began copying out the final sentences that she'd scribbled in her rough book the previous evening. The fringe on her new pageboy fell forward and she could pretend not to see Queenie, arm in arm with Tash and lusting over one of the pin ups of the boy wonder in Brian's latest comic.

'Very snogworthy.' (One of Tash's words.)

Queenie and her new friends had all been to a pub disco at the weekend: worn bowling shirts, drunk Pernod and blackcurrant, won erections from beardless boys drenched in after shave as they shuffled round the hall to slow soul music (the food of lurve).

Baker crunched a new blue cartridge into her fountain pen and began copying.

She lowered herself into the cold chair and quivered with misery

Damn: 'quivered' again. She tilted her head back, closed her eyes and breathed deep: *Shook? Trembled? Oscillated?* Perfect: vintage Gleet. The English mistress was giving a prize to the best novel. Baker opened her eyes and squinted up at the ceiling. Every single one of the drawing pins had gone . . .

. . . *oscillated with misery: never to see him again, never again feel the dread heat of his quick, dark hand. She looked across to the window sill with its urn of desiccated snapdragons, the blossoms an emblem of all her withered hopes. She felt rather than heard the slam of the taxi door, the fearless, bright step on the crushed cinder path – an intruder? But it was a step she knew, a step she loved and dreaded. In a moment his nerveless hand had swung the oak barrier clear of his path and she was locked in the maximum security of his imprisoning arms.*

'*You came back!*' she quivered.

'*Yes. Yes. Yes!*'

Baker crossed a few Ts, then took a set square from her smart new tin and drew a short line under her work with a red felt-tip. All done. Double tennis later.

Acknowledgements

This is a novel about friends, parents and teachers but it is not about my own friends, parents or teachers and any similarities are entirely coincidental. It is essentially a story about growing old, about shrinking horizons and the gradual death of the angry teenager inside.

Kyran Joughin and my husband Peter Mulvey kindly read the early drafts. My agent Anna Webber has been hugely supportive and Helen Garnons-Williams, my editor at Bloomsbury, improves every text she touches. Thanks also to Oliver Holden-Rea, Ros Ellis, Elizabeth Woabank, Imogen Corke and to my dear son Ed Mulvey.

Many dear friends helped me relive the teenage years. I would especially like to thank Ismene Brown, Caroline Davidson, Fiona Green, Caroline Griffiths, Susannah Herbert, Caroline Miller, Victoria Merrill, Victoria Pile and my beloved daughter Lily Mulvey for sharing their thoughts and memories. Most of all I would like to thank the poet Helen Buckingham, a girl who refused to follow and to whom the hardback edition of this book was dedicated.

A NOTE ON THE TYPE

The text of this book is set in Adobe Caslon, named after the English punch-cutter and type-founder William Caslon I (1692–1766). Caslon's rather old-fashioned types were modelled on seventeenth-century Dutch designs, but found wide acceptance throughout the English-speaking world for much of the eighteenth century until being replaced by newer types towards the end of the century. Used in 1776 to print the Declaration of Independence, they were revived in the nineteenth century, and have been popular ever since, particularly amongst fine printers. There are several digital versions, of which Carol Twombly's Adobe Caslon is one.

A VISION OF LOVELINESS

Jane James *knows* she was born to better things than a dingy bedroom in her Aunt Doreen's house in Norbury and a job as junior saleslady in a cashmere shop in Piccadilly. And then a chance encounter leads her to Suzy St John, a girl-about-town with the glamour and irresistible allure that Jane has rehearsed for so long. Taken under Suzy's wing, Jane becomes Janey, a near carbon-copy of her new best friend, who catwalks effortlessly through a sleazy world of part-time modelling and full-time man-trapping. But she can never quite drown out the nagging doubt that there might be more to life than a mutation mink jacket or an engagement ring . . .

'This immensely readable book is so full of period atmosphere that reality actually pales when you put it down'
VIRGINIA IRONSIDE, INDEPENDENT

'I loved this book. It wonderfully evokes the essence of the 1960s'
JOAN COLLINS

'Biting social satire, drenched in extravagant shoes, jewellery and clothes. Levene has a pitch-perfect ear for dialogue'
OBSERVER

B L O O M S B U R Y